I dedicate this book to Nora and Rick Fisher who died in a wreck in 2002. They play a key role in my books especially Nora who plays Nora in *The Key Club Murders* and Dora in *Who Killed Tom Solo?*

By putting their characters in my novels, keep them alive in my heart. I see Nora's face in every word I write and it makes me smile as I know how she would handle the situations or what she would say. She was a character and I miss her still.

Who Killed Tom Solo?

Interior Print Design and eBook Interior Design:

Dayna Linton, Day Agency

ISBN: 978-1-72284-444-8 Paperback

First Edition: 2018

10 9 8 7 6 5 4 3 2 1

Printed in the USA

Who Killed Tom Solo?

CHAPTER 1

3 A.M.

I WAS JARRED OUT OF a sound sleep by loud sirens blaring and flashing lights coming through the window. I joined my employer, Mike Farren, and his mother, Katherine, who were up looking outside to see if they could figure out what the commotion was all about. The phone started ringing and startled Mike.

"This is Mike," he answered. There was a long pause. "Thanks for the heads up."

Katherine and I looked at him, waiting anxiously for a response.

"That was Ben," he said. "Mary found her husband Tom dead beside their house. The police are going from one neighbor to another. It doesn't look good. They're questioning Mary."

Just then the doorbell rang in quick chimes. Someone was leaning on the doorbell. Since I'm the kids' nanny, I ran back to check on Mike's two children. Thank goodness they were sleeping through all the chaos. When I came back, there were several police officers standing in the entry waiting for the detective to arrive. He entered with a big booming voice and bellowed, "Sara Carlton?"

I turned toward him and said, "Yes, I'm Sara Carlton."

"I'm Detective Zackery Zanders. Where were you about two hours ago?" he asked, flipping through his notebook.

Mike stepped closer to me while Katherine stepped toward the detective and said, "Since it's Fourth of July, I stayed all night with my family. We were all in bed and asleep by then."

"I was asking Miss Carlton," he stated.

"I was in bed asleep by then. Why?" I asked.

"Several people witnessed you shoving Tom Solo into the swimming pool. Why?" he asked.

"Well, if several witnessed me shoving him into the pool then you know why," I answered sarcastically through clenched teeth.

"I want to hear it from you," he smirked.

"Look, Detective Zander Zackery, I didn't push him maliciously. He wouldn't stop bothering me. He was slobby drunk and kept reaching for me. He kept telling me he wanted to get better acquainted. He wouldn't listen to me or stop, so I pushed him into the water to help cool him off. It didn't work."

He laughed and said, "Miss Carlton, it's Zackery Zanders."

And I soberly said, "And it's Mrs. Carlton."

"Touché," he mumbled.

Since they had no search warrant, the officers walked through the house taking in all they could with their eyes.

"Okay, Mrs. Carlton, I'm taking you in," he said, reaching for handcuffs.

"Wa, what, taking me in, for what?" I asked.

"You're a person of interest and suspected of murder," he said.

"You can't just arrest me without reading me my rights or without some kind of evidence. You have to have probable cause," I almost yelled. "This is, crazy."

"Oh, I have probable cause," he replied.

About that time my best bud and partner in all things, Dora, came bursting through the front door. Everyone turned in shock, including me, watched her enter in her Micky Mouse pajamas with every single red hair in place. Even from where I was I could see her false eye lashes. *Never goes without them*. I started to walk toward her, but Detective ZZ put his hand on my arm to stop me.

"How did you get in here?" he asked her.

"I lied," she snorted.

"What? Lied?" I said, along with the detective in unison.

"Well yeah. I just told the officers I lived here. They tried to stop me, but here I am. Now what's this taking my girl in for suspicion of murder?" she snapped, getting rather loud. "Should I call an attorney?" my almighty protector Dora said.

"That's your call. Meantime go put some clothes on, Mrs. Carlton," he said still holding onto the handcuffs.. "Go with her, officer."

"Really?" I asked, looking back at him. "What evidence? What proof?"

"I'll go over all of it as soon as we get to headquarters," he said.

Dora started to walk with the officer and me, but the great detective stopped her.

Officer Rose Raven accompanied me to my bedroom. She looked around picking up my picture of my husband Jerry that I had just kissed good night a few hours ago. "Nice," she said setting the photo back down. "Is this a picture of your hubby or boyfriend?" she asked.

"My husband. He was killed in a hit and run a few years ago." I sighed. "They never caught his killer."

"I'm sorry about your husband," she said. "Better hurry up; Detective Zanders has had a bad day and is not real patient with any of us right now. Although, I have to say I've never heard him tell anyone to go get dressed before. That's a first. So, hurry up in case he changes his mind."

Since I just showered Tom Solo's touch off of me before going to bed, all I had to do was pull my hair back into a ponytail and put a scrunchie in it to hold it in place, then throw on some clothes and shine on my lips.

"You won't need any lip gloss in interrogation," Officer Raven said.

"Habit," I replied, as I grabbed my purse and threw it over my shoulder and sashayed out of my room like I was going to a movie instead of jail. But I was plenty scared. What evidence did they have against me? I could still hear Dora making demands as I walked towards her.

"What about the children?" I asked Mike.

"I got it covered," he said.

"How? Who?" I asked him.

"I'll call Clancy in the morning. Tomorrow's Friday, and she's due to work tomorrow anyway."

"Where's Katherine?"

"Oh, the detective sent her to her room," Dora said, sarcastically. "He told her to be in for questioning at 8 A.M. and Mike's to come in, too. He said he was taking me in with you."

"What? What do you mean taking you in?" I asked. "What for?"

"You heard her, I'm taking her in as I am sure she has a lot to add as she hasn't shut up since she waltzed in here," the detective said.

"I was able to call Richard before the detective confiscated my phone from me. Richard's bringing my things to the police station, so I don't have to remain looking like I just climbed out of bed. He's calling our attorney and will meet us there in the morning," she said.

"You'll need more than a brother-in-law studying law for an attorney," I said.

"I'll call my office and ask our corporate attorney to recommend a defense attorney," Mike said . . ."for all of us!"

"Okay, folks, time to call it a night," the detective said, turning back to me. "You have the right to remain silent . . ." as he took both Dora and me by the arm leading us out to the patrol cars finishing the Miranda to me. Though I didn't have handcuffs on, he still pushed my head down to get into the car.

It would all be comical if I wasn't about to tear up. Besides, nothing was funny about murder. They wouldn't let Dora and me ride in the same patrol car. This was serious.

CHAPTER 2

I SAT IN THE INTERROGATION room tapping my fingers on the table impatiently waiting to be, well, interrogated. I think this was a way the police tried to make you sweat. Then I smiled to myself and thought how many people swore their innocence, that weren't?

While waiting for Detective Zack Zanders to come in, I drifted back in time to Jerry, my sweet, sweet husband who meant more to me than life itself.

It was the day we were getting ready to go camping. Jerry had to run a quick errand to get one more thing for the camping trip, and I was expecting him back any minute. Our friends who were going on the trip with us would soon be there. I continued packing and would be ready to go when Jerry got back home. I was humming and half giggling at how Jerry grabbed me, and threw me down on the bed to make baby before he left on his surprise errand. He always called it make baby, especially since we were now ready for a baby. Our plans were coming together.

I was carrying our bags to the front door and just put Jerry's jacket on top of the camping gear when the doorbell rang. I ran to the door and swung it open and said, "Did you forget your key?" Only it wasn't Jerry. Two police officers were soberly standing there when I swung open the door. I stumbled back losing my balance and dropped to the floor crying. I felt Jerry's jacket falling with me when I fell against the camping gear. I pulled the jacket close to my chest and buried my face in it, smelling his cologne.

"Mrs. Carlton, there was a hit and run and your husband has been rushed to the hospital," one of the officers said, as they both helped me up.

"I, I heard the sirens, but never thought for one second it involved Jerry. Oh, my God, what happened?" I asked, as I felt my legs trying to fold again.

The officers steadied me, and one said, "We need to head for the hospital. We'll tell you on the way."

"You mean he's alive?" I asked.

"Yes ma'am, but we need to hurry."

I clung to Jerry's jacket, picked up my purse and about collapsed teetering back and forth and toward the wall. Again, I was held up by the two officers. As we headed to the patrol car, the friends of ours who were supposed to meet at our place for our camping trip just pulled up. As they got out of their car looking bewildered toward me, one of the officers rushed over to them and gave a brief summary of what happened to Jerry.

I just got the car door shut when the officer came back and got in the front seat. He turned to me and said, "Your friends will stay to tell the rest of the group what happened to Jerry and then they will head to the hospital."

Finally, on the road one of the officers told me a witness was looking out their window, waiting for their dog to come back in when the crash happened. He said, "It looked like your husband just started to move from a four-way stop when an older car, perhaps a convertible, ran the four-way speeding through it and T-boned your husband's car. The witness said the old car just kept going, and it was traveling so fast they couldn't get a license plate number if there even was one. They rushed out to your husband and called 911."

Dora and Richard didn't like anything outdoors, no camping, no hiking, no fishing, no outdoors anything so they weren't part of the group going. Crying but trying hard to hold it together, I called her to let them know what had happened. She was surprised and upbeat to have an unexpected call from me. Immediately she knew something was wrong. She listened without saying a word. I told her everything I knew to that point. She said she and Richard would be there soon. And they pulled in just as I did.

The officers escorted me with Dora and Richard into the hospital where Jerry would be. The nurse in charge saw me and rushed to me. "Sara, we're doing all we can for him. But you're a nurse so you know it can go either way. Jerry's tough and strong and has a will to live so I feel good about his recovery."

"Thanks Nita. Where is he?" I asked, pulling myself together not for myself but for Jerry.

"Oh Sara, you can't go back there," Nita said, looking at Dora and Richard, "Stay with her.

I'll get an up-date and be right back." Then, looking back at me, said, "You need to stay here until we know something."

"No!" *I yelled. "I want to see him."*

"I realize you work with the whole staff here including me, Sara, but this time you're the patient's family. You need to give us a chance to help your husband."

"Nita, I know the protocol, but I am going in. I have to see Jerry," I insisted.

Nita started to argue but gave in to me and led me back to where Jerry was being operated on. We walked into the scrub room and put on the gown, footies, mask and gloves. I recognized so many people milling around in there and was on a first name basis with most of them. I was amongst friends. As I passed by each one of them I could see sadness and care in their eyes. We stepped just inside the operating room, and Nita caught me as I started to sink when I first saw the ER staff working on Jerry. I had been there on the other side of this scenario so many times doing my job, but this was the first on this side. Nita helped steady me, and I sucked it up and took a deep breath and walked closer to where I could see Jerry. I didn't recognize him. His face was so bloody, and it looked like his nose was broken and swollen. His blond hair was matted with blood and he was covered in it. The doctors noticed me, nodded, and kept working. Doctor Kent Delmar was one of the best in his field, and Jerry was lucky to have him. I had worked with him for a couple of years now, and I trusted him. I couldn't get close enough to Jerry because the staff had him surrounded, each doing what they had to d. Save my husband.

I returned to Dora and Richard and told them, "I'm not sure it's him. It doesn't look like him." And then I broke down and sobbed until the doctor came out four hours later.

"Sara," I heard his soft voice say. "I'll be all right."

I looked around looking for Jerry. I smelled his after shave and heard his voice but I couldn't see him.

"Sara, Sara, the doctor's coming." my best friend said to me.

"I just heard Jerry."

"No, baby, you didn't. You dozed off for a few minutes. You must have dreamed."

"It was so real," I said.

"I know, baby. I know," she said.

"Sara," the doctor said.

"How's Jerry?" I asked him, as I stood up.

The doctor told me that Jerry was holding stable, but it would be touch and go for a few days. "He's in intensive care. You can go be with him in a few minutes. They'll come and get you."

"Thanks, Dr. Delmar," I said to the doctor as I felt a calm come over me.

Dora went with me, and she was shocked when she saw Jerry. I sat down by my man and my best friend sat beside me.

I stayed by Jerry's side day and night for weeks. Dora stayed by mine. She would keep the family and friends updated. Richard was great too. He ran all the errands and brought us clean clothes and did everything for Dora and me so we didn't have to leave Jerry's side. We prayed and prayed for Jerry to recover, but at the end of the fourth week Jerry just couldn't hang in there any longer. His internal injuries were just too much. I thought I saw a little smile come across his face as he faded away. A peaceful smile, I guessed, for he was now at peace.

CHAPTER 3

I WAS STILL IN DREAM mode when Detective Zanders came through the door, jarring me from my memories. He acted like he was in a hurry to get this over with. Could I be that lucky? I glanced at my watch and it was 7 A.M.

"Detective, may I go to the ladies room? I need to use the facilities and I need to eat something," I stated as sweetly as I could. *Anything to go pee.*

He didn't say anything just stood and motioned for me to get up, and he led me to the ladies room. When I was through I washed my hands and splashed water on my face to wake myself up. I walked out where the detective was waiting with a bag from McDonalds and coffee. I looked at my watch, *how long was I in there*?

On the way back to the interrogation room I saw Richard approach Dora and walk her out just as Katherine and Mike walked in. I saw them stop and talk to each other briefly.

"So, Dora gets to go home?" I asked.

"Yes, she was very cooperative. She's very fond of you and she considers you family and her best friend," he said, opening the door to interrogation room three and leading me in. He spread the McDonalds out and handed me a coffee.

"I asked one of the officers to pick this up for us just before I came in to interrogate you. We have a McDonald's around the corner," he said. "I hope you like it."

"Detective Zanders, I know how serious this is. You hauled me in here without just cause or motive. You read me my Miranda and I still don't know the proof that you claim you have." I shrugged my shoulders and took a breakfast sandwich and hash browns.

"Mrs. Carlton, we have evidence, and I will go over it with you shortly."

"So, Detective, why did Dora get questioned and I waited forever?"

"Sara, may I call you Sara?"

"Yes." but I thought *no.*

"I was shorthanded, and you drew the short straw."

"I drew the short straw!" I said, sarcastically. Then reconsidering my attitude, thanks for the food and coffee, Detective." I took another bite.

"I have a confession," he said. "I made Dora wait while I went back to the crime scene. I only questioned her for an hour or so. She had to wait too."

"May I ask you why you took her in in the first place?" I asked.

"She just made me so damn mad when you were getting dressed. She kept badgering me over and over again, "take me in. Sara and I do everything together. Take me in." So, to shut her up and teach the bossy butt a lesson, I took her in. She just got under my skin. I'm not proud of it, and it's a bit unorthodox to haul someone for just plain aggravation, but she needed a quiet place so the interrogation room was the right place. She was asleep when I got there. Meantime, I interviewed several people before getting to you. But now here I am. Let's get started. Tell me about the Fourth of July pool party. And don't leave anything out."

"Well, did ya?" I asked.

"Did I what?" He answered.

"Teach Dora a lesson."

"Probably not. She's strong-willed, but she was helpful," he said. "Start telling me your side of the story."

"It'll take a while."

"That's fine. I have all day," he smiled, taking a sip of his coffee.

I rolled my eyes.

"Start with how you came about becoming a nanny after being a nurse. So, start from the beginning."

"I lost my husband in a hit and run a few years back and had a very hard time of it. Oh, and, by the way, the police never found the killer."

"Sorry, "I'll check on it," he said, writing something down.

I continued, "Since I couldn't help Jerry and God sure didn't, I gave up both my nursing and, God. Although," I said, taking a sip of coffee, "recently I started letting God back in."

I paused then continued. "Jerry left me in great financial status so it was easy to just exist. Finally, last spring I ran into an old friend who told me of Mike Farren needing a caregiver for his two small children. He lost his wife to cancer several months before. His mother helped out but needed to get back to her life so Mike started looking for a caregiver and in walked me. Dora insisted and even called Mike herself and told him I would be a good fit. She has a way about convincing people, you know?"

"Yes, I noticed. But a nanny?" he said.

"There is nothing a bit wrong with being a nanny. It's an honorable profession," I half scolded him.

"Mr. Farren liked you and hired you immediately. Why's that?" he asked.

"I found out later when Dora spoke to Mike, it was basically a done deal. I fell in love with those two kids. And it was through the kids playing in the back yard that we became acquainted with the neighborhood parents chasing after their kids. After a while, they became Dora's and my friends."

"Why's Dora there so much? It's your job." he asked

"We used to laugh and say, "where I go, there goes Dora." But even I was surprised to see Mike allowed Dora there all the time. He just said she was always welcome.

"Yes, Dora told me. So far, your stories match," he said. "But I don't imagine Mr. Farren meant for Dora to be there as much as she is."

"Probably not," I sighed. "Then you know we spent a lot of time together with the neighborhood ladies and planned the Fourth of July pool party."

"Dora said you all got pretty close to each other. So, tell me about what happened at the pool party."

"We invited all the neighbors and any family of theirs to

come and join in the festivities. If you invite everyone then no one can complain it's too noisy. Anyway Mary, Tom Solo's wife, had been drinking two to everyone else's one. She was feeling it. She was already slurring her words early on and feeling sorry for herself. Tom was already three sheets to the wind and it was ugly. He was loud, sloppy, and just an all-around bad drunk. I was trying to take care of Mike's kids, but Mike told me to relax, that he and his mother had the kids covered and to enjoy myself. And, since it was my first real social activity in a very long time, I tried to enjoy it.

We were eating and visiting when I felt someone staring. Since it made me feel uncomfortable, I turned looking every which way but didn't see anything. A little

while later I felt it again. This time Tom didn't turn away and let me know he was staring."

"So, what did you do then?" the detective asked.

"I moved away from his line of vision but he just moved too. It didn't stop him from watching my every move. After a while, thinking he gave up, I let my guard down and was getting another drink when Tom approached me and tried to hug me, spilling my drink all over me, and then he wanted to help me wipe it off, only he got pretty handsy." I paused.

"Go on, Sara, what else happened?" he asked, looking down at his notes.

I thought, *I was trying to tell him everything, but he kept interrupting me.*

"I tried as nice as I could for his wife's sake to keep my cool and let him down easy. He didn't give up. He tried a couple of more times, and the last time he was pulling me to him and tried to kiss my neck. I was able to get a bit of space between us, but it didn't stop him, and on his last grab for me, I admit I was tired of it, and I wanted him to leave me alone, so I pushed him and maybe, just maybe, I pushed a little too hard. I was hoping it would cool him off. I guess it did because he stopped bothering me but stared holes in me the rest of the afternoon. He was angry."

"How angry were you? Were you angry enough to kill him?" he asked.

"I could never be that angry. I would never. I'm a nurse and my job's to help people live."

"But you gave up nursing, so you gave up helping people live," he said.

"Oh, I watch cops on TV and I know how you twist words around and try to trip up people."

"You got me. Mrs. Carlton."

"Oh brother, Mrs. Carlton again," I sighed, "I didn't kill Tom Solo. Nada, zero, zilch," I said. "There's no way, no matter how upset I was, that I could harm another soul, not anyone."

He brought out an evidence bag and asked, "Does this belong to you?"

I started to pick it up but didn't.

"You can look at it but don't open the bag," he said.

I looked at it closely and said, "It looks like part of my swimsuit scarf. Why?"

"We found it in Tom Solo hand," he said.

"What on earth? You found this in his hand?" I asked."

"Yes. Now can you tell me why he was still clutching it in his hands hours later?"

"All I can say is, when I pushed him he had a hold of my scarf I had wrapped around my waist. When he grabbed it, he tore a piece of the corner of it as I held onto it tightly. He fell backwards into the pool. But I was able to keep most of my scarf intact. It was only a corner piece. Okay? Never dreamed he clasped and held on to this piece," I said, setting the bag back down.

"Mrs. Carlton, where was the scarf again, when Tom Solo grabbed it from you?"

"Around my waist to help cover my tush," I said.

"Old fashioned isn't it?" he asked.

"Not for me. "Sometimes a girl just doesn't want it all hanging out, therefore a scarf. So

why was it still in his hand hours later?" I questioned.

"Souvenir?' he said.

"That's just plain sick.'

"Here's another piece of evidence." he said, as he again presented another bag pushing it across the table.

Again, I picked up the evidence bag and studied it. "What's this?

"Your hair barrette."

"I have never seen this before in my life," I said, with a lot of disgust. "Who said this was mine?"

"A witness said you wore this the day of the pool party." he said.

"Was your witness even at the party, because if they were they would know I never wear barrettes? Ever! That, my dear detective, needs to be checked out further. Someone's lying. You brought me in as a suspect and read me my rights on extremely flimsy evidence. I spent all night and all day going through such tripe and in the meantime the killer's getting away with murder. You have the wrong person. And it looks like hair is hooked into the barrette and when you test it; you will find it's not my hair."

"Well, we've convicted on less evidence." he sarcastically said.

"I'm sure. Check out the DNA on this, 'cause this isn't my DNA and it's not going to stick," I said, tossing the barrette back to him. I was really getting tired. The coffee didn't help, and I wondered how much longer this was going to be.

"Sara, it's two in the afternoon and I think I have been misled. I think we both need a rest. I'm going to let you leave and go home, but since you are a person of interest, don't leave town."

"It means because you lack evidence and you know I didn't murder Tom Solo, I can go home," I said irritable.

"Well, Sara, a person of interest is still a person of interest. But you are right; we lack evidence to hold you. I need further testing on the barrette and the hair stuck to it. You can go, but I will be talking to you again, soon."

I didn't hesitate, and I got up and walked out of interrogation room three, right into Mike.

"You going home?" I asked him. "Can I catch a ride?"

"Let's go," and he guided me out the precinct door.

"Is Katherine still in there?" I asked.

"The best I can find out, they let my mother go home an hour or so ago.

Since we were all brought in for just questioning, we didn't need an attorney. Mary already has one."

"I really feel bad for her," I said, in an undertone.

"Apparently, you're free to go, and you didn't need an attorney either. So, everything's looking up." he said.

"Except someone's pointing their finger at me and lying. The detective's reaching for straws. He thought he had evidence against me, but the jokes on him. He has nothing. But I wonder why Tom Solo was clutching a piece of my swimsuit scarf still in his hand hours later. Why?" It just dawned on me I didn't need an attorney. One should have been there first thing this morning since I was hauled into the police station. What happened to my attorney? Things were a bit . . . unorthodox. Later, I found out I had one, but no one knew where I was. *The ladies room.?* Talk about Mayberry?

CHAPTER 4

I WAS DEAD TIRED WHEN I walked through the door. Mike was okay since he was able to go back to bed when they hauled Dora and me in.

Clancy, the housekeeper, slash emergency baby sitter, had a pot roast with all the fixings headed for the dining room table when she heard us come in. It was a welcome sight. The children came running to their dad, hugged him and then came to me. They were singing 'Who's Afraid of the Big Bad Wolf?' as they turned to climb up onto their chairs to eat. Immediately the song stopped at the first taste of mashed potatoes.

"Thanks, Clancy, this meal hits the spot. It's really good," Mike said, as he took a sip of wine. "You know the police will call you in before long; they are talking to everyone who was at the pool party, so you and Mr. Clancy will be called in for interrogation."

"No doubt, I'm ready to talk to them," she answered. "I would like to get it over with."

"Well, Clancy," I said, as I slid my chair away from the table patting my tummy. "That was just what I needed and, as usual, it was good."

"No problem, missy, you had a long day. I didn't mind helping out with the kiddos and dinner."

"Go ahead and take a nap," Mike said. "I got this handled," as he swooped his hand toward the dirty dishes and the dirty kids.

"You guys are so nice. I think I'll take you up on it," I said as I started toward the bedroom, only to be stopped by the constant doorbell ringing. I made a U-turn to go to the front door. I opened it and there was Zackery Zanders, the detective in charge, standing getting ready to ring another series of rings. Oh, great. No nap!

"Yes Detective?" I asked, as I let him in.

"I need to speak to a Mrs. Anita Clancy. Her husband said she was still here," the great detective said, looking around for her.

"Clancy, you have a guest," I yelled back toward her and Mike. "It's Detective Zanders."

"Well, that didn't take long," she said, taking the end of her apron and drying her hands then putting a strand of her hair behind her ear, taking a double take on the detective as she walked toward him.

"Aren't you a hotty?" Clancy said, as she reached for his hand shaking it with gusto.

I looked at Mike; Mike looked back at me, and we both shrugged our shoulders. Clancy acted and talked like a generation and sometimes two ahead of us, but the truth was she was forty-something and has an old soul.

"You were a witness to Sara Carlton pushing Tom Solo into the pool, so . . ." he said.

"Well, actually I didn't see her push anyone," Clancy said. "I heard a splash, and "you bitch," coming from the water."

"Is there somewhere we can talk? I have several questions and . . ." he said.

Mike said, "Sure, you and Clancy can go into the den for privacy." They were in there for around an hour or so, and finally the French doors opened, and they walked out.

The detective said, "I'll be back to question you again so don't leave town." And with that he left.

It was too late to take a nap so I knew I would have to tough it out a couple of hours before turning in. Mike told me to just kick back, and he would bathe the children and get them ready for bed. I hunkered down in a recliner, and my mind went to my hubby. But before I could get into my memories, my cell rang and, since I am of the generation who sit with the phone in their lap, I answered it. "Hi Dora," I said.

"Boy, that detective hunk had a lot of questions about you."

"Well, I am a person of interest," I replied, lackadaisically "However, because the lack of evidence, I think I'm off the 'who done it' list." That got a tiny giggle from Dora.

"You sound beat, really tired. Didn't you get any rest?" she asked.

"Nope, didn't work out. Clancy had dinner ready, and ZZ showed up with more questions."

"ZZ?" She asked.

"Yep, ZZ. Zackery Zanders."

"Cute!" she snorted. "I got a great nap and am raring to go. By the way, what did ZZ want?"

"He wanted to question Clancy, and he did for a lengthy time. I just hate it that that drunk tried to push himself off on me, and out of desperation trying to get him to stop, I pushed him away from me," I took a deep breath, "not knowing it would get him killed."

"Oh, I don't think it had one bit to do with you. I think it was an opportune time for someone. And we need to help the police find out who." my best friend rattled off to me.

"So, you want to get involved in this murder and clear my name once and for all," I asked her.

"You bet yah! Plus, we're good at snooping so we need a plan of action. I'll be over in the morning so get a good night rest."

"Yes, mother, good night," I said.

She laughed and hung up.

CHAPTER 5

Finally, I climbed into bed, and, just as I laid my head on my pillow to go into a deep blissful sleep, my eyes popped wide open. I tossed and turned then finally gave up and went over to my desk and pulled out my old diary full of memories that I used to keep. I turned to the first page and read.

Dear Diary,

Today I met the man of my dreams. Our eyes met and locked in on each other. We were in the parking lot of my nursing school where I had just graduated, packing up my rental van and saying goodbye to classmates when I saw him.

He walked over to me and said, "Where have you been all my life?"

I giggled and just as I started to answer, the sky opened and it poured down rain with thunder and lightning.

"Your place or mine?" he asked.

I replied, "Starbucks."

We sipped our coffee and talked for what seemed like hours. We exchanged numbers and left. I no more than pulled into my driveway when my cell rang. I answered, and he said, "This is Jerry Carlton, when can I see you again?" He drove up behind me and never left. It was love at first sight.

I closed the diary and wiped the tears from my eyes and wondered how did I get here? I was so tired but still couldn't sleep. I put my robe on and walked to the kitchen, running smack dab into Mike.

"Couldn't sleep either?" he asked.

"Nope," I said without enthusiasm, as I had none.

"I just made some hot chocolate, want some?" he asked me.

"Sounds good," I answered. "Mike, I'm so sorry you, your family and friends are going through this. I should have walked away but no, I pushed Tom in the pool."

"Number one, Sara; you didn't kill Tom and neither did Mary. And number two, we don't know the why or the who. So, let the police figure it out."

I put my head down, resting my chin on my chest, too tired to raise my head and said, "First, my husband was killed, and now I am a person of interest in another murder. Tom basically ruined my life in one night, and I'm tired of all of this. I don't want to talk about him anymore." I took a deep breath. "What the hell's going on in my life?"

Just then flood gates opened, and I cried uncontrollably. Mike walked over to where I was sitting at the breakfast bar and handed me a box of tissues. I wiped, and I blew, and I wiped, and I blew again. "Oh Mike, I'm so sorry. I normally don't cry like this; I guess it's just that I am so tired."

I could tell that Mike wanted to put his arms around me to comfort me, but he slowly pulled his arms away and just patted my shoulder instead. I guess that's appropriate, but I sure could have used a good hug. Instead, he offered to top off my cocoa.

I held out my cup, sniffled again and stood, and he refilled it. I said good night, taking my hot cocoa back to my room.

I sat back in my recliner and snuggled under a throw, sipping my hot chocolate, and the next thing I knew, my cell phone ringing woke me up. "Yes, mother?"

"Get up, get up, get up, it's morning and time for work," Dora said.

"*No!*" I whined. "Leave me alone."

"Nope, I'm on my way over to work on a plan of action."

I hung up.

The phone rang again, "Do not hang up on me."

I hung up. And I let the phone ring while I climbed into the shower.

It was Sunday morning so Mike was home. As I rounded the corner into the kitchen I wasn't completely surprised to see Dora and Richard drinking coffee with him. We did a fist bump.

"Well, you look better this morning than you did last night," he said to me. "I'm making

pancakes for breakfast. You two staying?" he asked, pointing his question to Richard and Dora while he handed me a cup of coffee.

"What else you having?" Dora smiled.

"*Dora*," Richard said, "That's rude."

"Sausage and eggs," Mike replied.

"Alright, we'll stay," she said.

"Glad it suits you, queenie," Richard said.

I am always amazed at the banter that Dora and Richard do on a constant daily basis. That's just who they are.

"Hey Rich, we can go play a little golf while Sara and Dora do whatever," Mike said. "I feel the urge to drive a golf cart. I haven't played in a very long time."

"Sounds like fun." Richard said.

"What about the kids?" I asked.

"Mother picked them up, and they're probably sitting in church about now. They're spending the day with her."

"What time is it?" I said, looking at my watch which had apparently stopped.

"That's what I was trying to tell you when you kept hanging up on me" Dora said. "Time was ticking away. Now it's quarter after nine."

"Really?" I stated, looking up at the kitchen clock. "Well, how about that?"

After we ate, Dora and I cleaned up while Richard and Mike left for a nine-hole round of golf. We sat down at the table with our pens and pads, scribbling down a few things we remembered from the party.

"Looks like Mike and Richard enjoy each other's company. Now golf?"

"I like it," my feisty friend said. She brought in the newspaper, unrolled it where it lay, wide open on the counter.

"I purposely hadn't turned any news sources on," I told her. "I didn't want to hear or watch how the media butchered the truth." Just as I suspected. My picture along with Tom's wife Mary, were front and center with "Mistress and Wife" in bold letters under the pictures.

Dora started to read, "Who did it? Which woman was that angry? Mary Solo and Sara Carlton are leading the *Person of Interest* list."

I was devastated. *No, I was pissed.* Now I know why I didn't want the news on. They are just a bunch of vultures and write whatever about whomever just to get a story, true or not. They are thrill seekers and not truth finders. That's why I hate the media. I don't think there's one newsworthy reporter left in this world." I hung my head and was about to tear up when my buddy took me by the shoulders and yelled, "Snap out of it."

I looked at her and tilted my head to one side, and then about the time she started to yell at me again, I stood and yelled back "Okay."

For some reason, we both started laughing like two school girls. I grabbed my side that was riddled with pain from laughing so hard. Finally, the pain subsided, and I was able to straighten up while Dora was still uncontrollably snorting.

At last. Calm.

"So now that's over with, let's read on."

We skimmed through the pages and then turned TV on to see any updates. Of course, the murder of Tom Solo was plastered all over the news, including cable news.

Because Mike suspected the phone would be ringing off the hook, he turned the land line off for the day. But my cell phone wasn't off. I could choose who I wanted to talk to with caller ID. I could tell it was my mother calling, so I answered.

"Sara, you okay honey?" my mother asked.

"Yes, I'm fine, Mom, just frustrated about it all."

I explained to her exactly what happened, and that we hadn't killed Tom. Okay, maybe Mary, but certainly not me. I told her that everyone who had been at the pool party weren't only witnesses but suspects as well. No one was exempt.

"Your dad says hello, Sara. I'll fill him in. Tell Dora hello for us."

"Here, you tell her yourself, love you guys," and I handed the phone to Dora.

She spent five minutes on the phone with my mother explaining what happened all over again.

"Your mom's okay now."

"What do you mean now?" I asked.

"Oh, she just had to have this old murder thing explained to her again. Done. All better."

I hugged my buddy for just being her; then we broke from the hug, and I pulled out the list

of neighbors with their friends and family who were invited to the Fourth of July party. So, with no idea who might have done the deed of killing Tom Solo, we decided that we needed to interview all of them ourselves and whoever had a beef with him. We started today, but silly me didn't want Zanders to know what we were up to. The first house we went up to we ran smack dab into the two junior detectives, Allen and Edwards who work closest to Zanders, doing their jobs. That was a bust.

MARY AND I BOTH were called in to take a lie detector test. As suspected, we both passed. Yet the police kept knocking on my door asking the same questions over and over again. I also had to go down to the station regularly. I'm sure others had to, too. As irritating as it all was, the police were just doing their job. They had a murder to solve. *So, did I!*

The problem was this little Midwest town didn't see a lot of crime, let alone a murder. The town had all the amenities of a big city with a fire department, police department, with detectives, a nice sized courthouse with a nice sized jail, two hospitals, several schools, a couple of large shopping centers and everything a bigger city has to offer, but not the crime. In such a case as murder, they had to use the resources available in the big city surrounding us.

In walked Detective Zanders, who was a striking man with good, rugged looks who probably has more years in his face than his age. Very slight graying appeared around his temples. He's very attractive. I guess him to be in his late 30's. He has interviewed me from the first night on. A lot! And here he was again, leaning on the doorbell.

"Yes Detective?" I asked, swinging the door open. "What now?"

"Where were you the night Tom Solo was killed?" he asked.

"Look Detective, your questions are redundant as are my answers. I refuse to respond to the same ole questions and giving you the same ole answers anymore so I wrote it out in different languages. I also answered in the same languages," I said, as I handed him the two sets of papers. "You can now read the questions and answers in English, Spanish, French, German and Mandarin etc. It all says the same."

"Clever," he said, and then it dawned on him, "Mandarin?"

"Okay not in Mandarin," I confessed. "Look, I took a lie detector test and passed both times. I answered every single question the same every single time from the first night on and," I said, "that's why I wrote the questions and answers in French, Spanish, German, and English so you would have a better, clearer, and more precise understanding of my answers to your questions.

Look." I pointed to the sheets of paper in his hand.

"I'm glad you find this so amusing," he said, adjusting his stance from one foot to the other, starting to show a little agitation.

"I just don't know how else I can answer the same thing over and over again," I said, "Or how many times more."

He got a call and nodded to Dora, passing her coming in while he left. She brought back our lunch and handed it to me. I complained to her about the constant interrogation that I was getting and hardly anyone else was now.

"I think Detective Zanders considers you a person of interest and not necessarily in Tom Solo's murder case. The interest is you." she said.

"Hmmm," I said. "He does have that Tom Selleck 1980s Magnum thing going on, without the mustache. He does have that certain *je ne sais quoi*. But, I . . . no way, no how can I be interested in him."

"But you're thinking about him."

"Nope, nope I'm not."

CHAPTER

6

SINCE DORA WAS HERE so much, Zanders got a two-for-one just about every time he came by. He was often accompanied by his junior detective partner, Alex Edwards, who appeared to be younger by about ten years and more my age. Clearly Detective Zanders was the lead on murder investigation, but the department was out in full force working every angle they could think of. I felt the pressure lifting with each of his visits with me. Dora felt it too.

She and I went out almost every day ourselves with a list of people who were at the Fourth of July party. We took Jeffey in a stroller that turned into a two-wheel tyke bike, so he could peddle or ride while Karen Anne ran a head of us. When Mike was home he wanted to care for the kids, so I often had free time to investigate then.

Dora and I were sitting in the back yard going over the suspect list as we now referred to it when we watched one of our friends, Sherrie, with her daughter, Grace, walking through the gate towards us. Karen Anne was swinging with Jeffey on the new swing set, and Karen Anne let out a shrill scream of excitement when she saw Grace. The giggling intensified a couple of octaves.

We were talking in general conversation about the kids starting school and the upcoming teacher's conference next week. School would start the week after that.

"Sherrie, I know you have to be tired of me asking, but can you remember anything new about that night Tom was killed? Anything else at all that could get this case moving forward."

"Oh, I don't know. Who would want to kill Tom?" she asked.

We looked at each other laughing and said, "Who wouldn't?

After thinking, Sherrie repeated the story to us the same as she had told the detectives several times already. She couldn't think of anything else. She put her head back to face the sun, and it looked like she was asleep. We sat there in silence listening and watching the kids.

"Wait," Sherrie said, sitting up straight. "I didn't think it important then and it probably isn't anything. I heard a horrific scream and ran out to the side of the house. I saw Mary all crumbled on the ground and Tom lying there not moving. I checked him, and he wasn't going anywhere so I went to Mary, and while I was holding her in my arms before the police came, I felt something and looked around and saw a tall figure in the shadows on the other side of the fence. When the sirens got closer the figure disappeared."

We looked at each other. "You didn't tell the police?" I asked.

"No, I only just remembered about the tall shadow. It just now appeared in my mind's eye. I'm sorry. I was remembering holding Mary, and, and it just now appeared to me so vividly. I'm sorry." She said, over and over again.

"If you told the police now, they would think you made it up. It's been weeks since Tom's murder. Zanders wouldn't believe you now and would probably arrest you for aiding and abetting."

Tears streamed down her face. "What do I do?"

Sherrie was upset with herself for just now remembering a very important detail. She wondered if she should mention it to Detective Zanders or not. She was in turmoil. Then she stood up and said she had to go home and think.

She had to ask her husband what he thought she should do.

"Sherrie, I think you must tell Detective Zanders" I said.

Dora chimed in, "If you tell Zanders, he'll have to put it on record whether he believes you or not."

"You're probably right. I'll think about it," Sherrie said. "Grace, come on, honey, we have to go home and talk to Daddy."

"For Mary's sake, please say something to Zanders," I pleaded, "and for my sake."

She took her daughter's hand and walked across the back yard to her home.

THE NEXT DAY KATHERINE came and got Jeffey to take him to the park for a grandmother / grandson day, and Karen Anne was with her friend Grace for a tea party. Dora wasn't even coming by. I wasn't expecting to have free time on my hands, and thinking what I could do, I headed for Tom Solo's house. Mary Solo was surprised to see me. She still looked as bad as she did the day after her husband's murder. Her eyes had black circles all the way around them and they were still puffy. It was the saddest thing I have ever seen. She stepped back to let me in and offered me coffee.

"Mary, how are you and the kids doing?" I asked, as she handed me a not-so-fresh cup of coffee. It smelled like it had been sitting there awhile on the hot serving plate.

"I know the police wanted us to stay away from each other, but I just can't anymore. I want to know how you're doing."

"The kids are having such a rough time. You know how mean kids can be, and they're mean to mine. They've been in several fights defending my honor. I hate to think what it's going to be like when school starts. And then there's the worry how we are going to survive on no income. Tom was a good provider but didn't save much. He did leave me a nice insurance policy, and we can make it if we watch it. That's if the insurance company gives it to me. They're holding off until the case is solved. Or so they say. I don't see a college fund anywhere," she sighed, looking past me.

"I didn't know the insurance company could do that." I said. "Is there anything I can do to help?"

"No. Maybe bring Tom back."

I didn't understand that. She definitely saw something in him no one else did. I told Mary what Sherrie had said about seeing a dark tall shadow while she was with her.

"Mary, can you remember anything, anything at all? Maybe something will come back to you like it did Sherrie." Mary closed her eyes and tried to search her mind and tried to remember that awful night. At least it was an awful night for her. *And, as it turns out, for me.*

Mary opened her eyes and said, "I was crying so hard I'm not sure what I saw, but I felt the presence of someone. I can't be sure. Oh, I, I smelled a cigar. Yeah, a cigar," she slightly stuttered.

"Are you sure?" I asked.

"Yes, I am sure. Now that I think about it, I can still smell it. Yeah, I'm sure."

"Did you tell Det. Zanders?"

"Well no; I didn't think of it until now."

Mary went on to say she and Tom had another terrible screaming match and were fighting before they came to the party and just about didn't go. Tom was already ten sheets to the wind. She knew she would be embarrassed. But Tom was going to that party come hell or high water. "Wish we had stayed home and maybe Tom would still be alive," she said.

I thought; *wish you had stayed home too.*

She continued, "Tom and I had another fight after we got home. He slammed out the door, and I yelled don't come back. He didn't come back, Sara." she said, sobbing. "Oh God, he didn't come back." She paused again. "I started looking for him and stumbled over him. Oh, my God Sara, it was terrible, just terrible. I'll never forget it."

I held her for a while, and then I told her with a sorrowful hug, that I needed to go. Man, I felt so bad for her.

Though it was a long shot, I walked around the side yards of Mary's and Sherrie's looking for a cigar butt. I went over it with a fine-tooth comb. Not finding anything in the side yard, I slipped through the gate to the backyard. I walked around looking down and moving grass and toys, determined to find the cigar butt or anything that would help clear Mary and me. I need a clue, I shouted in my head. I was so frustrated when Sherrie walked out of her door into her backyard with Grace and Karen Anne.

"Hi Sara," Karen Anne yelled out.

I waved to her and threw her a wind kiss.

"What are you doing, Sara?' Sherrie asked.

"You said you saw a dark shadow by the fence. I asked Mary about it, but she didn't see anybody. However, she smelled cigar smoke. I was looking around for a cigar butt or anything to help."

"The police really scanned the yard and what they came up with was a kid's baseball bat that was covered in blood that they believe was the item that bashed Tom's head in. They checked it out and it belonged to Tom's boys. They found a bloody knife lying next to the bat; that was the knife that was shoved into Tom's heart. I don't think they found anything else," Sherrie remembered.

"I just want to find that cigar butt," I stated.

"I'll help," Sherrie said, and then she told the girls to play on the other side of the yard.

After going over every blade of grass and dog poop, Sherrie found the tiniest of butts. It was brown and about an inch long. "I found it," she yelled with excitement.

I rushed across the yard and looked down. "Or is it dog poop?" I asked.

"I'll go get a sandwich bag," she said, as she turned and ran to her back door. Within minutes she was back handing me the bag.

"Oh crap," I said.

"Nope, I think it's a cigar butt," she said.

I turned the bag wrong side out and picked up what I thought was a cigar butt then flipped the bag back out and zipped it.

"Yeah, its dog poop," I said, disappointed. Just then the sun came out, and I caught the glitter of something shiny close to where the dog poop had been.

"Sherrie, do you have another sandwich bag?"

She ran back into her backdoor and returned. "Here," she said, handing me another bag.

I leaned down and picked up a cigar wrapper that was tied in a knot.

"Hmph! I tie straw covers like this," I said, looking at the wrapper. "Could be something! Oh, did you tell Zanders about your shadow yet?"

"He's coming over this afternoon after lunch," Sherrie said.

"Good, send him my way," I directed.

"Will do."

"Come on, Karen Anne, time to go," I called.

"Oh, do I have to?"

"Yes,' I said, and motioned for her to come on. She reluctantly did but not without kicking dirt with her foot as she lumbered along.

Life is rough!

We had our work cut out for us since so many people couldn't stand Tom. The only reason he was invited to the Fourth of July party was because of Mary. She was a great neighbor. No one wanted to leave her out of the party because of her husband. Everyone always included Mary, which meant they put up with Tom for her sake.

Katherine had just brought Jeffey home and left already. Sitting on the patio watching the kids play, I was lost in thought. I was going to have to try to figure this thing out. Dora walked up, but I didn't hear her or see her as I was so deep in emotions which were making my head spin every which way. She cleared her throat and got my attention.

"We have to step it up if we're going to solve this murder," I said, looking at her.

"What's going on?" Dora said, pulling over a lawn chair. "I thought we had a break through."

"Depends on Zanders," I said, as I straightened my sunglasses back up on my nose. "I asked Sherrie to send him my way."

"Why?" she asked. "He'll end up here sometime today anyway."

That's when we heard a series of doorbells blasting. I stood and reminded the kids not to go out of the yard. Dora got up too and followed me in the house. Detective Zanders did indeed drop by. As he stepped in from outside, I handed him the cigar butt wrapper. He looked at it and said, "What's this?"

"I found it while searching Sherrie's and Mary's yards. Mary had a strong feeling that she smelled cigar smoke that night. I thought it could be a clue, though a long shot."

"A long shot's an understatement. Why didn't I hear about this then and why is Sherrie conveniently remembering a tall shadow now?"

"I don't know, except so much was happening, and so many people were upset and overwhelmed. And you and your cohorts were pretty pushy. You guys scared everybody to where they couldn't think. And . . ."

"And what, Sara?" he asked, giving me a chance to regroup.

"And it's hard to function when you're under a cloud of suspicion. And it's taking so long."

"Sara, we have a job to do and no leads."

"But, Detective, I just gave you a possible clue," I smiled, pointing to his hand. Then I glanced out the window to check on the kids.

"I doubt this is a clue, but I will have the lab test it for brand and DNA. Who knows, we might just get lucky," He said, as he turned toward the front door. "Sara, call me Zack, and one more thing. Stay out of the investigation and let us do our job."

"Okay, Zack," I answered.

He was turning to leave when he did an about face and said, "Okay Zack, what?"

"You said to stay out of it and I said okay."

"Hmph! I can't stop you, but you have to tread lightly. You have to be careful not to interfere with our investigation, and you can't knock on doors. You have to keep me informed," he said.

"Okay."

"Okay what?" he asked.

"Okay, Zack," I said as he shrugged and left.

"But I cannot just stay out of it. Someone, somewhere has gotten away with murder, and I do not like it one bit. Therefore, I cannot and will not stay out of it. I won't!" I remarked.

Dora stood back, smiling with her arms folded across her chest, taking it all in, but, my buddy didn't say a word. Unusual.

CHAPTER 7

KATHRINE, BEING A PROUD grandmother, wanted to be there for Karen Anne's first day of school that finally arrived. The little girl was so excited to get on the school bus for the first time with her girlfriends. Jeffey was beyond sad about his big sister leaving him behind.

The neighbors planned on carpooling, but the girls wanted to ride the bus the first day. Silly us followed the bus. The girls arrived at the school okay and went to their classes.

Katherine was entertaining some of her old classmates and needed to go back home to pull the luncheon together; otherwise she would have taken Jeffey for the day and let me get back to investigating.

Dora was waiting for us when we pulled in, and we started the first of many walks around the neighborhood. We put the little guy in the stroller that turned into the bike, but since he was sad he wanted to lay back and mope and just ride in the stroller. We walked around the neighborhood wanting to catch someone in their yard. After all, Zack said not to knock on anyone's door.

The neighbor at the end of the block was working in her front yard on her fall flower garden. We said, "Hi," and walked right up to her.

"Gosh, Donna, we haven't seen you since the Fourth of July party," I said, but I barely remembered her.

"Oh, I've been around. Just haven't been doing much since the police are around all the time." She looked at me and said, "How are you doing, Sara? I was there and I can't believe the police still have you as a person of interest."

"There's not as much interest in me as before," I gladly said.

"But still," Donna said, "Mike's such a private person and, with just losing his wife, now the police are always knocking on his door, not to mention it blasting all over the TV. I thought Mike would have asked for your resignation." Then, regretting what she had just said, she sorta apologized. "Oh, that came out obnoxious. I didn't mean to sound that way."

"Yet you did," Dora corrected. "That was hateful."

"I'm so sorry. I wasn't thinking." Donna hung her head briefly, but it seemed so fake.

"If you know Mike so well, then you know he thinks Sara's an angel in disguise. Mike knew Sara was the right person for the job and, furthermore, Mike and everyone knows what went down Fourth of July including you. Shame on you," Dora said. *Why is it that no one, I mean no one, thinks I can take care of myself?* Dora always gets caught up in defending me.

"I would like to reiterate what Dora said. Like you, Mike was there and knows I am innocent." I said, trying to keep calm. "I was wondering, Donna; can you remember anything at all that might clear Mary of being a person of interest?"

Dora added, "Donna, please think back and search your memory. Who knows, maybe you will remember something. If you do think of anything, let us or the police know. It could potentially be helpful."

"There was a tall older guy who was watching Tom very closely, but it probably wasn't anything. Heck, everyone was watching Tom and his obnoxious drunk stupor," Donna said. She looked at me. "I'm sorry, Sara, I shouldn't have reacted that way.

Shoot everyone probably thought that way. Donna just said it out loud.

"Call if you remember anything," I said, as I handed her our contact information.

"Will do," Donna answered. "Again, I'm sorry."

We said our goodbyes and walked on, pushing a sleeping Jeffey.

"I don't care for Donna," Dora said

"Why? Because she said what everybody thinks?" I suggested.

"Well, yeah, she didn't have to be so hateful while saying it."

"Hmmm," I mumbled.

Dora and I continued to interview people as neighborly as we could without suspicion. We had to make a lot of trips around the block, and a lot of days were spent just waiting for people to walk out of their house or catch them in their yard. We did a lot of walking and Jeffey loved it. This was no easy task, "helping the police." Clearly, they need help.

CHAPTER 8

THE MURDER HAPPENED ON the Fourth of July, and it's now September fourth, and no one was closer to the truth or solving Tom's murder.

I don't think Mike had any idea that Dora and I were playing detective with Jeffery in tow. Although I mentioned it to him before, it was never brought up. I wondered if I should say anything to him again. He took on a big project that would last a few more weeks and was working long hard hours so he wasn't home all that much. Why bother him with things we were still trying to figure out? I didn't see much of him, but neither did the kids, and I could tell they were missing him.

Mike was still leaving fresh coffee for me in the mornings. Thank goodness for the Bunn Thermos coffee pot. The coffee was always hot and always fresh when I reached for a cup. Apparently, his project was taking longer than he thought or, perhaps he moved on to another project. At any rate when I got to see him on the occasional way to bed, he didn't talk about his work. He mostly said, "Good night."

Clancy, the housekeeper, and sometime babysitter, was still coming in on Mondays, Wednesdays, and Fridays. She was the nicest lady. She often asked me how I was holding up. I would say I was hanging in there, and she would go on with her cleaning. Brief, but thoughtful. I remember when she first came. I was new on the job and was surprised when Clancy showed up. I thought I was to clean and do laundry. Mike forgot to tell me about a Russian-size shot putt specialist coming to clean, so he was surprised when I called him at work to question about some woman claiming to be the housekeeper. He explained that my job was the children and some cooking. His children were priority. Clancy's priority was the house and laundry. And she made it clear every time I tried to help.

Katherine came over for visits off and on, but no over nights since the Fourth of July. She came to give me a breather every so often and watched after Jeffey and waited for Karen Anne to get home from school if I wasn't home on time. It wasn't expected of her, but since she loved being with the kids, it gave me time to snoop.

Katherine still had her love interest that she brought to the pool party. But Jax wasn't around as much as she would like; he seemed to disappear for weeks at a time. She never knew when she would have the honor of his company again. He was a hard man to keep up with. She was still in-like with him, and he always made up to her tenfold when he finally came around. She wasn't sure what and where Jax was during the times he was gone. Not yet anyway. She thought the export business. But since he didn't talk about his private life that much, Katherine could only guess.

Whatever he was into, it took him out of town often and for long periods at a time. She didn't want to be pushy. I think I would be inquiring, but that was me. While things were back to normal for most of the people who were at the Fourth of July party, Mary, the wife, was still under suspicion. Mary clearly grieved for Tom. She said at this time in her life she was glad that she and Tom had children early on as they would remember their dad. They were ten and twelve now. It was hard enough to be under suspicion and have the police hanging around week after week. She was grateful for her neighbors who still stood by her and they all did.

Of course, we hadn't seen the last of Det. Zanders or his sidekicks Det. Edwards and Allen. They were around all the time. It seemed like every time I turned around there they were. They were clearly no further along with Tom's murder than us girls.

Dora and I thought one of the neighbors, Harper Daniels, had it in for Tom. Harper lived two doors to Mike's left if you were facing the front of the houses and caddy-corner to Tom Solo's back yard. They were seen the day before the party having a heavy, heated discussion across their backyard fence. People said they heard them raise their voices but couldn't understand their words. Dora and I would follow Harper while Kate, the neighbor, took the kids home with her. We followed Harper and watched intently. Harper had something going on and we were determined to find out what.

As we had been around the neighborhood many times asking questions, most of them knew what we were doing the first trip around. Some were fed up with our snooping and, since they were fed up, we pinpointed on a couple of them. We thought they had something to hide and therefore we concentrated on them. Suspects. *Our persons of interest.* And that is how we pinpointed in on the agitated Harper. He had become *our* #1 suspect. He was a very mysterious man and we had to find out why.

"What were Tom and Harper so intense about?" I thought out loud, looking toward Harper's house.

"Hmmm, I wonder myself," Dora replied.

One or the other of us would take turns watching his house. The street just slightly curved so we were able to stay in our yard and see Harper's driveway and garage door go up and down.

It was easy for the most part to watch Harper and his activities, which were unusually weird. Our neighbor Kate would keep an eye on the back of his place since she lived where she could see the back of his house. He appeared to have a lot of activity coming and going. What was he doing and how were we going to find out? Hmm! We took turns watching and working on Harper.

Detective Zack Zanders was still nosing around the neighborhood, but we didn't let him know the suspicion we had about Harper.

Zanders followed up on Sherrie's conversation again about the tall dark shadow. I guess he thought that it could be a possibility. Maybe! He said to her, "It seemed far-fetched, like you were reaching to clear your friend Sara when you first told me. Then all of a sudden Mary Solo smelled cigar smoke. It's just all too convenient."

"But it was true then and it's true now," Sherrie said. "I only thought of it because Sara told me to close my eyes and just think back and maybe, just maybe I would remember something, and that's when I did, for what it's worth." Sherrie had tears in her eyes. "It's all true. *It's true.* I am not making this up." She started crying hard. Sobbing with a sniffled, "I don't lie. I don't."

The detective couldn't wait to wrap up with her, so he said goodbye and went straight to Mike's. He just barely missed Dora and me snooping around Harpers garage.

Whew, that was close. Not only that but we just made it back to our yard when Harper came up the street toward his driveway.

"We have to be more careful and watchful when we're snooping, or we might get caught," Dora said, pretending to wrap sweat from her brow from our fake strenuous workout as she knew Zanders was watching us as he walked toward us.

"Just in time, Detective," I said, taking a tissue wiping my brow. "We were speed walking."

"Uh huh!" he smirked.

CHAPTER 9

"So, Detective?" I said, as Dora and I joined him, "How can I assist you?" Then I laughed.

"You can assist me by butting out of this investigation, Mrs. Carlton. Sara." He was not happy. "And do you think you can help your friend Sherrie stop crying?"

I said, "And do you think you can stop making her cry? Sherrie's crying was because of you are always badgering

her." I paused a few seconds, then I continued. "The investigation's taking so long and dragging out and not any closer to being solved. We decided we could help," I said, pointing to Dora who was smiling from ear to ear. "You said not to knock on doors. We haven't. We had no choice but to investigate under the radar. No offense to you, Detective."

"I also said to butt out. But it always falls on deaf ears," he reminded us.

"We helped Sherrie remember seeing a dark shadow of a tall man on the other side of the fence who fled as soon as she looked up and he heard sirens. We know Mary felt the presence of someone lurking, but she couldn't see anything through all her hysterical tears but smelled cigar smoke and we informed you. We also know that Donna down at the end of the block said she saw a tall, older man watching Tom's every move at the party. That's what we found out to date. That's it, Detective."

"I think you're holding back," he suggested.

"Did you find anything out about the cigar wrapper yet?" I asked.

"No, and if I did, it is of no concern of yours," he pointed at me.

"Oh, Detective," I said, but stopped short of saying anything.

"Yes, Mrs. Carlton. Sara?"

"Oh, I was just going to say 'good luck' and I hope you have better luck than Dora and me on finding Tom's killer."

"I talked to your neighbor Donna before, but I better follow up with her on my way out of the neighborhood," he said, as he walked to the door then turned and pointed to Dora then me and said, "Butt out." He started back out the door and stopped one more time and looked at me. "I was wondering, would you like to go out to dinner some time?"

"Whatever would my husband say?" Dora giggled.

"Huh, I meant just Sara," he said, looking at Dora. Then he turned back to me. "Would you like to go to dinner?"

"Well," I stuttered, "Thought I was still a person of interest."

"I'll question you over wine."

"Well, then, that would be nice, Zack."

"I'll call you," he said, and went out the door.

"*What?* Dinner? Zack? What's going on?" My buddy asked me. "When did you start with a first name basis? Are you going to go out with him? You should and maybe you can catch him off guard and ask him questions."

"Oh, for Pete sake, Dora, give it a rest. He only just asked. You'll be the third to know."

I thought, *what just happened?*

"Third?" she asked.

"Zack, Mike, and you."

CHAPTER 10

I called Dora. "You never will guess what just happened," I yelled into the phone. "Zack was just here, *again*. He came by just to ask me out to dinner."

"Zack? Are you pulling my leg? That was quick." Dora stated rather than asked. "Oh, my gosh! Are you going? When?"

"Well," I shrugged, but she couldn't see me over the phone. "He asked me out for Friday, if it's okay with Mike. I haven't been on a date since Jerry," I said, drifting in thought.

"What's the holdup, Sara?" My crazy redheaded friend questioned me.

Still in thought, I mumbled, "Detective Zack Zanders is nice looking in a rugged sort of 1980's Tom Selleck sort of way, I believe he's a bit too old for me."

"No, he's not," Dora argued.

"It did take me by surprise when he showed up at the door when he said he would call me. I don't know why I was so surprised that he asked me, so I don't know yet what I'll do. But if I go, you will be the third to know."

"Whoa horsey who's the first?" She asked. "And who is the second?"

Really! Didn't I just tell her? "Zack, Mike, then you, of course."

"Wonder what Mike is going to say." she said.

"Mike?"

"Your boss, you ditz."

"Why would Mike care?" I asked.

"You are a ditz. He has feelings for you," she said.

"What are you talking about? Mike's too busy to be interested in anything or anyone. So, no way Jose. No!"

"It's so obvious. Didn't you notice how he came to your beck and call at the pool party?" she said.

"That's been months ago, and I have hardly seen him since. He leaves early and comes in late. So, no, he has no interest."

"I have to go. See you tomorrow." She hung up. *She hung up!*

I pushed the on button on my cell and called my neighbor Kate. We have grown close over the summer, and we became even closer friends since the disastrous pool party at her house. She helped out with Jeffey and Karen Anne when Katherine's not available if Dora and I need to sleuth. I told her about Zack and the dinner invitation.

"Whew! I thought Detective good-lookin' was hanging around you above and beyond the call of duty. He has knocked on your door more than everyone else put together. Maybe six to one. You going?" she asked.

"He does come around all the time now that you mentioned it. I thought he knocked on everyone's door as much as this one."

"Nope."

"Hmph! Six to one. Hmmm, I'm just so excited about being asked out. So, I'm going." I said, like a school girl. "I have to talk to Mike to see if he will be home early that night, and if it's okay to have a night out since I haven't had a night out since I moved in here. It depends on Mike."

She paused then said, "Mike, well that's another problem."

"Now what do you mean 'another problem?' I asked.

"Oh, Sara, we have watched how Mike looks at you when you're at church with the family. How he acted at the pool party. Yes, he's enamored with you," Kate said.

"It's not apparent to me, and you girls have to stop imagining things. Like I just told Dora, I hardly see him. He works too much."

"And why do you suppose he works so much? Well, I can tell you. He's torn. If he shows attention to you he might feel unfaithful to his dead wife. So, he works. And you live in his house where he sees you all the time. He has to work to function," Kate took another long pause. "You really need to go out with the Detective. You can drill him for a change."

"More like he'll drill me," I muttered. "I'm not sure I agree with you on your summarization of Mike and his guilt. He's never shown me any personal interest. No interest there."

"You just haven't paid any attention to Mike. And as far as Detective Hunk, I bet you will come away with more than you started with," she went on to say. It was her week to pick up the kids from school so she had to run.

Jeffey came in and said, "I'm hungry, Sara."

"Karen Anne will be home shortly and I'll fix a snack then."

"Okay, Sara," he said, sounding so grown up in his little husky voice.

CHAPTER 11

A FEW DAYS LATER, ZACK called to confirm our dinner date. "We still good for Friday night?" He asked, "It will be a much-deserved evening off, at least for me."

"I haven't asked Mike yet if he'll be home Friday night, or if it will be okay to get a sitter. I'll have to call you back."

"I thought you would have asked him by now," Zack said.

"Not yet Detective. I had to make sure we were on before I said anything to him."

"Call me Zack. And why wouldn't you think we were on?'"

"You're a cop, and I wasn't sure it was cut in stone since things change all the time in a cop's life. I'll call you back, Zack."

"I'll stay by the phone for your call," he laughed.

"Really?"

"No," he said.

I called Mike. "Sorry to bother you at work but I was wondering if you could be home early Friday evening?"

"I can arrange it," he said.

"Good, I have a date with Zack Zanders for dinner."

Silence on the other end. "Mike, are you there?" I asked waiting for his reply. "Mike, are you there?"

"Yeah, I'm here. I'll be home early Friday in time for your big *date*," he muttered.

"Mike, you sound upset; what's wrong? If it's any trouble I don't have to go out. It's just I haven't been out for so long. But I don't have to go." I said.

"No, you're right. You haven't had any real time to yourself, and I should have realized it. No, no, you go." He went on to say. "I just wished . . ." but he stopped short of finishing the sentence. "Talk to you later."

Somehow that didn't go down as I expected. *What on earth?* I thought.

I called Zack back. "Okay, I got it worked out. It's a date. What time will you pick me up?"

"I'll be there at seven."

I was back in the dating game. I called Dora and Kate.

The next thing I knew, Kate and a couple of the other neighbor friends popped in with their kids who weren't in school yet. They were ringing the doorbell, *impatiently.* When I opened the door they practically fell over each other rushing in. The kids went one way and the girls, with toddler Ben, headed to the kitchen. Then Dora walked in all calm and put together, as always.

Since it was mid-afternoon, I started setting out chips and dips on the counter. The group sat around the kitchen island and started snacking and the questions started to roll out.

"Wow, so Detective hunk?" Dora beat everyone to the first question. "I told you, Sara, Detective Hunk was considering you his own person of interest."

"He was hanging around you more than the rest of us. A lot more," Kate said.

"Could be I'm the only one NOT married. I wasn't sure he meant it when he asked if he could take me out to dinner sometime. I thought he was just talking."

"*Right!*" they all chimed.

"Well it's sometime," Kate said.

"Wow," they all said, like moon-sick teenagers making fun of me.

"So, I called Mike to see if he could be home early Friday. Mike almost acted disappointed when I told him why. He hesitated with his answer when I told him I was going out with Detective Zanders. After a pause, he said he'd be home early to watch the kids so I could go *out*."

The girls all looked at each other and Kate said, "You still don't get it, Sara?"

I went, "*What?*" stretching my hands out. "I don't get what?"

"Mike's falling for you, you nut," Dora finished for Kate. "Mike's falling for you," She repeated. "He doesn't want to have feelings for you and that's why he works so much. He's still getting over Lizabeth's passing a year and half ago. Then here you are, right here all the time. This has gotten to be difficult for him." Dora said, with all the girls agreeing.

"Nuh-uh. You guys are dreaming. Mike has never shown any interest. He's just kind to me and loves his kids."

"And you," Kate said, with the other girls nodding yes.

"What are you saying?" I asked confused.

Sherrie said, "He could hardly keep his eyes off you clear back on July Fourth. He was never more than twenty feet from you. He was watching Tom trying to slobber all over you, making a fool of himself. Mike was always close by and ready to defend you, then you handled Tom and Mike back away. We all noticed."

"Well, I never noticed," I said, surprised though by now I shouldn't be. "Now it makes sense the way Mike reacted as he did about my date. But still," I wondered.

"Mike's uncomfortable about being interested in you for all kinds of reasons. All of which he has to figure out before he lets his feelings be known to you. Example: you and Jerry, he and Lizabeth, you're the kids nanny. Is it too soon? Is it not soon enough? He has a lot to deal with for both of you. But now that Mike knows you are ready to date, then he has to figure out what's too soon or will it be too late. A lot to take in," Dora shared.

"Wait a darn minute, how do you know all this stuff?" I asked.

Sherrie went on to say, "We all observed and have been talking about this since the Fourth of July. It's what we figured out."

"Who are we?" I asked.

"Just Kate, Dora, Holly and me," Sherrie replied. "We." She pointed her finger to each one of them.

"You didn't say anything to Detective Zanders or Detectives Edwards or Allen, did you? Did you?" I panicked.

"I don't think so. No," Kate said, as they all shook their heads in agreement. "But any fool could see how Mike looks at you." Kate continued. "Besides Zack's an investigator and can figure things out."

"I now wonder if asking me out was an ulterior motive to check out Mike's emotions and put him on the *Person of Interest* list again. Or was Mike ever off the list if what you girls are saying is that apparent," I started to tear up."

"What? Tears? There's no crying in baseball," Dora giggled. "Don't be ridiculous; Mike was probably never off the list! You worry for not." She swung and missed hitting my arm.

Sherrie, being younger than the rest of us, looked around and said, "What is no crying in baseball?"

"It's an inside joke between Sara and me from back in the day. But to you, it is something Tom Hanks said in the movie "A League of Their Own." We watched it on TV when we were kids."

"Oh," She said. "Do I need to see it to understand?"

"Yes," we all answered. "Try Netflix."

"In the movie one of the women baseball players started to cry and Tom Hanks was basically telling her to suck it up. His quote was, "There's no crying in baseball." Baseball was typically a man's game back then before World War II broke out. Then women stepped in and became the American pastime baseball players while the men folks went off to war," Dora continued with quotes signs, to explain like she was from the movie.

"Oh," Sherrie once again stated.

"Again Sherrie, go on Netflix and watch it. It is a good movie and will explain everything," Kate said.

Meantime, I was thinking Mike should be prepared. But how on earth am I to tell him everyone thinks he's into me and if the detective thinks he is, then it could stir unnecessary feelings or problems for him. And to top it off, I'm dating the detective. I decided I would tell him, but I sure didn't know how or where to get the words that wouldn't sound ridiculous either about me or his feelings for me, or the lack of feeling for me that I am thinking or any of the girls. Would it be embarrassing for either of us? And hopefully Detective Zanders wouldn't see it on Mike's face if it's true. I decided to decide later on what to do. I sure didn't want to sound *full* of myself.

Everyone noticed I was deep in thought.

"What are you thinking about, Sara?" Dora asked.

"I was thinking what on earth I will wear on my date."

"Not so fast," Dora said. "Spill the beans."

"Really, nothing," I smiled, "nothing."

Dora wasn't buying it, and I knew she would definitely ask me about it later.

"Ok, girls; help me pick something out to wear." I said, as they followed me to my room. "I know this is only Wednesday but since you're all here you can help me. I don't want to dress up since I have no idea where we're going. And I don't want to dress down because again I don't where we are going. I want to wear something that can go either way. What do you think of this outfit?" I asked, as I pulled a dress out of my closet that hasn't seen the light of day in, I don't know. Years. I took off the dust cover.

"No, it's outdated," Dora's voice rang out.

I tossed it on the chair and got out several other outfits that ended up on the chair also. Finally, one met with Dora's approval. It didn't matter what the rest of the girls thought, only Dora, mostly because she's the most opinionated and has the biggest mouth.

Since it was September, though it was still warm, the girls agreed with Dora on a green sun dress with white piping with a little white cap sleeve shrug that was still in style. I would wear multi-color heels and hand bag. Though the white after Labor Day didn't apply anymore, I went with the multi-color anyway. There, the job's done.

All of a sudden Dora poured her things out of her bag on to the bed and tossed the bag to me. "Here, this bag will be better."

"No, I don't think so." I tossed the bag back to her.

"Yes, take it." And she tossed it back to me.

"Just once I wish I could win," I said, laughing. "But it is the perfect bag."

Dora didn't want to use my no-name bag and chose a grocery bag to carry her things home.

"Thanks everybody for helping in this *big* decision. Or I should say thanks, Dora."

"Just take the rest of these things to Good Will or somewhere," she pointed to the chair that was full of rejected clothes. "Don't hang them back up. Bag them today and get rid of them tomorrow.

The girls left with their kids, and Dora hung around longer, I am sure, to advise me.

I was fixing dinner when I heard the garage door open. Mike walked through the door. I looked surprised and he looked pleased.

"Wow, to what do we owe this pleasure?" I said, surprised.

He said, "I was able to wrap up early today. The project I've been working on is winding down. I should be home earlier from now on."

Dora raised her eyebrow grinning. After saying hello to each other, she waited until he went to the other room to surprise his kids to say, "I told you so, he's marking his territory," she smiled and said good night before I could respond, but turned and said, "I'll be by tomorrow to help you take the clothes to Good Will." And she slammed the door.

Mike, with the kids hanging all over him walked back into the kitchen. "Where's Dora?"

"She went home. You're in time for dinner. The kids wanted Mexican tonight, so we are having tacos. Can I fix you a drink?" I asked him.

"Tacos sound great, and I will make myself a drink. Chianti for you?" he asked.

"Yes, thank you."

"Daddy, I missed you," Jeffery said, hanging onto Mike's leg as he tried to pour the wine.

"Me too," Karen Anne said, as she ran to jump on her dad's lap when he finally sat down.

Mike asked Karen Anne about school, and they chit-chatted about the teacher and her new friends.

Jeffery put his two bits in about what he had been doing with Andy, who is Jeffey's age. Ben kept getting in our way and knocking over the building blocks, Dad. And he keeps trying to sit in my lap. Dad, Ben's a pain," he said, in his little husky voice.

Mike explained, "You know, Jeffey, Ben's still little and, Jeffey, he's learning from you and Andy. So, he wants to hang out with you now. Isn't that okay?"

Jeffey nodded his head, "Yeah dad, it's okay, but he's a pain."

Mike laughed and said, "Ben will grow out of it, Jeffey."

"Yeah," the cute kid said.

"Dad, I love Sara. Is she in trouble?" Karen Anne asked.

"Why would you ask that? What happened?" Mike asked.

"Well," Karen Anne said, "I heard some kids talking at school. They were saying Sara could be a murderer. That she could have killed that Tom guy. And that Detective comes over a lot."

"Karen Anne, in this country you are innocent until proven guilty, and Sara is not guilty. As far as the Detective goes, he is just trying to find out all he can about the case and he knows Sara didn't kill anyone. He just likes Sara. *A lot.*"

"Really?" Karen Anne said, sounding disappointed. "He likes Sara? Does Sara like him?"

"I hope not." Mike replied.

"Come and get it. Dinner's served." I yelled, acting like I didn't hear one word they had just said and like they were in another room. The kids came skipping in from the hearth room, which was right by the kitchen, while Mike followed.

"Karen Anne has a question for you, Sara," Mike said. "Go ahead Karen, ask Sara."

"What?" Karen Anne asked, as she had forgotten what they just talked about.

"Remember, Karen Anne, you wanted to know if Sara liked Detective Zanders?" Mike continued.

I ignored it.

"Well? Karen Anne wants to know," Mike looked at me, waiting.

"Guys, I hardly know Detective Zanders. I just know him as a detective."

"But you are going out with him Friday. That sounds more than knowing him as a detective." Mike said.

"Well, it's a first date and there may not be a second. I think he wants to pick my brain on Tom's murder over dinner. He's nice enough, even though I think am still on the Person of Interest list. There are a few people on the Persons of Interest list. I believe there's a person added back on that list. Mike, I would like to talk to you about that list. There's a theory and I believe that it's interesting. I would like to talk to you about it after dinner, if that's okay with you?" I asked.

"How many people of interest is the detective taking to dinner?" Mike continued ignoring my question.

"I am sure I don't know," I answered.

Our taco dinner was good and now over. I started cleaning up the kitchen and Mike pitched in. He poured me a second Chianti and fixed himself a second scotch and water. We sat at the kitchen table while the kids were off in another room playing.

"So," Mike asked, "who is this other *Person of Interest*?

"It could be you," I said.

"What?" he asked.

"Well, the police have been questioning me about your feelings for me and do you have enough to kill for me. I think it's a ridiculous notion. I think the dinner is to probe me for information on your feelings for me. So, it should be a cake walk. I definitely don't want you to be a *Person of Interest.* One in the house is enough."

There I said what needed to be said, or did I? Am I full of myself? Oh my God, I should have not said anything. Too late!

"Well, that is an interesting theory, all right. I wouldn't want to give off a wrong impression," he shrugged as we joined the kids dropping the subject.

CHAPTER 12

MIKE MANAGED TO COME home early Thursday night as well, and, as promised, he was home in time for my date with Detective Zanders on Friday.

While waiting for me, Detective Zanders was speaking with Mike and the kids. *No interrogation.* When Karen Anne asked, "Do you like Sara, Detective?" *Out of the mouths of babes.*

Mike immediately glanced at Zack and waited intently for the detective's answer.

"Well lil' missy, I sure think she's interesting and yeah, I kinda like her."

"Hmph," Mike murmured, with a grimace.

They all looked at me when I walked in. Karen Anne said, "You look beautiful, Sara."

Jeffery said, "Yeah"

Both Mike and the detective said, "Yeah" too.

I thanked everyone, gave the kids a hug and said goodbye to Mike.

My date had started. Right off the bat, Detective Zanders reminded me to call him Zack.

We arrived at the middle of the road mom-and-pop Italian restaurant, Lydia's Pasta Place.

I ordered a glass of Chianti as did Zack. We sipped our wine and shared small talk while waiting for our salad. I could smell the aroma of my chicken alfredo fettuccine as the server set it down in front of me.

"I hope it tastes as good as it smells," I said, picking up a piece of garlic toast and taking a bite. "This is a quaint little place. It's wonderful, and it's so charming." I looked around. "How did you find this place?" I asked, now taking a fork full of food. "Oh, this is delicious."

He smiled and was pleased I liked it. "A friend of a friend told me about it years ago. I hadn't been here in a while. I haven't had time. Glad you like it," He said, twirling the spaghetti around on his fork taking a bite. "Hmm, just like I remembered it."

About that time the restaurant owner's son, Gino, came over to greet us. He stuck out his hand for Zack to shake. "Detective, Detective, so nice to see you. It's been a long time," he said, looking over at me.

"Working hard catching bad guys," Zack said, and they both laughed.

"Gino, this is my friend Sara."

"Welcome, welcome," he said, giving me a kiss on one cheek, then the other. "The detective used to be a regular at Lydia's Pasta Place, but he stopped coming in. Now here he is," he said, "Dinner is on me."

"Oh no, Gino, I can't let you do that," Zack said.

"It's my honor. Just don't be such a stranger, Detective, don't be a stranger." Before Gino left our table, he filled our glasses again.

After dinner we finished off the Chianti as we were having the dessert of the day, homemade Spumoni ice cream over ladyfinger cookies. And like our dinner, it was delicious, too.

Zack asked, "So, what about Mike and your relationship?"

Uh, oh. Zack didn't waste any time, I thought.

"First of all, there is not a relationship. It's like I said when you interrogated me the first dozen or two times before. I told you then about the loss of my husband several years ago and how lost I had become. Mike was the answer to my prayers for me to snap out of it with his wonderful children. The children, for the most part, are well behaved, but occasionally they get crabby. I explained to you that Mike worked long hours and I barely saw him. I explained all of this to you before."

"I think things are changing," he said.

"What?" I asked. "Changing?"

"I do believe Mike and the kids are closer to you now," he said.

"Of course, they are. I'm close to them also. After all, I've been around them for months now," I answered.

"No, there's more than that," he said.

"Mike said he will be home earlier for a while. The long project he's been working on was done. The kids are thrilled. That's the change. The kids will see him more."

"What about you, are you thrilled, Sara?"

"What?"

"Are you glad Mike's coming home earlier now?"

Where is all this coming from? Am I that dumb? Men!

"Well, Zack, Mike just started coming home early on Wednesday. So, I really can't answer that question at this time," I smiled. "But I know the kids like it."

I continued with the story in case he missed it the first twenty times I told him on how I applied to be Mike's kids' caregiver.

"His mother Katherine needed to get back to her life, and Mike needed to concentrate on his job. It was win, win. Plus, Mike liked that I was an RN in my other life. He knew I would know what to do for the kids if needed."

"Enough Sara, I know how you got here and I understand the history, but clearly you didn't notice how Mike looked at you tonight," Zack said. "He looked like he wanted to punch my lights out and all the while admiring you."

"That's because he doesn't have to worry about his kids, and he's more comfortable about the whole arrangement of my living there. Up until lately I barely saw him. So, there's no interest."

"You're in denial," he mumbled. "If you don't see it, then you need to open your eyes."

"Maybe you're the one who is reading more into it than needs to be," I said, with a little more disgust than I intended.

"We'll see," he said.

I pretended not to hear. We sat in silence for a few minutes. Finally, Zack rose up out of his chair, tossed the tip down on the table and waved to Gino while he walked to my side of the table. In an old-fashioned way, he pulled my chair out for me and offered me his hand to get up to leave. He was a gentleman that you don't see much these days, only in old movies.

Zack brought me home in silence about 11 P.M. And I must say, over all, it was a pleasant evening. I wondered if the table had been bugged to record our conversation at the restaurant. I've never been paranoid before, but I was wondering the motive for the dinner date. I stuck out my hand to say good night, and Zack leaned in and kissed my cheek and said, "We'll talk later."

"I don't know what more I can add," I said, but thought, *haven't we talked enough now?* "I didn't kill the Neanderthal, Tom Solo, and so far, I don't know who did."

"Good night, Sara," he said, as he turned away from me.

"Good night, Zack."

I opened the door, and Mike was waiting up. Or he was up. And I didn't make a big deal about it. After all it was only eleven.

"How did the evening go?" he wanted to know.

"I hope I took the pressure off you being a suspect. I would like to believe that it was just a dinner. Zack was very pleasant; I was surprise to see he was quite nice."

"Now it's Zack, not Detective?" With that, he said good night and left.

Mike seemed, well, jealous. I don't mean to seem oblivious to his feelings, but I don't think he's as interested in me the way others have mentioned, or am I that oblivious? Duh!

It was Saturday morning, and I was already up when Mother Dora called me for a report.

"How did it go? Where did the detective take you? How did he act? What did he ask you? What did you talk about?"

"Whoa, horsey," I said, "One question at a time. I think I made it clear Mike wasn't interested in me. I told him about Jerry's death again and how it affected me, again. Oh Dora, I really had a good time and a wonderful meal. It was very nice, and Zack kissed me goodnight on the cheek. I stuck my hand out, and he leaned in to kiss my cheek. He was a sweet gentleman." *I paused,* "Mike was up when I came in."

"Well? How did Mike act?" Dora wanted to know.

"Have you and Richard ever eaten at Lydia's Pasta Place? It was so good."

"Yes, and don't change the subject. How did Mike act?" Dora insisted.

I lied and said Mike was okay. "I have to go. Katherine's coming over early, and we're all going out for breakfast."

We said goodbye, but not before Dora said, "This conversation is not over with."

Probably not.

"Gotta go," I replied and hung up.

CHAPTER 13

IT WAS PANDEMONIUM WHEN the kids heard Mike say their grandmother was coming over and we were all going out to breakfast. They were so hyper. Apparently, they had a good night's sleep. And to add to the chaos, Mike thought we should all go to the zoo after breakfast. That did it. There was no possible way to calm the kids down now. The excitement was overwhelming. I was exhausted already, and we hadn't had breakfast yet.

We went to the new IHOP, now called IHOB, that had just opened three weeks before. I recognized Detective Alex Edwards, who came in with another detective, Scott Allen. They were laughing, but I couldn't quite hear what they were saying. As they were being seated, I did hear something about college football. So maybe they weren't here spying on *me*, or perhaps Mike. We ate our pigs in a blanket, drank our orange juice, Mike paid the bill, left the tip, and we headed for the zoo.

We were having such a fun day walking along the zoo path toward Nikiah, the polar bear exhibit, when I notice Detectives Edwards and Allen fifty or so feet back strolling along behind us. Either they were spying on us, or they had a thing for each other. They seemed to like the same things we did. This time I begrudgingly stomped over to them. Mike didn't see me at first and probably wondered, "What the hell?" He watched but kept his distance as he could tell I was on a mission, as did Katherine.

"Okay, numb-nuts," I said. "I let the IHOP thing slide when I saw you, but *now* you're intrusive. What are you doing following us here at the zoo, and don't say you aren't because clearly you are?"

Both detectives smiled from ear to ear and chuckled.

"What the hell's so funny?" I asked. *I am clearly getting back to my old self.*

"Well, Ms. Carlton, we are not following you, but since we are here we thought we would tag along, so to speak." Edwards said. "For appearance sake."

"Appearance sake? What's with you two?" I grabbed my cell phone out of my back pocket and called Zack. He answered. "Yello."

"What is going on, *Detective* Zanders? Why are the two gung-ho detectives following this family and me?"

He knew I was pissed. "What? Put Edwards on," I repeated him with disgust, and handed my phone to Edwards.

When they were done, Edwards explained. "We aren't following you, but," he nodded his head toward a couple of men just ahead of us. "They also had been at IHOP, and it's a coincidence they came to the zoo," which the detectives clearly thought was amusing. They assured me it wasn't me and the family, but the two dick heads strolling in front of us.

"Is that right?" I asked, as I walked more and stomped less returning to the family. I looked over my shoulder at them, and they were still standing there with smirks on their faces.

Mike and Katherine were curious about what was going on, and so I filled them in. We were moving along by the lion exhibit now, and the kids were making growling noises and pretending to be the big giant kitty cat as Jeffery referred to the growling lion. Jeffey had his face plastered against the window growling when the lion charged where Jeffey was standing, scaring the bejesus out of him. While we were trying to comfort Jeffey, I could see out of my peripheral vision the two detectives were on the chase. The two dick heads had just met up with a third guy, and we saw an exchange of envelopes.

"Look," I pointed. We watched in amazement how one detective tackled one guy while the other detective pulled down one of the other guys. But one guy got away and started running our way. Knowing Jeffey was okay in his dad's arms, I instantly clothes-lined the run-away guy and grabbed him as he went by. I flipped him down on the ground and pulled his arm around behind his back and pinned him down with my knee in his back. I held him until Det. Allen caught up. He said thanks and lifted the perp up. Det. Edwards, with his two in cuffs, caught up with Allen.

The detectives marched off as backup arrived helping get the three in the patrol cars. Allen and Edwards nodded their heads and with a smile said, "Thanks Mrs. Carlton for your help. You folks enjoy the rest of the day. We'll see you later."

"Not if I can help it," I mumbled and threw up a wave to them. I turned around to Mike and Katherine who stood there with their mouths open.

"What was that?" Mike asked, putting Jeffey back down.

Katherine concluded I was nuts. "That was dangerous, Sara. What were you thinking?"

"I wasn't thinking, just reacting," I replied. "But now that I am thinking, you're probably right. I had taken self-defense years ago and even taught a class, but this is the first time I used it. I could have done that to Tom, but I was trying to be polite." I said.

"I'm dumb founded," Mike said. "You forever surprise me."

"Nice move though. I would have never done that, training or not. I am impressed," Katherine said, still shaking her head in wonderment.

The kids never even noticed as Karen Anne was busy growling with the lions. And Jeffey had his head buried in his dad's neck. A kid's life!

We continued on around the zoo, and we all had such a good time, even though Mike referred to me as, "Killer," a couple of times, but with a laugh.

When we got home, Katherine got a call on her cell from her beau, Jax. "He'll be back in the states this week," she beamed.

"Katherine, what does Jax do that he leaves the country and is gone so much?" I asked, curiously.

"He's in the import-export business. I'm not sure what he imports or exports. So far that's all he has shared with me."

Hmph, interesting.

Since Jax was a tall thin man, I wondered if he smoked cigars. *Always investigating.* So, I asked.

"Katherine does Jax smoke?"

"I have never seen him light up. Why?"

"I saw a pack of cigarettes on the deck on the Fourth of July and thought they belonged to him since none of us smoke," I lied.

"No, not his," she replied.

"Some people don't consider smoking cigars the same as smoking cigarettes."

"No, not Jax," she said again, as she cocked her head to look at me strangely. "What's going on, Sara?"

"Okay, I'll be up front with you. Someone was smoking where Tom was killed, and Mary smelled cigar smoke when she found him. And Sherrie saw a tall shadow for a brief second at the same time. So, I'm just checking everyone out who was at the party."

Mike turned to see me and listened to the back and forth between his mother and me.

"Thank goodness, it wasn't Jax," she said, with a small laugh. "He doesn't smoke and he had gone home long before Tom was found."

Mike said, "Mother, why don't you invite Jax over next Saturday night for a barbecue. We haven't seen him since the Fourth."

"That sounds like fun. I'll let you know," Katherine replied, sliding her cell phone into her jean pocket. She didn't wait around for the pizza delivery to arrive; she just went home.

"That was curious," I said.

"Not really," Mike said. "I heard her tell Jax she would have to call him back. So, she probably wanted privacy. She's in-like you know."

I smiled at the thought, but then, I wondered, *how about you Mike, are you in-like. With me? That's what I keep hearing.*

Mike caught me looking at him and said, "What's wrong?"

I lied and said, "I'm pleased for your Mother being in-like."

"Yeah, it's not like her. But it has to be good for her to find someone after all this time. Night cap?"

"That sounds good. It's been a hectic day with a wee bit of stress, thanks to the Bowery boy detectives, Mutt and Jeff,"

While he poured our drinks he asked, "What's this about cigars and thin men?" What are you getting at, Sara?"

"I hope Katherine was okay about my questioning her about that," I said.

"She doesn't let anything like that bother her, but I'm curious."

"Oh, it was just a thought. Jax was the only tall thin man at the party, and several people brought it up, is all," I said.

"I didn't pay any attention to tall or thin anybody at the party, *hmph!*" he said.

We sipped our drinks and talked about the day's events and then back to the July 4th party.

"You know Sherrie witnessed a shadow lurking in the dark, and Mary smelled smoke the night of Tom's murder," I shared with him. I went on and told him the rest of the information that Dora and I had gotten so far, though it wasn't much.

"Geez Louise, I didn't know you girls were investigating."

"Yep, we are thinking about getting business cards with all our numbers and names. I think "Sleuthing for Rea. PIs."

"For real?" Mike asked.

"Well, PI doesn't stand for Private Investigators yet," I laughed. "It stands for Pretty Intense. Past Intelligence. Pistol Idiots. Whatever."

We both belly laughed.

"But for real, we are determined to solve this murder. Not for Tom, but for everyone else. I want to find out about the mysterious tall dark shadow. Who is he or she? What was he doing lurking around after the party was long over? And was he the killer? Possibly a witness, what? Then there's your neighbor, Harper Daniels. Apparently, he had a couple of run-ins with Tom, and so we started investigating Harper, though he's far from thin."

"We?" he asked.

"Dora and me, with Kate's help. All we have found out so far about Harper and Tom was that they had quite a few heated arguments. Something wasn't on the up and up. Boy, how we wish we could find out what, and if, indeed, he was the one who killed Tom."

"You are really putting a lot of time in to this, aren't you?" Mike asked.

"Oh, more thought than foot work. I hope not too much time, I don't want you think I am not doing my duties. I try to investigate with Dora when Karen Anne's at school and Jeffey's playing with Andy while Kate watches them for an hour or two. Or I watch them, and Kate and Dora go sleuthing. Or Kate and I go sleuthing, and Dora watches the kids. Or sometimes Katherine comes over to watch the kids, or we all go out around the block pushing the kids in strollers which Jeffey likes. And we research on the internet. We work it out so we can stay on top of it," I rattled off, feeling the wine more than usual.

"I see that, but Mother's helping out?" he asked, as he looked at me with amazement.

"Yes, but she doesn't know exactly what we're doing. If we are shopping, snooping or what? She just loves spending time with the kids."

Thinking to himself he wondered, who is this amazing woman who has changed so much in the short months she has lived here? She's no longer a drab, mousey and quiet nanny, that's for sure. Which he didn't think was so bad; in fact she was cute. But now she's alive, energetic, and an investigator of all things with no bars held. Why heck, he just that day witnessed her take on the detectives at the zoo. Then take down a runner while he and Katherine just stood with their mouths agape, stunned. Sara was different, confident, and outward and downright beautiful. No, not like any nanny he ever knew. And now she's dating *Zack*.

He knew he had feelings for her but didn't realize how much feeling he had until now. Or was Zanders "the great detective" waking him up by showing his feelings for Sara. He knew he shouldn't let Zanders bother him. What would people think, and was he mentally cheating on Lizabeth, the love of his life, his children's mother? What are these feelings he wasn't quite sure he should have now, if ever? Were the police right? Was he that obvious when he looked at Sara? What the heck? I am not ready for this, but yet here she sits across from me talking about investigating Tom's murder, and my feelings are stirring. She is beautiful with her green eyes, her tan skin, her dark blond hair that curls around her face, and that body. He smiled to himself.

"Mike? Mike, where are you? You look deep in thought. Do you have any ideas on this case?" I asked.

He snapped to. He had thoughts all right, but it wasn't about any murder case.

"Yeah, yeah, I was thinking we, you, should focus on anyone at the Fourth of July party who is a tall and slender man or woman." he suggested. He gave himself a head slap and thought, *Well duh! That's what she just said.* He drifted off again and went back to Sara. He had fallen for her. But he had to be careful. Couldn't rush into anything and certainly didn't want to run her off. He would play it safe. Give it some time to see where it would go. *Forgive me, Lizabeth.*

CHAPTER 14

I NOTICED THAT MIKE CAME home early all the next week. I also noticed he was changing; he's chattier and not so serious. He's not so hum-drum just going through the motions. He was more outgoing and alive. The kids noticed it, too.

Wow, Mike was really good looking, especially when he smiled, and he smiled a lot lately. Hmm. I don't know why I hadn't noticed before.

I jarred to when my cellphone rang, and it was Zack. He heard of another restaurant we should try. It was a little place over in the city that was supposed to have great Greek food. He asked if I was up for it for Saturday night. I told him I would check and get back to him.

"Who was that?" Mike asked, then apologized, "Sorry it isn't any of my business." But he could hardly contain himself. On the other hand, he thought, she was the kids' nanny, so it was his business. But on the other hand, she does have a life outside this house. *Wow, I'm losing it.!*

I turned to Mike and said, "That was Zack and he would like to take me out to dinner Saturday night. Do you need me?"

Mike acted strange. He dropped his head for a few seconds then perked up again and said, "Sure, go ahead, I've got it covered here. Enjoy yourself," he said, and walked out of the room.

He is completely indifferent to my dating Zack. He showed no emotion. Darn. And why do I want him to? What's wrong with me all of a sudden?

I called Zack back in private and told him I would be happy to go out for a Greek dinner. He said he'd pick me up at seven.

I joined Mike and the kids to watch a little TV. Mike was quiet, he didn't say a word. I tried to start several conversations but had no luck. He wasn't having any of it.

Mike was deep in thought with his head leaning on his fist staring at the TV. He decided since he couldn't or shouldn't show his interest in Sara yet, *yet* being the key word, then he shouldn't care if she dated the lead detective in the murder case that was changing all their lives one way or another. Just how interested was Zack in Sara? Were his feelings for Sara the same as his? Surely, not the same. If they were, Mike thought, I am going to have to act sooner than later. Man, he wasn't counting on this. And, if he acted too soon, would that put him back on the *Person of Interest* list? Was Zack that interested in Sara? Was Zack a jealous type? Am I jealous? I can't get her off my mind. But I can't act yet, and when I do, I hope it isn't too late.

"Who wants ice cream?" Karen Anne shouted, like we were all hard of hearing.

It woke Mike up. "You don't have to yell, K," Mike said.

"Yes, Daddy, I do. You or Sara didn't answer the first time."

"Yeah," Jeffery said.

"Well, I for one would love to have some ice cream," I said, clearly not hearing her before. "Let's go," I said with vigor.

Mike looked at his watch and said, "Okay then, we're going out for ice cream."

Kids have a way of bringing a person back to reality.

When we got back, I saw Harper getting something out of his white Ford 350 big ass truck.

"What?" I said, out loud. Mike looked at me looking at Harper.

"Mike, watch the kids," I demanded, as I pulled out my cell to call Kate. "Kate, Sara, can you get over here quick?" I whispered in my cell phone.

"What's up?" Kate asked.

"See if your hubby can watch your kids and get over here quick," I said.

"Okay, okay, I'll be right over. This better be good."

"It will be." I hung up and turned to Mike.

"Oh Mike, I'm sorry, I should have asked first if it was okay with you before calling Kate."

"I saw the look in your eyes, and I knew there was no way I would interfere with you, especially after I witnessed what you did at the zoo. No problem, I got the kids."

Kate was there in a heartbeat, and I pointed in Harper's direction.

"What on earth?" Kate said.

Mike watched as Kate and I strolled over towards Harper's house. I was sure he was wondering what on earth? I didn't want to take time to explain to him, so I just waved and strolled off with Kate. We were talking and fake laughing when we walked in Harper's direction.

"Hi, Harper," We both greeted him. "What's going on? Moving out or moving in?" I asked, looking at Harper's F350 truck bed.

"What are you two chicks up too?" Harper asked.

"Oh, we're just taking a walk around the block to try to build some endurance for a marathon we were thinking about getting involved in later this month," popped out of Kate's mouth.

"Looks like you need to walk faster than that to build endurance," Harper snickered.

"Whatcha got there, Harper? Having a garage sale or something?" I asked again, as I walked closer to the bed of his truck. Kate joined me, and Harper rushed over to throw a tarp over the bed to stop us from snooping in the back of it.

"What's going on, ladies? Can I help you?" as he tried to edge us away from the truck.

"No, just walking by," Kate said. "Saw you and thought we would say hi."

"Well, you did, so keep moving," he said.

"Where's Joyce?" I popped out with. "I haven't seen her in a while. In fact, I don't remember seeing her since the Fourth July party at Kate's.

"Joyce left me," he said. "Not that it's any of your business."

"Oh, what happened?" We both asked at the same time.

"Joyce found out I was cheatin' on her, so she left. I tried to convince her it was just a one-time thing but she didn't believe me."

"Oh, poor baby," Kate said, as I elbowed her.

"What?" She asked.

"He was cheating, that's what," I scolded her. "Looks like someone moving in." I looked back at the truck.

"Alright ladies, enough chit-chat. You need to get back to your *endurance* walk," he said, as sarcastically as he could.

"Okay, you don't feel like talking. See ya later," I said, as we threw up a wave and we both strolled off. We went a couple of houses down and ducked behind one of them. Dogs started barking, and we tried to shut them up by speaking softly and calling them by name since we knew them. It worked. We looked around to see if anyone was watching us. We crept along the side of the house for a better peek.

"What's going on at Harper's?" I said.

"Don't know."

"What's he up to?"

"Don't know." I can't see a darn thing," I rattled off.

"I need to walk, so let's go around the whole block this time," Kate said.

I begrudgingly said, "Okay."

As we came back around closer to where we started, we still couldn't see anything. Once again, we walked around the block and Harper noticed. He was for sure keeping track of us.

We went around the block several times, and it ended up to be an hour and a half exercise trip that we hadn't planned on. On our last trip we stopped back by Harper's just to see if he had a change of heart.

"Lookin' good, ladies, but you need to step it up," Harper heehawed, "if your endurance is going to kick in."

Gasping for air, I said, "This is just our first day, Harper." I growled, knowing we would have to keep this up for a while to have a reason to spy on him.

We got back home, and Kate cut across the back yards to her house. I walked in and Mike was standing there with his arms folded a crossed his chest.

I went. "What?" I said, throwing my hands out and up.

"Okay, fill me in," Mike said. "I see you made several trips around the block."

"Kate, Dora and I suspect Harper. He could be the killer. He's into something and up to his neck. We need to find out. This isn't over." I explained.

Mike smiled and started laughing. "Where's the nanny I hired? What happened to the almost shy, timid little lady?"

"No guts, no glory," I told him. "We can't get over the feeling Harper's involved somehow," I said, bending over trying to gasp for air.

"Uh-huh." he smiled.

Mike found all of this very amusing but also intriguing.

"So, what can I do to help? Shouldn't you call your buddy detective, uh, Zack with your suspicion?"

"No, not yet. We have to be sure, and if we do find out what's going on, we don't want the police blowing it."

"The police blowing it? What are you thinking? You three girls shouldn't take this on alone. I wish you would call Zanders. I don't like him, but he's a good cop and you need his help," Mike said. "He won't blow it."

"Well, that's nice of you to say, Mike. Just give us a little more time to investigate. We only just found out about Harper. He's suspicious-acting, and we need more before we go to Zack. We need to, oh, I don't know, more." I pleaded.

Mike agreed to give us more time, but he wasn't thrilled about it. "Luck is with you, and I'll try hard not to talk to your detective. Just be cautious."

CHAPTER 15

It's October, and the Halloween decorations are up all over the neighborhood. All the kids are excited, and my second date with Zack was over. I guess I passed his test *again*.

Kate and Sherrie suggested that we get together for a Halloween party at Sherrie's house, which was one of the biggest in the neighborhood and can hold a lot of people.

I spouted, "Good grief, we haven't solved the last party murder."

She reminded me that we did the Labor Day thing, and it went off without a hitch. She was right.

"It was a smaller number of people that attended," Sherrie said.

"But Halloween means dressing in costumes," I said.

"It will be fun," she muttered. "But this time we have only adults and no children. We'll plan a little party for the kids for another time." We all agreed and started planning.

"We should invite Ryan Paulsen and his wife Renee again. The Paulsen's fit right in. Their daughter Bridget can come to the children's party. The children have become good friends.

"Meantime, Kate, Dora and I have several more tall, thin shadows to check out," I reminded them.

"We don't have any more tall, thin people to checkout. It's redundant," Kate said.

"I know it's tiresome going over the same ole leads. Maybe a party would give us something else to think about," I said. "I have lost five pounds with all the endurance walks! So, I guess it's okay."

"I know how dedicated you girls have been to trying to solve Tom's murder, and, if we can still help, let us know," Sherrie said, pointing to her friend Holly. "I, for one can still babysit for you, so you can concentrate on the case. I'm not into the investigation part of it."

"That's so nice. But I'll have to ask Mike if you still can and see how much time I can dedicate to this crime solving, I'm on Mike's payroll, you know, though he said he trusted my judgement, and he said I wasn't on the clock 24/7. He's home early every night now and we talk more, but I don't want to step on his toes," I said as they all looked at me with a big smile.

"Really?" Kate asked.

"Yes, really," I grinned. "It's comfortable now."

"Comfortable is a good way to express your feelings," Kate said, winking as she got up to go pick up the kids from school.

Karen Anne just got home from school and was waving at Jeffey and me as we walked across the yard from Sherrie's to meet her. I was surprised Mike was home already. He didn't hear us come in, and he looked like he was deep in thought. I found out later that some of his deep thoughts were of me.

I've also been studying him a little too often. I have to be more careful as I was almost caught watching him several times. I think I'm falling for him. I just know I couldn't pursue him as I had to give him time to get over Lizabeth. I knew a lot of his deep thought was of her. He was struggling to move on. When he wasn't deep in thought, he was a happy guy.

Zack hadn't called for a date lately but did come around to ask tons more questions. I think he was thankful in a small way that we were "sleuthing" and feeding him ideas, such as they were. He totally dropped me off his *Person of Interest* list. The truth isn't hard to remember. He knows I am innocent and knew it long before he said he took me of the list.

It has been over three months, and the leads were further and further apart. So, we three sleuths needed to step up our game. It's been awhile since we were told not to knock on any doors; maybe Zack forgot he told us. So, we went door to door talking to everyone again.

Some of the neighbors were curious as to why it was our business to investigate a crime the cops were doing.

"We're just helping them. If we find out anything we missed before, we have no problem giving the information to them to follow up on," Kate said.

"Aren't you dating that lead detective?" I was asked. "That should clear your name," she smirked.

"We had dinner twice. They were more like business dinners. He was picking my brain, so to speak."

"Sure, sure," she grinned a Cheshire cat grin.

I put my hand on Dora's arm to hold her back and calm my protective mother down just as she was about to say something to the neighbor for being so flippant. It worked, but Dora grunted and said "We're not inviting her to the Halloween party."

"*Dora*." I said. "Be nice."

"She wasn't," my redheaded friend said.

"Sticks and stones, kiddo. Sticks and stones," I laughed.

Walking to the next house, I started thinking. *So, half the neighborhood thinks Mike has a thing for me, and the other half knows I had a couple of dates with Zack. Oh Brother!*

We walked to the house just across the street and at the end of the block. Susan and her husband Troy were working in the yard and waved. We waved back. "We'll be over later," Kate yelled to them.

On the second knock, Karla and Glenn Frederickson both came to the door. They invited us in, and we talked about the upcoming Halloween party before Kate said that we wanted to pick their brains about the Fourth of July party once again.

"I know this is getting old, but is there anything you can think of that struck either of you as strange?" I asked.

Glenn said, "We told the police everything we know or could remember. So, no, but we look forward to coming to the Halloween party."

"I can't help but remember there was this older man watching Tom a lot. We didn't think it strange as everyone was fed up with Tom's behavior. We knew most everyone there, but we didn't recognize this guy. He must have been a guest of one of the neighbors," Karla said.

Then Glenn said, "I remember that guy. Wasn't he with Mike's mother?"

"Why yes, Katherine has a new beau. We don't see him much, so we haven't given him a second thought." I replied.

"We saw Tom arguing with a couple different guys. Harper was one," Karla said.

"Yeah, we know that. But who else was Tom having words with?" Kate asked.

"I noticed a couple of guys that were at the party, but after a few minutes they left. They were talking with Tom, and it appeared they weren't happy," Glenn added. "It was at the beginning of the party. People were still arriving when they left. They looked like they wanted to break Tom's legs or something."

"Did you know or recognize either of them?" I asked.

"Nope, they're not from around here," Glenn said. "Meaning, not from our neighborhood.

As we headed down the street, I told the girls maybe Jax was the mysterious tall shadow, and we laughed at how ridiculous that sounded. After all, all eyes were on Tom, watching his absolutely bad behavior. We didn't give Jax another thought.

We wandered over to Troy and Susan Allen's. We were sharing pleasantries and talking about the upcoming Halloween party when Det. Scott Allen walked out of their house.

No way!

"You remember my brother Scott?" Troy asked.

I never connected the dots before. He's the Mutt of Mutt and Jeff, and the brother to Troy.

"Nice to see you again, Mrs. Carlton. You been to the zoo lately?" Scott laughed. "Oh, thanks again for your help on apprehending that drug dealer."

"I didn't know he was a drug dealer," I said, surprised.

"Oh, they were small time, or more cops would have been there, but we didn't need them with you there, Ms. Carlton. We'll just call you for back up from now on." He just heehawed.

With Dora and Kate listening, he told the story to Susan and Troy, laughing out loud about how I chewed him and Edwards out, then slammed the perp down on the ground. "It was so funny," he said.

I also found out that Mutt and Jeff, otherwise known as Det. Alex Edwards, and Det. Scott Allen, were cousins as well as being each other's sidekicks. Will wonders never cease? And each one took turns working with Detective Zack Zanders.

CHAPTER 16

We walked home via Harper Daniel's house. His whopper F350 was there but nothing was in the bed of it. Harper was closing his garage door. He walked back out toward us when he saw us.

"Ladies, how are you today? Sorry for my rudeness the other day, but you know some things are private. And I thought you a little nosey. If you have something on your mind, spit it out." Harper said.

"We did spit it out, and you said we were a bit too nosey," I stated.

"What's on your mind?" he grunted.

"As a matter of fact, there's a question I would like to ask you, Harper. We were curious to know what you and Tom were fighting about before Tom was murdered on the Fourth of July."

"Well, now there you go again, being nosey. Don't see as it's any of your business," he replied.

"You asked what was on our mind and that's it," Dora said."

"It was personal," he shouted, getting angry.

"Well, Tom was murdered and that's everyone's business. We just want it over with," Kate responded.

"What's that got to do with me?" Harper burst out in laughter. "I didn't kill him."

"We are checking everyone who had a run-in with Tom. You know they still suspect his wife, Mary," I went on. "So, it is very important to check out everyone. You did have an argument with him, and I would like some information whether it's my business or not." I was getting angry myself.

"Hold on there, toots. It is no big deal. He owed me money and I wanted to collect." He didn't have it, *again*." Harper said. "So, we argued."

"How much money did he owe you?' Dora asked.

"Well, again, it's none of your business, but right at fifty grands." He yelled, looking at all three of us.

"Well, why on earth did he owe you that much money?" Dora questioned.

"A little business venture, and that's all I am saying for now. You ladies have a nice day." He turned and walked away.

"But," I yelled after him.

"But nothing," he yelled back. He walked back to his garage and opened the door. Now we know why his truck bed was empty. He emptied it into his garage.

"Man, I would love to know what he is hiding in there." I said.

"Me too," Dora said.

"We'll have to watch for Harper to leave," I said. "Then sneak over there and check it out."

We got back to Mike's, and Kate walked through the house saying hello and goodbye to Mike and walked across the backyards to her home. Dora also left without coming in.

"So, what did you girls find out?" Mike asked.

I told him about the exchange between Harper and us just now.

Mike said, "Where's your side kick, Dora? I haven't seen her in a while."

"Ah, she had to get home and pack."

I explained to Mike that Dora was going out of town to visit her parents in Cleveland. Then I went on to tell Mike who we talked to.

"You're suspicious about Harper? So, when are you planning on checking out his garage? Mike asked.

"Soon."

"You have to?" He didn't sound too happy about it.

"Well, *yeah*, got to. We'll check it out the first thing when Dora's back in a few days. When she's back we'll figure a way to see inside his garage. But we have to be very careful. Meantime, Kate and I can keep an eye on Harper," I said.

Mike was grinning from ear to ear, then said, putting his hands to his ears, "I don't want to know. Though I'm getting a kick out of you and your friends snooping around like real detectives, but didn't I tell you to call *Zack* for help?" he emphasized Zack's name, loudly.

"I'm helping *Zack* as are my friends and unless he arrests us, we're going to get to the bottom of this. I myself don't want Zack's help, yet"

"I just want you safe," he said.

"Why Mike?' I asked, "Why do you care if I'm safe or not?"

He thought for several seconds and smiled, "Who else will I get to watch my kids?"

I was thrown completely off guard with that statement.

He thought, *Clearly Sara wasn't expecting that kind of comment.* He chuckled to himself.

"Funny, Mike." I paused, and then said, "Dora's got my back."

He smiled, but then got grim, "That's what I'm afraid of."

"She's had my back all these years, and we made it just fine. Oh, there's going to be a Halloween party. Will you be able to go? I believe it is going to be an adult party. Sherrie's still planning it. I will stay with the kids, so you won't have to worry." I said.

"Wait a minute. We'll get a sitter. You and I will go

together. It'll be fun." Mike said.

"You wait a minute. You pay me to sit, and now you will pay someone else to sit while I go to a party without the kids?" I questioned.

"Well, I will deduct that couple of hours from your pay if that makes you feel better," he laughed. "When you sleuth, I don't mind because I am home, and I need that time with the kids. Otherwise, you trade off sitting with your friends. So, it all works out. I don't mind at all how you work it out. I just know you make sure the kids are covered. And I know you don't sleuth that much on my dime. One more thing, Sara, no one expects you to work 24/7."

"Don't you think this is a somewhat unusual arrangement? You pay me to take care of your children, and then I come and go as I want," I said.

"Well, all I know is, you always have the kids' best interest at heart. And you shouldn't have to be on the job 24/7. So, if you aren't gone too long at a time, and Jeffey's with one of your friends, or you have him with you, it works out. You're always home by the time Karen Anne comes home from school. I don't see a problem. So, I'll get a sitter, and you and I will go to the Halloween party together. Is that okay?" Mike asked.

"Yeah, if you want," I concluded.

"I want," he said.

We went to join the kids, who were watching the Halloween movie, *It's a Great Pumpkin Charlie Brown* and Jeffey's eyes were so big with excitement. Karen Anne was teasing him about being a ghost. And when a little fight broke out, Mike stepped in and told them if they couldn't get along, the TV would go off. They hugged each other, and the TV stayed on.

I got everyone a snack, and then it was bed time. We put the kids to bed without a story as they both were so tired.

Mike and I went back into the family room and talked about my bossy buddy, Dora, and how much she means to me. I told him how she absolutely drove me nuts early on in our friendship, but, as time went on she became my protector, and our friendship blossomed from then to now. I told him that Dora was a better sister than my real sister, who I hardly heard from or barely saw.

"My sister and my relationship have never been that great. But my brother and I are close. My brother and Jerry were best buds, and we did a lot with him and his family. He now has two sons, William and David. They are cute boys but ornery as they can be. Bill got a promotion and sarcastically transferred to Denver, so I don't see them all that much now, maybe twice a year. But we talk all the time. It's the same with my mother and dad. I miss them all even mean Jean, my sister. I am the only one who stayed here in Grandville. I had no reason to move. I guess I want to stay close to Jerry."

"What business is your brother in?" Mike asked.

"He is an architect with Smithgreen and Dawnitt, but they had more business in Denver and surrounding areas than here. So, they just moved the firm to Denver. They only have a small satellite office here now. Bill was one of the key players, so he moved. I think that's why Bill and Jerry were so close and had so much in common. Both were architects, though different firms."

Mike smiled and listened to me with interest, but since he didn't say anything, I asked him about his mother.

"Well you know my mother. She looks one way and acts another. She confuses people all the time. She and my dad were so much in love, the real thing. Everyone thought they were the perfect couple," he said, leaning back in his chair.

"I almost had a brother when I was three. He was stillborn, and the doctor told my mother she shouldn't get pregnant again. It would be hard on her. So, she gave up on having any more children. Sure would have liked having a brother. I guess it wasn't meant to be. So, I am an only child but not treated as one. I had a great childhood. Mother was the same then as she is now."

"My dad, on the other hand, was strict with me and I didn't always like it, but I managed okay. Though dad was strict, he was there at every football, baseball, and basketball game throughout the years. When I was 16 he helped me put in a transmission in my old 51 Chevy pickup truck. The old classic was my first vehicle. We should have paid to have the transmission put in, but dad wanted us to experience a manly thing and work on it together. Boy, that was fun, and I learned a lot and so did Dad. But we never got it running and ended up paying for a transmission being put in anyway. I drove it about a year before it gave out and we gave up.

"I do have a lot of good childhood memories. Mother was devastated when my dad died of a massive heart attack a few years ago. We all thought she would collapse, but she held it together for me. After a year or so, she bounced back as you can see. She just decided one day that life goes on.

"I had a lot of cousins and friends growing up. Of course, I have a longtime best buddy from childhood, Ray Williams. He's like Dora is to you, but he moved away to Idaho before Jeffey was born. We went back and forth to

Idaho, and he and his family came back here too, until Lizabeth got sick. We couldn't go there anymore, and they didn't want to impose on us while she was trying to get well. I haven't seen him since the funeral. We talk about getting together all the time but haven't yet. Maybe soon."

"Wow!" I said. "You and I haven't ever had this kind of conversation before. It's nice to see this side of you."

"Yes, it is nice to share above and beyond, but I'm beat." He said. "It's time for bed."

He got up out of his chair and started walking away, and he turned and said, "We need to make plans for that Halloween party."

"Okay, like what?" I asked.

"That's why we need to make plans is for what," he laughed, heading for his bedroom.

I was confused about what Mike just said, but since I couldn't get him to elaborate about it, I decided to just sit for a while longer and enjoy the fire Mike had started after dinner. I reflected on my life watching the fire go down to a flicker. I dozed off thinking of Jerry.

I awoke two hours later and forgot where I was for a minute. The fire had gone completely out, so I turned out the light and headed for my bedroom falling into bed where my eyes popped back open. I pulled out my old diary again and skipped ahead to a favorite part.

Dear Diary,

Today was one of the most special days of my life. Jerry and I went on a hiking trail and had a little scare when we spotted a couple of bear cubs playing. We stood perfectly still watching them frolic. Though it was really cute, I have to admit I was clearly not comfortable. A bit of fear hit me. Finally, the momma bear came and scolded her twins and led them away. I guess that bear repellent worked. She didn't smell us. It helped that we were at a good distance away from them. When we felt it safe again, we continue the climb up the hill. We reached a clearing where a large arbor covered in yellow and white daisies with streams of yellow ribbon blowing in the wind. In the middle of it was a round table with fine china sitting on a white table cloth. Wine was sitting off to the side chilling. Three Violinists were playing softly while a gentleman seated us and brought out duck under glass. He poured our wine. I was surprised and couldn't find the words to say anything. Finally, Jerry got down on one knee and the violinists switched volume and songs. Jerry reached under the table and pulled out a little box and the music went louder "Come Fly with Me," followed by "You Light Up My Life." Tears filled my eyes when Jerry said "Sara, you light up my life. Come fly with me and spend the rest of our life together as my wife."

"Oh Jerry, I will fly with you, and you lit up my life from the day you walked into it. I will."

He slipped a beautiful engagement ring on my finger. I held out my hand and kept looking at the sparkly diamond. It was the most special day. Good night, Diary.

I closed it and put it back into the drawer. There's something about reading my diary that makes me feel so good. After reading a little of it I am either sad or happy. But almost always can sleep. *Almost always.*

CHAPTER 17

DORA CALLED ME THE next morning, and I told her how relaxed Mike had been the night before.

"We had such a good conversation. I never knew he could talk so much. Mike's getting a sitter for the kids so he and I can go the Halloween party at Sherrie's."

"Mike's finally making his move," Dora said.

"Oh, for Pete's sake Dora, it is just a Halloween party. There's no move. I'm just not seeing what you guys are seeing," I said.

"For someone not seeing what I am and everyone else is, you sure get frustrated when we mention it."

"You, and even Zack, read too much into his kindness." I said. "But I am looking forward to the Halloween party. It should be fun. It's a costume party. You guys are coming, right? Oh, the kids are up. Gotta go but think about the party." And I hung up.

Just then the phone rang again, "I have things to say so hear me out and don't, I repeat, don't hang up on me again," She said.

I pushed the off button and said, "Hi kiddos. Breakfast is almost ready. Eat up and then I will help you get ready for school, Karen Anne. So Jeffey, what to do want to do today?"

"I want to uh, I want to uh, go to the park and uh, see my buddy, uh, Spencer. Can we take Andy?" Jeffey finally got it out.

"Well, I will check with Kate. Maybe she can go too." I replied.

I called Kate to see if she and Andy would like to ride along to take the kids to school and then go to the park. And she said they would.

We dropped off the big kids at school and headed to the park with the little ones.

"Wait!" Kate said. "That's Harper? Who is he talking to?"

We pulled around for a better look. We circled around again. Andy and Jeffery were singing along with a Tim McGraw song, "*I love it, I want it, I want some more of it. I tried so hard, I can't rise above it.*" Good beat. I was glad the boys didn't understand the meaning of the words they were singing.

We tried to see who Harper was talking to, but every time we thought we could see his face he would turn away from us. It was so frustrating. Finally, we got to a parking spot that we could get out and be rather close to Harper. We started walking to the playground and circled around to a swing set closest to Harper. He and the guy seemed to be arguing, but we couldn't understand their words.

"Did you see that?" I asked Kate. "That guy just handed Harper an envelope. Watch the boys a minute."

I threw the ball over by Harper, who ignored it. I acted like I was chasing it down. It landed close to the men, so I ran over and bent down and picked it up.

"Oh hi, Harper." But the other guy had turned and walked towards the parking lot so I still couldn't see his face, but something looked familiar about him. Tall, a little thin, but I couldn't tell who it was.

"Well, fancy seeing you here, Sara. Day at the park, uh?" Harper smirked.

"Yup, the boys wanted some park time," I said, pointing to the boys.

"Who's your buddy?" I asked.

"None of your business. You don't know him. Gotta go." Harper turned and started walking away sliding the envelope into his pocket. He yelled back to me, "You have a good day now. And quit following me."

"But I, I'm not fol—" I yelled after him, but he was already in his big hunk truck.

I was bewildered and disappointed in that bit of a conversation. Harper completely shut me down. I went back to Kate and the boys with disgust on my face.

"What just happened, Sara? You look like you were hit with the ugly stick."

"I was and his name's Harper. He just cut me off like a pro."

I told Kate what was said, and that I couldn't get a look at the tall guy's face.

Jeffey's new buddy never did come to the park. We let the boys play for a little over an hour then headed for McDonald's. The boys loved it.

Just as we got our food, Detective Zanders walked in. He saw me then looked over at Kate and the boys, and smiled, "What are you guys up to today?"

I started to explain leaving out the part about Harper.

He laughed, "I saw you trying to pump Harper at the park. It doesn't look like you got much."

"You were at the park? I, we didn't see you." I chimed in.

"That's what surveillance is. No one's to know you are watching them. We have been watching Harper ever since you told me about him. It's a good lead, but I can't find out anything on the other guy. I didn't recognize him, but he was older. I, however, really enjoyed watching you try to get information from him," he smiled.

"But I didn't tell you about Harper," I said.

"You didn't come right out and tell me about Harper, but it didn't take a brain surgeon to figure it out," he laughed.

"*But!*" I sputtered.

I asked him, "Did you see the envelope pass between the two men? Do you have any idea what was in the envelope? Money or dope?"

Zanders raised his eyebrows when he read who was calling him on his cell. He answered it and turned his back and, while walking away, he threw up his hand in a wave and left.

Kate noticed how Zanders looked at me. She gave me a nudge in my ribs and said, "The hunky detective can't keep his eyes off you. You are so lucky, Sara. You have two men who are clearly interested in you. Detective Zanders' more like Tom Selleck when Tom was in his 30s including the mustache, and, Mike, who's more like Chris Hemsworth without the Australian accent but with the blond hair and chiseled chin. Both are hot in their own right, in every way. I would love to have your problem."

"Well," I replied, "Zack isn't as tall as Tom Selleck. I can see where Mike favors Chris Hemsworth. Both guys are hot. I can't figure it out why, in my life, I have one guy interested in me, let alone two. And I know Mike is slowly coming around. He is showing more interest without feeling guilty now. But he's still careful. I still don't see what you and Dora do."

"Oh, Sara, you are blind if you can't see what we all see with Mike having feelings for you. Blind!"

"I guess I am then. Did I tell you Mike's getting a sitter for Halloween? He wants me to go with him to the Halloween party. I have to say I am looking forward to it."

"No, you didn't mention you and Mike are having a Halloween date".

"I think we are just going together but not as a couple dating." I went on.

"Right!" Kate mumbled. "Blind."

We called the kids from the play area to come on and headed for home, but not before picking up Vicki and Karen Anne from school, that got out early for a teacher conference.

Karen Anne didn't act like she felt good. She wasn't talkative, and she wasn't her bubbly self. When we got everyone home and I checked on Karen Anne, she started coughing and was running a slight fever. I gave her some soup followed up with baby aspirin and cough syrup. She lay down and went to sleep.

I called Mike to tell him about Karen Anne and what I did to help her. Mike said he was sorry his daughter was feeling so bad, but he knew she was in good hands and he wasn't worried.

I thanked him and went back to check on Karen Anne. I felt her head. It was still a little warm, but she was sleeping soundly, with an occasional cough.

A little later Mike walked into the house and gave Jeffey a big hug and kiss. He asked how his day was and Jeffey told him all about it. Mike went to check on Karen Anne. She was just waking up but sounded worse and hoarser. I checked her temp again and it had gone up a degree. I was getting a little worried as she hadn't improved. I doctored her up again and Mike sat with her for a while. I was able to get her to drink some chicken broth with a couple of crackers, and she went back to sleep.

Mike and I took turns checking on her. She was as comfortable as a sick little girl could be with coughing.

In between, we paid a lot of attention to Jeffey who was clearly worried about his sister.

"Is Karen Anne going to be okay?" he asked me.

"She sure will. She is going through the worst of her cold now, but she will be just fine," I answered.

"Yeah," he mumbled.

I sat up with her all night so Mike could sleep as he needed to go to work. He checked on both of us a couple of different times through the night. Sitting in a lounge beside the sick little girl, I must have dozed off, as I woke up with the touch of a blanket going over me. Mike whispered, "Karen Anne's sleeping, so close your eyes and rest, Sara."

For a couple of days, I slept when she did. Thank goodness Katherine took her grandson to her house for the next few days.

Just as I thought Karen Anne was getting better she had a coughing fit and her temp spiked with her nose drippy like a faucet. I held her and gave her more warm chicken broth. She felt so bad I was a little afraid it was turning into pneumonia, but it didn't as her fever finally broke. She hated she had to miss school and her friends. I told her that school and her friends would still be there when she got better.

On the fourth day Karen Anne was on the mend. It was Friday, so if she continued on the right track, she would be back to school and her friends Monday.

Mike said, "You went way beyond your duties, and you deserve to be off all day Saturday."

About that time the phone rang, and I answered it, walking out of the room. It was Detective Zack Zanders. "I feel like dinner and a movie tomorrow night. Are you up for it?"

"That would be great. Mike gave me all of Saturday off. Dora's back from vacation so I'm going to call her to spend the day with me. It's long overdue."

"I'll pick you up at five so we could go the movie then dinner or vice versa," he said.

"What movie would you like to see?" I asked.

"You decide. I don't have a clue," he said.

I told Mike of my busy day. He was glad I could spend some quality time with Dora. I was so looking forward to the whole day that I forgot to mention my date with Zack to Mike. *How insensitive of me.*

Dora picked me up after I had breakfast with Mike and the kids. Karen Anne was doing so much better. She was full of energy again with only an occasional cough. Dora came in to say hello and we left for the girl's day out.

Dora and I looked at each other and sighed. "What are we going to do first? We haven't done anything in such a long time that was just us. I want to make every minute count," I said.

We headed for the mall. Dora collected Precious Moments, so we headed for the Hallmark store to see the latest ones. Dora spotted one she had not yet seen so she bought it. It was cute.

We came out of the Hallmark store and ran smack dab into Detective Edwards and Detective Allen as they were just walking by the Hallmark Card's door.

"Are you two following me again?" I asked them.

"No, Miss Carlton, we're not. But we are following that guy over there, and we might need your help again." They both snickered.

"Just let me know," I said, as I slapped Edwards on his back.

Dora wanted to know, "What the heck did that mean?"

"Remember, I told you about what went on at the zoo in the summer. Apparently, Mutt and Jeff haven't forgotten how I took down a runner for them, and now it's an on-going joke."

"Oh yeah, I remember," Dora mused.

I tried to find out who Mutt and Jeff were following but straining as much as I could, I couldn't see who it was yet.

Dora and I went into Macy's to check out their sale. We both liked Macy's. It's one of our favorite department stores.

Dora never passed a lingerie department without looking at underwear. She liked matching panties and bras. Dora's law. Heaven forbid we would be in Macy's and not stop off in the lingerie department. I, on the other hand, thought panties were panties and bras didn't have to match. *Sara's law.*

Dora talked me into buying a couple of matching sets. Not thongs. My ass will remain covered. However, she could sell ice to an Eskimo. I must admit my new underwear was pretty nice. Maybe someday I would actually wear them.

Dora suggested I wear them tonight on my date with Zack. "I double dog dare ya," she teased.

I clearly said, "*No*. Absolutely not."

She smirked, looking me up and down, "I double dog dare ya," she said, again. It seemed there was a lot smirking going on lately.

We moved to the ladies' slacks. Now that's something I could use. My slacks were wearing thin in the seat and outdated. I paid for my slacks, and we started into the general mall area when I saw Mutt and Jeff chasing a rather hefty thirty-something perp. Though the guy was hefty, he was fast. Mutt and Jeff were losing ground. I handed Nora my packages and stepped out just has the guy started by me. I tackled him and brought him down like a lassoed cow, which was feat in itself as he was one big guy. I flipped him over and twisted his arm behind him and then sat on him and waited for the detectives to arrive.

Dora was amazed.

"I just saw a whole new side of you I never knew existed," she said. "Glad you remember how to do self-defense."

"I just started using these skills since those two came into my life," I explained, pointing at the two detectives running up to us while I checked my fingernails.

"Miss Carlton, you saved our butt again," Detective Edwards said, out of breath.

"Thanks, Miss Carlton. Sure glad you're on our side," Detective Allen blurted out gasping for air. "Glad you were here again to lend a hand." Then he went on to say, "Or in this case, your body."

"Well, glad to help, *again.* I just wonder what would you two do if I weren't there to catch the bad guys for you," I asked, as I smiled from ear-to-ear.

"Believe it or not, sometimes we can do our jobs without you," Detective Edwards said, "You sure have been a big help though. It's just hard to explain it in the reports, especially for a second time."

Dora just stood there laughing at the comedy of it all. Detective Allen helped me up and then helped Detective Edwards heave the hefty guy up. Dora handed me my packages.

"Oh, Miss Carlton, you will need to come in to the station to sign the report or at least make sure we wrote it up right, like you did before," Detective Allen mentioned.

"Will do, and while I am there, I am going to punch the time clock. I want to get paid for all this help," I suggested, grabbing my side that was started to hurt from laughing not to mention I twisted my knee in the take down. "Oh, and boys. It's Mrs. Carlton."

They nodded their head yes and yelled, "See you later, and for the record, its men."

I waved goodbye to the dynamic duo and turned to Dora who was clearly entertained.

Now that the excitement was over, and the gawkers strolled away, we thought we would go ahead and grab some lunch. We headed for a little sea food restaurant. I knew Zack would take me for Greek or Italian tonight, so I wanted anything but Italian now.

"Oh my gosh, I love these cheddar garlic biscuits," Dora said.

"Yeah, me too, but butt fattening," I replied.

"I don't care; they're worth it. And I love the grilled plank salmon."

"I think I'll have the shrimp-crab potato casserole. It's new on the menu."

"How do you know it's new on the menu?"

"Uh, it says so," I said, pointing to the menu item.

"Oh yeah, good choice," she chimed in. "It looks wonderful."

And it was.

We finished our meal and went to a flea market nearby. Dora likes to look for older "Precious Moments" that she might not have yet. She found one that she didn't have but decided it hadn't been taken care of very well, so she passed. Then all of a sudden, she spotted a Precious Moments painting she just had to have. Dora collected the paintings as well, though I never once saw one displayed.

"Now this is a good buy," she said.

CHAPTER 18

DORA DROVE ME HOME in time for me to get ready for my date to pick me up. Mike didn't know Zack was part of my day off until the doorbell rang. He answered the door and was surprised to see Zack on the other side of it. Zack nudged himself through the door past Mike and turned to me when he heard me walk toward them.

"You look nice, "Mike said, as he looked me up and down. "New blouse? I haven't seen you in Orange before. Very festive."

"No, no new top. New slacks though." I responded.

"Nice color anyway," Mike continued.

"Thanks."

Finally, Zack chimed in, "You do look nice, Sara."

The two men glared at each other and finally Zack said, "Shall we go?"

Mike looked at me and said, "I didn't know you had plans with," he took a deep breath, "him."

I forgot to tell you I was going out tonight. It's still my day off, isn't it?" I said

Mike said sarcastically. "Don't be too late."

I took a gulp of air and hugged the kids, threw up my hand to Mike and turned and walked out with Zack.

"Well, that was thoroughly awkward. You still don't see how Mike feels about you?"

Until now, I thought. "Mike's just feeling better and more comfortable about me being here. Really, he has never come on to me or showed interest. He just seems more relaxed."

"I find that hard to believe; you're fooling yourself," Zack said. "No one's that naive."

"I'm not naïve; I just don't see him having that much interest in me. *Until now*. We are going to a Halloween party together, but it's not a date."

"Really? What about the kids? Are they going?" he asked.

"As a matter of fact, Mike's getting a sitter."

"A date," Zack snarled.

"Not really, just going together." *Okay a date.*

"Come on, Sara, get real," he said. "Don't play dumb."

"Well, Zack, it's less complicated not to let myself think that way. Okay, if Mike started to have feelings for me, he hasn't acted on it even a little. I just can't go there. Right now I have a *date* with you. What movie are we going to? Or are we having dinner first?"

He said, "Thought we could see the old classic, *Gone With The Wind.* They brought it back for a limited time. Then I'm taking you to a little Italian restaurant that just opened a month ago and is open late. Or do you want to eat first?" he suggested.

"What? No Greek?"

"Italian," he said.

"Of course, it is," I mumbled.

"What?"

"Movie first sounds good. I've never seen, *Gone with The Wind.* I'm excited about seeing it and what a great idea. I had a big lunch with Dora, so I am not hungry yet."

"Good," Zack said. "Oh, and Allen and Edwards said you were recruited today to help them."

I laughed holding up two fingers "Yup, twice now."

Dropping the chitter chatter about the Bowery boys, we headed to the early movie. We got popcorn and coke, and he added butter to the popcorn. A lot of butter. We found seats half way up and, while waiting for the movie to start, we noticed something going on in front of us. Someone yelled, "Help."

Zack and I rushed down to see a sixty-something squeezed between two rows of seats. We went right into action. Zack rolled her over, and she barely had her eyes open and was laboring for breath. She was having a heart attack. I started giving her CPR. "1,2,3, *Staying Alive, Staying Alive, Staying Alive.* 1,2,3, *Staying Alive,"* I sang under my breath pumping her chest. Zack called for an ambulance. In twelve minutes the paramedics reached us and took over. The paramedics told me I basically saved her life.

"You haven't lost your touch, Sara," Zack said. "Good job."

"I couldn't have done it if not for your muscle. You got her in position for me to help. It's been awhile since I used that skill. *Staying alive, uh, uh, uh, uh, staying alive.* That rhythm works every time," I said. "Or every time I've had to use it."

We took our seats and the movie started. I enjoyed the whole thing. As we were on our way to a very late dinner, I put my hand to my head and said, "As God is my witness, I'll never be hungry again."

"Miss O'Hara was indeed dramatic," Zack said.

"Oh, my gosh, Zack, that movie was everything everyone ever said it would be. Good choice. Clark Cable. Hmmm."

"Vivian Leigh, hmmmm," He rebutted. "I enjoyed it too! I did make a good choice," patting himself on the back.

We arrived at Mama Mia's.

"Are you kidding me? Mama Mia's? Really?" I laughed. "How original."

"It's quaint," he said.

We went in and saw it had a theme from the movie "Mama Mia." It actually fit, and it was cute as it could be. Even the servers dressed the part. The music was from the "Mama Mia" sound track, and the servers would stop serving and start singing along with the music that was turned up louder for that particular song, to let the servers know to belt it out at that time. They broke out four times while we were there, dancing along as they sang. It was a fun experience. Zack and I both sang along with the parts we knew. I must admit Zack had a decent voice. He was no Elvis, but on the other hand, I was no Carrie Underwood. I sang okay. Zack knew how to show a girl a good time. He was a fun date.

He walked me to the door and leaned in and planted one square on my lips. *Wow*, I thought. *Wow*. I was surprised. That was one great kiss. I didn't want him to stop kissing me. It was long and tender. And my legs were starting to get weak.

He apparently thought, "Wow" too. We parted and we both smiled. He stepped back. I wanted him to step back in. It was my first kiss since Jerry. It was so nice.

Then all of a sudden, he stepped back in, and I thought the first kiss was great, but this time it was a little passionate. No. It was a lot passionate. Mike's face appeared in my mind. *Woah.*

I stepped back with Mike's face still there. *What's going on?*

"Well, Zack," I said, as I fanned myself. "Thank you for a great evening. I had so much fun."

"The ending wasn't bad either," he said.

I turned and put my hand on the door handle. "Yes, the ending was great," I blushed.

He said, "It will give you something to remember me by just in case I have a chance. I'll be in touch." He smiled a half cocky smile and walked to his car then turned and waved.

I walked through the front door, and Mike was nowhere to be found. Clancy was there with the kids.

"What's wrong?" I inquired.

"Mike was called on an emergency with his job," Clancy explained. "He called me about seven to come over. The kiddos are in bed. Everything is cleaned up and put away. Now that you're here, I reckon I will go. Oh, by the way, how was your date with that sexy detective?"

"My date was a fun-filled evening. I had a really good time," I said, feeling guilty.

"Oh Missy, I don't mind taking care of the kiddos. Mike made it clear that you earned a well-deserved day off after a rough week with Karen Anne being so sick and everything. But I got to tell ya, Missy, he was disappointed that you finished the day off with that sexy detective. He didn't say so, but it doesn't take a blind man to see he wasn't happy. He also told me you had a date with him on Halloween. Well, good night now," Clancy said, turning on her heel to leave.

"Ah, yeah, a date. Halloween. Thanks Clancy. Good night," I said, before she shut the door; then I mumbled, "why would he tell her about our Halloween date?"

I checked on the kids and they were sleeping peacefully. Karen Anne had a book lying on top of her. I took it from her gently as not to wake her, and a picture of her mother fell onto the bed. I quietly took the picture and placed it on the night table facing Karen Anne. Jeffey had his baseball player teddy bear tucked under his arm. I kissed him lightly. He smiled and said, "Hi Sara." Then went back to sleep.

I was wide awake and once again I couldn't sleep. I reflected on my date with Zack and how I enjoyed his company. He knows how to date, but I wasn't in-like let, alone in-love. I thought of him only as a date. Okay, a good date but a friend date. And the dates got better and friendlier each time and then there was the kiss. *The kisses*. They were *wow*. Or was it just that I hadn't been kissed in a very long time? Not since the day Jerry went to do one more errand. That's it! I had just forgotten. Maybe it wasn't so Wow. Maybe I only thought it was and it really wasn't. "Oh, who am I trying to kid? It was *wow*," I said, out loud.

One more very important detail came up. Mike. Why did his face pop up in Zack and my kiss?

Still running the evening through my mind, I went in to the kitchen for an after-midnight snack.

"Oh, I didn't know you were home, Mike," I said, startled when I saw him.

"I just got here. How was your date?"

"I had a nice time. The movie was great, a classic. The dinner was good. It was a good time."

Mike was staring at me. He was thinking of the next thing to say. He didn't understand why it bothered him so much that she went out with the detective! He thought to himself, *am I jealous? I have no right to be.* He was confused, damn, then shook his head and said, "Glad you had a good time. What movie did you see?" He gave himself a mental head slap. He was not glad she had a good time and wondered why she was really getting under his skin, *again*. Still. What was it about the detective that was making him want to double up his fist and haul off and slug the guy? He wanted to grab her and kiss her right there and right then. Whoa, what is going on with me? What's with all these emotions? He tried to compose himself.

He moved close to me, reaching around me pretending to get a banana off the counter just barely touching me.

Oh. I felt his slight touch. I could tell emotions stirred in us both. A shiver ran through me from head to toe. My libido was going out of whack. We looked at each other and smiled.

Mike felt an unsettling arousal. The first since Lizabeth.

"We saw "Gone with the Wind." It's really good. I now understand all the hoop-la about it."

"Yeah, I heard it was worth seeing. I haven't seen it yet, but I would like to," Mike added, still brushing my arm as he placed the rest of the bananas back.

"Oh, and I saved a lady's life. Don't want to brag, but she was having a heart attack just before the movie started."

"You never cease to amaze me, Sara," He smiled, shaking his head. "She make it?"

"Yes, she's going to be okay."

There was a long pause between us. Then I said, "So did your work emergency get handled?" I asked him, still feeling the thrill of his touch.

"I got there, and it didn't take long to figure out what the emergency was. It could have waited until Monday. It pissed me off to be called in on a Saturday night on a project that should have waited," He said, still thinking he wanted to take her and take her right there on the table, right then. "But I took care of it and came back home."

"Wild goose chase, huh?" I suggested.

"Kinda," he said. He brushed my arm again and I wanted to swing around and kiss him hard and deep.

We looked at each other and waited for the other to make their move. Finally, I said good night and walked away. This was getting awkward. But I knew this was more than in- like. It was real and I was no longer going to ignore my feelings.

He said softly, "Good night, Sara." He watched me walk out of sight. "Damn." he said out loud. "So close. Why can't I just seal the deal?" He spilled water on himself.

I turned and asked, "What?"

"Nothing, I just spilled water down the front of me," he mumbled.

I was in the dark hallway so he didn't see me turn and watch

him take his wet shirt off. "*Damn!* I had no idea he had a six pack. *Woof!*

"Sara, did you say something?"

Rushing further down the hallway I yelled back, "No. Good night."

CHAPTER 19

MIKE WAS STRUGGLING WITH thoughts of Sara. He couldn't stop thinking of her. He reminded himself to slow down. He lay down in his bed. "*Damn!* Slow down, Mike," he said out loud. He hit his pillow and rolled over and tried to sleep, but all he did was toss and turn.

I could hear Mike ever so slightly down the hallway. I lay there listening to him. I was having trouble going to sleep too. I went from the wonderful date I had with Zack to the mixed emotions I was clearly having for Mike and I kept seeing him without his shirt. One thing for sure, the emotions I felt were only for Mike. I was up and down all night watching TV to try to get my mind to relax. Not even reading my diary helped.

I just dozed off when Dora's phone call woke me as it so often did.

"Oh, Dora, I just got to sleep. Can I call you back in a couple of hours?" I asked her.

She wouldn't have any of it. "*No!*" she demanded.

"Please." I pleaded.

"Oh, alright," She said, as she hung up. Thank goodness.

But the harm was done. I lay there fifteen minutes wide awake. Giving up I called her back.

"Thanks a lot. I really needed the sleep." I yelled at her.

"Well, why were you up all night? What's going on? Is it Detective Hunk?"

"No!"

Then I told her of my date with Zack and how much fun we had, that ended up with two amazing kisses, but I saw Mike's face pop into each kiss. Then I told her of Mike's and my awkward encounter.

"I just couldn't get *him* off my mind. He was stirring things in me that I forgot were there. His scrape against me made me feel feelings I never thought could feel again."

"Who? Zack or Mike?"

"Mike, you ditz, keep up," I scolded her.

"You mean he hasn't been that close to you before?"

"He has, but this was intentional. He did this on purpose. And it worked, and you know what I did? I said goodnight. I said *goodnight.* Can you imagine?"

"You vamp, you. You have those two hunks after you, you lucky duck," She laughed.

"Yeah, but only one stirs me up. I don't know what to do. And on the other hand. Zack's kiss was . . . *Wow!* Then Mike's face popped in to my mind's eye. Well, that's the update. Gotta go, the kids will be up soon, and I need to be ready for them."

As I was turning off my cell I could hear her say, "*Wait!*" Too late.

I got my shower over, brushed my teeth, combed my hair, slapped a little mascara on my tired eyes as they needed help after the night I had. I got my clothes on and walked down the hall to check on the kids, but they weren't in their beds. I glanced in the living room for them. Hmph, no one there. I headed for the kitchen. I turned and looked into the hearth room right off the kitchen. No one. *Hmph!*

Where was everyone? I poured myself a cup of coffee that was thoughtfully left for me. I was sipping it and watching a little TV news when the door opened. Mike was helping Jeffey in while carrying a big bag of McDonalds and a box of Lamar donuts. Karen Anne was carrying the kids' drinks.

"Good morning, Sara, you finally got up? The kids were up early so we decided to go get breakfast. I hope you like egg mac's or breakfast burritos. We got plenty of them," he said, opening all the packages and displaying them on plates.

He clearly slept last night. Lucky guy.

"Help yourself." he said. "How was your night? Did you get plenty of sleep?"

"No," I blurted out. "I mean, Dora called early and woke me and that was the end of my sleep."

He smiled rather cockily. "We were up early and decided to get breakfast and surprise you."

"Thank you, everybody." I grabbed each of the kids and gave them a hug.

Now that my feelings for Mike were waking up, I wanted to hug him too, but I didn't.

Oh boy!

We finished our breakfast, which was a nice change. I reached over for one more donut choosing the apple fritter. It was my opinion that Lamar's was the best. Just as I finished my thought and was about to pick up the apple fritter, I felt Mike's touch. This time he wasn't so gentle. He wanted me to feel it. I did. Goose bumps formed, and tingles ran from my who-ha and up to my nipples and I felt my lips quiver. And Mike knew it.

Instead of falling into his arm, I said, "Oh, I am sorry, I didn't mean to crowd you," I moved away. *Idiot.*

"You didn't crowd me. But glad I got more than one apple fritter," He boasted.

We smiled at each other, and he knew he was under my skin. How could he not know?

Just then Dora called. She told me that Richard was going as Kenny Rogers and she was going as Dolly Parton to the Halloween party. We hung up and Mike asked me what I was laughing about. I told him what Dora said.

Mike laughed and said, "I can see Richard as Kenny Rogers with his white hair and goatee, and for sure Dora would be a perfect Dolly with her fake eyelashes and her really big . . ." Mike said, as he rounded off his chest to indicate a huge bosom. He continued by saying "All she will need is to change her big hair from red to blonde. All Richard needs is to trim his goatee."

Then Mike looked at me and asked, "So who are we going as?"

"Oh, I don't know, maybe Starsky and Hutch." I replied. *We?*

"I was hoping for something a little more girlie for you," he suggested.

I told him I would work on it, still feeling the chills he caused me to have. It may take me the rest of my life to get over it, if ever.

"So, what does everyone want to do today? It is Sunday and we need to do something fun besides watch football. Any ideas, kids?" Mike said, still smiling from clearly causing the chills he knew I was still experiencing.

About that time Kate called and suggested we get together today. The kids would love it. I asked Mike and he said, "Why not?" So, when noon came, Mike, the kids and I skipped over to Kate and Andrew's house for lunch. Okay, Mike didn't skip but the kids and I did. Jeffey was disappointed that it was too cold to swim, and the pool was closed for the season. The kids still loved being together. And it was still sunny and warm enough to sit out on the patio. It was nice and I could talk with others about other things and not the things I was thinking about. Mike. Chills. Tingles.

We were walking across the back yards toward home when I noticed some activity at Harper's. I thought I better find out what. Kate and family were headed to church so she couldn't help me, but Dora could.

I looked at Mike, and it was like he could see my head spinning and aching to stick my nose into Harper's business.

"Go ahead and call your buddy. I know you're anxious to investigate," he said.

"We have to investigate. When we were kids and we found a dead bird or squirrel or anything, we would have to try to find out why they died, how they died and 'who done it.' Though most of the time we didn't know the who or why," I said, as I pushed the single digit on my cell to call Dora, with Richard, rushed over. I explained what I wanted to do which was to go for a walk and stroll by Harpers house. It was the first time I could clearly see into his garage. It was half empty except it looked like a car was covered and boxes setting around. Dora and I walked past and saw Harper bent down and looking at something in the garage and he didn't see us.

We got back to the house, and I asked Mike if he could go borrow some kind of tool from Harper. Mike said he would play along.

He and Richard headed over to Harper's. They talked awhile and borrowed an electric drill.

The guys seem pleased with their visit with Harper and the tool of choice.

"So, doesn't every man have a drill? So, wasn't it odd to borrow one?" I asked.

"Not if you just burned yours up and saw your neighbor with his garage door up," he answered.

Mike said they struck up a conversation on sports and who would they choose for fantasy football. They had a beer with Harper before coming back.

I asked if they saw anything unusual.

They both said there were a lot of big boxes sitting around, and there was a car covered up.

I asked them to take the tool back in an hour or so and try to find out about the car because all of a sudden, I had a sick feeling.

They went back and were gone about an hour yet again.

They said they didn't want to be pushy about the car and boxes, so they took their time asking questions without being too obvious, but Harper wasn't forth-coming with information.

Mike said he asked Harper, "What's this?" reaching to uncover the car.

Harper quickly stopped Mike and covered it back up.

Harper said the boxes were toaster ovens and other small kitchen appliances. He was wheeling and dealing with a buyer. If the guy took them, Harper wouldn't have any extra to sell to anyone else.

Mike and Richard said they left with a friendly demeanor.

"So, what did you two ladies do while we men folks were poking around for answers?"

"We have to come up with our next plan of attack. So, while the kids watched Halloween cartoons on TV, we sat at the computer to research info on Harper."

"Well, what did you find out?" Richard asked us, looking at his bride.

"Nothing new. For some guy up to here," raising her hand above her head, "he sure seems to be clean. Or he's staying under the radar." Dora answered.

"Oh, we're just getting started." I chimed in.

With Richard and Mike going over to Harper's an hour at a time with an hour in between at home pretending to use the drill during that hour, the evening went fast. We said good night to Dora and Richard, and by then I was dead tired. We all were.

NO ACTIVITY WAS GOING on at Harper's, and, believe you me, we tried to find out. We did a whole lot of endurance walks, after all we had to keep up appearances.

A couple of days later I saw Harper come home, and he left the garage door open, but now it's full of boxes surrounding the car. Since Mike was at work, I called Dora and asked Kate to watch Jeffey.

"Okay, but the next time I'm going, and Sherrie can take care of the kids," Kate said.

She didn't want to miss out.

Dora arrived just about the time Harper pulled away. We sprang into action. We slipped over to Harper's garage. We looked into the window and saw the boxes and the covered car. The window was locked, of course. We grimaced.

"We need to get in there."

"I know, but how?" I said.

We walked around to the back and tried the door handle and it opened. We looked at each other with satisfaction and confusion, shrugged our shoulders and pushed the door open.

"Why would Harper leave the back door unlocked when he worked so hard in keeping his garage so private?" I raised my eyebrows. *Curious.*

"Go figure. Go on in," Dora said, giving me a little shove through the door.

"That's 'breaking and entering,' I said.

"But who is going to tell?" she replied. "Besides we aren't breaking anything while we enter."

"Bum de bum bum," I chimed in.

Since I went in first, I was barely squeezing by the numerous boxes. Dora had a little more trouble squeezing in. Her ginormous boobs got in the way, and she dusted everything that her boobs touched. Finally, we got in.

There were boxes everywhere. They were stacked about six tall and six deep. Different sizes. I took pictures with my cell phone as one would never know if it would come in handy.

Ole eagle-eye Dora spotted a stack of cardboard file boxes, and one in the very middle had a small X on it. But before we could investigate, we heard Harper's truck and his cell phone chime that he had left behind ringing off the hook. We slid back through the back door and just got out when the garage door went up. We were safe.

We ran to the front of the house to the sidewalk just in time to see Harper walking back out carrying his cell phone.

We yelled, "Hello," to him and he looked up unamused.

"I see you are *not* coming along with that power walk," he smirked.

"Oh, that's Kate and me. Dora isn't up to it," I spouted.

Dora hit me. "I can do it," she said.

Harper heehawed and said, "Keep up the good work. Looks like you have a way to go." He got in his truck and drove away.

We slipped back into the garage and could clearly see where Dora had dusted. I looked and her chest that was covered in dirt. Too late.

We looked around in the boxes and mostly there were small kitchen appliances, but then we hit the jackpot or so we thought. The box Dora had spotted with an X on it had file after file with peoples' names and information. We thought, how odd. One of the names was Tom Solo with information about him and Mary. Something about payments and apparent blackmail or so we thought. I snapped a couple of pictures.

We raised the cover up on the car. It looked like it had an unfinished front end that was replaced but still needed painting. I snapped more pictures. I opened the glove box and the pink slip had Tom and Mary Solo's names on it with a different address than their current one. What on earth?

"Dora, look. This pink slip has Tom and Mary's name on it. And there's a paint bid and it's dated a little over four years ago. It looked like somebody was going to have some work done then, too."

"Let me see," Dora tried to take it from me.

"No," I said as she yanked it out of my hand.

"Oh my gosh, Sara, do you think this could be the car that was involved in Jerry's hit and run?"

"Yes, I do." I said, as I got nauseated at the possibility of that car being involved, let alone Tom or Mary Solo. I have to find out.

I took pictures of the pink slip and paper work then carefully put them back in the glove compartment. We covered the car back up, closed all the boxes then snuck out.

Dora said, "I dusted things off pretty good back there. I think we need to get the vacuum cleaner bag and let some dust drift over the boxes and doorway."

So, we did. We grabbed the vacuum bag, went outside and sifted some of the dust bag into a paper bag and headed back to Harper's.

Using a hand-held battery-operated face fan, we lightly blew the dust over the places we thought we or Dora had dusted. We just finished, when Harper's garage door went up, and we darted out the side door. As we closed the door we saw through the window dust blowing.

Oops!

We ducked down just in time and waited for the all clear and the dust to settle.

We made it just in time.

We got back to the house and looked at each other and started jumping up and down with excitement at what we just did and discovered. Then landing on our feet on the last jump, I looked down the front of myself and saw the blow back dust all over me. I looked over at Dora who was dirtier than me, as she was the original duster.

I couldn't wait to tell Mike. But Dora said I should call Zack first.

"He needs to know our suspicions," she said.

Crap, she's right, I called Zack, and he said he would call the original officer who had been working the case.

"The case." Jerry's hit and run was *the case!*

Of course, Zack scolded Dora and me for snooping around in Harper's garage. But he said it was good information. I e-mailed and texted him the pictures. I wanted to be sure he got them.

"You know we have to go by the book on this and can't act rashly," he warned. "We need to be sure all the i's are dotted and t's crossed. We don't want to mess this up. We have to solve this without mistakes. And we need to know what Harper's involvement in this is and why he has hidden the car, if it is the car, after all these years. Please, Sara, do not get anxious and overreact. Let us do the investigation. We will find out what needs to be found out. You have to treat Harper the same. No red flags, promise?" Zack stated. "Oh, and that goes for Dora too, and tell your other sleuthing friends to butt out. Just plan your Halloween party. Be normal, okay?"

I had him on the speaker phone; we both said, "Okay," reluctantly. I knew it was going to be hard to do. It was killing me not knowing.

We called Kate, and she brought Jeffey home along with Andy. The boys went off to play and we filled Kate in.

"Oh, Sara, I so hope your detective will find all the information needed pretty quickly. I hope he can get Jerry's case solved without a hitch, and you can have peace of mind," Kate said.

We did a group hug, but I was thinking *your detective? Really!*

Dora went home, as did Kate. Jeffey and I waited for his sister to come home from school.

Mike came home, and I went and pulled him to me. He looked confused.

"I need a hug, badly," I told him.

Mike could tell I was very upset. He hugged me back and held me for a few minutes. I let go but he didn't. I explained what Dora and I found out.

He unhugged me, "You two might just have stumbled on to something. Thank God Harper didn't catch you. You need to be more careful."

"It'll all work out until Harper figures out Dora dusted a lot of things in his garage. She had a filthy chest when we left." I laughed. "But we went back with a little vacuum bag dust and tossed it all over everything. It worked."

"You're kidding? You took vacuum dust!"

"I know, but it was the only thing we could think of."

"I'm glad you called Zack," he said. "He needs to know everything you come up with."

"Yeah, he keeps saying "butt out." But he knows we can't."

"I watch your wheels spin every day. I recognize determination when I see it, and I have learned to step aside and keep out of your way," Mike said. He reached for me for one more hug when the kids ran in the kitchen and said, "Supper ready?"

"Sure is."

"You have a tear on your cheek, Sara. What's the matter?" Karen Anne asked.

"Oh, baby girl, nothing's wrong. Help me set the table."

CHAPTER 20

EVERY DAY I WANTED to call Zack to find out what he knew, but every day he put me off. He only said, "I'm working on it and when I know, I promise you, you will know." *Not very reassuring.*

We were no closer to solving Tom Solo's murder, but if he in fact had something to do with Jerry's death, then I wanted to know more than ever.

The wait and see was eating at me. I was convinced more than ever that Tom Solo and Harper Daniels had a lot to do with my husband's death. Just knowing that the car that killed my sweet man was sitting in a garage a couple of houses down from me was making things even worse for me.

Zack kept saying, "We don't know that for a fact. We haven't been able to prove it yet. We have to make sure to cross the t's and dot the i's. No stone unturned."

As much as I knew that was the truth, it didn't make it any better.

We were busy finalizing the Halloween party details. It was going to be so much fun, and fun was what I needed. I still didn't know what my/our costume was going to be. Since Dora and Richard were Kenny and Dolly, I thought it a good idea to follow with the country singer theme, but who?

The kids were watching another Charlie Brown Halloween movie. I thought, good grief, more Charlie Brown. Mike and I just looked at each other wishing we could be watching anything else on TV. *Anything else.*

Mike asked me, "Have you figured out a costume for us yet?"

I said, "Nope!"

"Well," he said, "How about an action hero. I could go as the Green Hornet and you can go as Cat Woman or maybe Wonder Woman."

"Oh I don't know."

"You'd make a great Cat Woman."

"Hmm. I was thinking of being Faith Hill or Shania Twain."

"Oh, sexy. I could go as Tim McGraw or maybe if I had another foot in height, I could be Toby Keith."

"I'll go as Shania and you go as Toby. You're tall enough."

Mike smiled and said, "That's a deal. I have an old straw hat, a bandana, jeans and a plaid cowboy shirt. I could pull it off. And you will make a *great* Shania."

"Okay then, it's settled. Just make sure your mom doesn't come as Shania." I laughed, remembering the Fourth of July party when she bought and wore the same exact swimsuit.

"Oh, I forgot to invite her. Better get on it." Mike picked up the phone.

"Mom, you're invited to the Halloween party at Sherrie's. Will Jax be in town?"

"Mom? You haven't called me *mom* in a very long time. What's up with that, Michael?"

"Good grief, Mother, I don't know, a slip of the tongue?"

"I don't know about Jax, but I would love to go. You know Jax didn't show up when you invited us for barbecue the last time, but he called. He said he was tied up in Hong Kong or some damn place." She paused then said, "Or, if you'd rather, I could babysit."

"Clancy volunteered to babysit. And Sara said don't come as Shania as she's going to be Shania."

Kathrine just heehawed. “Okay, I won’t come as Shania. I couldn’t pull it off like Sara anyway. And who are going as, Mike?”

“Toby Keith.”

“Nice,” Katherine said. “Okay then, next Saturday at seven o’clock. See you there.”

It was Halloween night, and we had just got back from taking the kids trick or treating. That in itself was fun. When we got home, Clancy was ready to take over with the kids.

I came down the hallway looking like Shania or the best I could. I wasn’t as skinny, but my navel showed from the midriff tuxedo shirt and the sexy tuxedo style shorts. I had on a skirt that was slit up to the waist, and I wore net stocking and stilettos which were working, but I knew my feet would be killing me within two hours. I stopped in the hallway to look into the mirror to place the top hat with a veil just slightly cocked to side of my head.

“There,” I said, giving the hat a couple of taps on the top of it.

Mike’s mouth dropped open when he saw me. He stared and looked me up and down. “Wow, you look,” he took a very long pause, “Amazing.”

“I didn’t overdo it, did I?” I asked.

But he kept staring. “No, you most definitely did not overdo it.” He felt a chill move up and down his body.

“You make a pretty good Toby, too,” I said. “You even have the long blonde hair sticking out from under your hat, and the bandana completes the Toby look.” *Really nice, indeed,* I thought as I straightened his bandana. Now why did I do that?

If I am ever going to make a move, then it’s now, he thought, as he took off his hat with the long blond hair attached to it.

I noticed his actual blond hair was a lot shorter and I said, “Clever hair and hat thing,”

Mike put his hat back on and surprised me by taking my hand and pulling me toward him. "This is nice, our first date." He grinned from ear to ear. Just as fast as that happened, he dropped my hand and gave the kids a hug and told them not to eat too many sweets. But I think it was *too* late. We gave a few more hugs and said goodbye but not before we thanked Clancy for being there.

Katherine and Jax pulled up just in time to walk over to Sherrie's party with us.

They were so cute. They were dressed like the 1920s flappers.

"Surprised to see you, Jax," Mike said, taking Jax's hand in his with a hardy greeting, then hugged his mother. "Mother."

"Michael," she said, hugging him back then patting his shoulder. "Break."

They laughed letting each other go.

"I just flew back home today and surprised your mother."

Katherine smiled. "Well, Jax called from Hong Kong and said he was on his way, and that's why his costume was ready. The surprise is that he actually showed up,"

"Surprise!" is all that Jax came up with.

"You guys are adorable," I said.

Dolly and Kenny were already there and *boom, boom*; Dora outdid Dolly on Dolly's best day. Dora's waist was cinched so tight, I thought it hard for her to breathe, let alone move. But she was doing okay; she looked awesome. Perfect. With her cinched waist, her boobs were even bigger. *everyone* noticed. How could they not?

"You two look great," Mike said, with his eyes glued on Dora's bosom. He couldn't help it as that's all anyone could see. "You look good too, Kenny," he said, as he tried to pull his eyes from Dora's girls.

"Well, Shania and Toby, you look pretty darn good, too," she giggled. "You look amazing, Sara, I mean Shania."

"Grr," Richard growled, "Sexy Sara!"

Karaoke was set up, and everyone had to sing when their character's song or the era they were dressed as came up, whether it was Micky Mouse or well, Shania. Kenny and Dolly were up first and did 'Islands in the Stream,' and it was so darn cute. Someone yelled, "Don't lean forward, Dolly, gravity will pull you over." Everyone laughed.

With everyone enjoying the different songs, finally Shania was up. Oh brother, the song was "I Feel Like A Woman." I got up on the tiny stage and started singing and did all the moves I could remember from different Shania YouTube videos I watched briefly just today. I heard whistles and wolf calls and, lord, the guys were having so much fun with me. I tried following one of the wolf calls. I spotted Zack and one of his sidekicks. My eyes immediately went back to Mike, who had watched me look toward Zack. The song was over, and, while I got a standing ovation for more, I declined. As I stepped off the little stage, Mike was there and pulled me to him and swung me around and around. It not only surprised me, but everybody in the room.

Next, they called Toby up on the makeshift stage. He stopped swinging me around and climbed on the stage when the music started. "How Do You Like Me Now?"

"Good song," he said, looking at me.

Someone handed him a guitar, and he actually played it, then shoved it behind his back and put his hands out looking at me singing "How Do You Like Me Now?

As Dora walked up beside me, she leaned into my ear, "How do you like him now?"

"*Oh, baby I do*," I said, giggling. "I do."

When Mike was done and walked over to me, Katherine dragged Jax behind her to Mike and me and wrapped her arms around, hugging both of us. "I am so happy that you found each other."

Mike asked his mother, "Were we lost?"

"Oh Michael, you know what I mean," she scolded, slapping at him.

He swung his mother around and then stopped, handing her off to Jax. He was having a good time, and I must say I have *never* seen him like this before.

Kate came over and told me, "Mike's acting like his old self. It's nice to see and it's about time," as she gave me a hug. "You're the difference."

"Ah, no, I didn't have anything to do with it," I said, liking what I see.

"Bet me," she replied.

Mike turned back to me and asked me to dance a slow dance with him. He took my hand, twirled me into him. I was feeling pretty good with my head resting on his chest when he pulled me closer and whispered in my ear, "You know, Sara, I hate to say this, but just maybe I should thank Detective Zack Zanders for waking me up. He woke us both up."

I raised my head and studied his expression, noticing just how handsome he really was. He pulled me close again, and I laid my head back on his chest smiling. Boy, things really started stirring in me. He snuggled his face down next to mine, and he started humming along with the song. I almost fainted, it was so romantic. Everything started to flutter and not just in my heart, but I definitely had a tingle where tingles happened.

Just as the song ended, Zack started to walk over to us, and I was still hanging onto Mike. I smiled and said, "Speaking of Zack, here he comes."

"I didn't know you were going to be here," I stated, still holding on to Mike.

"Kate thought it would be polite since I'm in the neighborhood so much and thought that it would be a good idea to be on the same level with all the neighbors. I am actually working under cover. Sorta. I'm looking for Harper. Is he here?"

"I haven't seen him. I know he was invited but don't know if he'll be here. Mary's declined her invitation. She's not ready to party yet," I said.

About that time another slow song started playing, and Zack looked at Mike reaching for my hand. "May I?"

Mike smiled a crooked smile and said, "Just bring her back."

Zack put his hand around mine and we started dancing. Mike was apparently unconcerned about what just happened and walked over to Dora and Richard. Or he's all of a sudden secure.

"That guy just makes me . . ." Mike said, and started walking back toward me, but Dora grabbed his arm holding him back. He stopped and looked at her.

"It's okay, Mike. Trust me. It's okay. She chose you."

Mike grinned.

Zack could dance pretty well, too. At the end of the song and before another started, Mike cut in.

"Excuse me, Zack." Mike pulled me away from him and twirled me around, then dipped me.

"Whoa," I mumbled, surprised.

"Look at that, the two roosters have started their cock-a-doodle-dooing over Sara," Dora said to Richard

Kate, who was standing close, overheard her and said, "Yep, this is going to be fun."

Zack stepped back and just smiled. He saw the writing on the wall. He thought, Sara can be in denial all she wants, but there it is, out there for all to see. Mike's very much in love with her and she loves him. I can only walk away and bow out graciously. Mike won, I lost.

He walked over to Richard, Dora and Kate and said to them, "I think I just lost out. Like I had a chance."

"Sorry, Zack." Dora patted his arm, and without a word he turned and walked to the other side of the room.

Katherine was watching all of this take place said to Jax, "It's about time my son made it be known that he cares for Sara."

Jax, a man of little words, just grunted, "Yes."

Later Zack walked over to me as I stood by the buffet table and said. "Still think this isn't a date? That Mike doesn't have feelings for you?"

Trying to decide on what to put on my plate, I looked up at Zack and said, "I guess you were right, Zack. You're a really nice guy and a fun date, but . . ."

"You don't have to finish that statement, Sara," he said, and gave me a goodbye hug. "I'll see you around on police business soon."

Mike walked over to us, and Zack reached out and shook his hand, "You won."

"Thanks to you, I had to step up my game," Mike said, with a sturdy handshake.

"Wait, you two roosters; I'm standing right here," I said.

"Yes, you are," Zack said. "Treat her right, Mike," and walked away while Mike hugged me tight.

Nothing unusual happened after that. Everyone was having a good time. Harper never showed.

Zack gave up and left.

It was about midnight, and Mike thought we should let Clancy go home. Katherine and Jax left earlier and were probably already home.

We started walking home, but the stiletto boots were killing my feet so I was limping. I bet Shania didn't have this kind of trouble walking. I leaned on Mike and finally took my boots off.

Mike offered to carry me, but I said it wasn't far and I could make it. About that time, he swooped me up and carried me home, anyway.

"Thanks, Toby."

"No problem, Shania."

I was so wowed. My hooha was doing flip flops. I didn't know if I could control the feelings stirring in me.

Mike sat me down at the door so he could get his house key out of his pocket. He unlocked the door and turned to me and put his hands on the back of my head, gently taking off my top hat. He tilted my face to his and kissed me long and hard. *Oh!*

We stepped away from each other just barely and walked into the house holding hands.

Clancy was sound asleep on the sofa. We decided to cover her and let her sleep. I went to check in on the kids while Mike went into another room to call Clancy's husband. He told him that we covered Clancy and were letting her sleep. Mr. Clancy was okay with the decision to let her stay the late.

My hooha settled down and I was glad. I sure didn't want to let Mike know how he affected me. But he had to know and he probably loved it.

He started towards me, and I knew it wasn't going to be a brush against my arm. He pulled me towards him again and ever so gently kissed me. Then he kissed me slightly harder and then harder, until it was a full blown passionate kiss that seemed to last for three hours. Of course, it was more like three minutes. *Okay thirty seconds*. Whatever it was, I went limp and was his for the taking. *But*, instead, he slowed the kiss down then he gently pulled away and just looked at me with my eyes crossed and my tongue hanging out. Or so it felt that was what I must have looked like. Mike smiled and gave me a tiny kiss and said, "Well, that was a long time coming."

"*Yeah!*" I mumbled. "Long time coming."

He turned around and said he was checking on the kids and going to bed. He would see me in the morning.

In the morning! I gave myself a mental head slap, yet again. I tried to compose myself and said, "Good night."

I couldn't sleep thanks to Mike. I started talking to Jerry. I wanted to feel it was okay to have feelings for Mike. Wasn't it time to move on? I felt Jerry heard me and gave me his approval. It was all good. I remembered a poem Jerry had written me that I had recently found in a box of mementos.

I recited it to myself.

Roses are red, violets are blue

When I met you, Sara, I knew it was true.

When we met and then we wed, I knew our

Love would never end.

Our love would forever glow with life, with

Laughter and overcome any obstacles with you as my wife

You make me long for you when you are away.

I can't wait to hold you and keep you safe.

Make love to you all night until the day.

And that you will always stay with me all the way.

You, my beloved, mean more to me than the air we need to breathe

Or the water we need to drink.

You, Sara, are my life.

I am so happy you are my wife.

I remembered our first winter we were married; we went on a sleigh ride on the coldest, snowiest day of the winter with only heavy Russian hats and gloves on, snuggled under heavy blankets. Jerry was enjoying the nakedness. *Men!* He wanted to be only in our birthday suits. We were, and we were warm as toast with our bodies touching, gliding through the snow. He stopped the sleigh under a block of trees where someone had started a bonfire for us with wine and cheese waiting.

Laughing and baring it all, we ran to the warm love nest that he had someone prepare and we made love. Oh boy, how we made love.

Jerry started the sleigh back up, and I think the horse was glad to move again. We laughed so hard and I still smile at the memory.

I still couldn't sleep, and my thoughts wandered to the time Jerry put tons of rose petals all over me and the bed while I slept. He said he wanted me to wake up in a bed of roses. I did. It smelled wonderful. I can close my eyes still today and see and smell those beautiful rose petals. My Jerry was a romantic man. I sure miss him and the love we shared.

Bam! Just like that my thoughts returned to Mike. I really cared for him, and I know I was falling in love with him, yet I was guarded somewhat. I didn't want to assume anything, though the kisses spoke volumes. And then at the party he made it clear I was his date. How he cut in on Zack and me dancing and didn't think twice about it. How he occupied my time at the party. How many of my friends made the cracks about Mike marking his territory. Dora especially made a big deal about it as she smiled from ear to ear. I know Mike had to have heard the comments and giggles.

I was actually pleased. I just wondered what Mike was thinking about now. Or was he asleep? I drifted off.

MIKE WAS ALL COMFORTABLE in his bed thinking of Sara. He had his arms up over his head, smiling. He knew Lizabeth would say it was time to move on. Heck, Lizabeth, being the gracious, wonderful person she was, probably sent

Sara to him. She wouldn't want Mike to go on without someone in his young life. Mike felt sure Lizabeth knew the kids loved Sara. That would also please Lizabeth. She never was a selfish person. She would want Mike and the kids to be happy and live a normal life. That was why Mike was so head over heels for Lizabeth in the first place.

Mike now shifted to Sara. He smiled bigger. Yes, indeedy, he was in love with her. He was glad he made his move and let it be known, especially with that pesky Detective Zack lurking around. Zack seemed to be an honorable man and he did back off graciously.

Mike thought to himself, "I am on my way to a new beginning, and Sara's going to be the biggest part." He was very pleased with himself. Smooth. He drifted off to sleep with a smile on his face.

CHAPTER 21

IT WAS EARLY IN the next morning, and after checking the kids, who were still sound asleep, I rounded the corner to the kitchen, excited to see Mike, but there was no Mike and no coffee.

What the heck, I wondered looking around? This is the first time in all these months that Mike didn't have the coffee pot on. Thank goodness Mike had a Keurig coffee maker with every imaginable K cup ever made. I have often sipped on a K cup on many occasions, but this was the first time I had to make myself a cup first thing in the morning; I shrugged. I was sipping a vanilla cinnamon while making a fresh pot of coffee. It had been so long since I made a pot, I wondered if I had remembered how. Ah, success!

"I could use a cup of coffee, Missy," Clancy said, walking toward me.

She got a *to-go-cup* out of the pantry and said, "Top of the morning to you. I'm going to go home in a minute."

"Good morning, Clancy," I greeted her putting her cup under the coffee-spigot.

"Oh, thanks for covering me up last night. I should've gone into the spare bedroom. That sofa was comfy though. I musta slept on my neck wrong. It's really hurtin'," she said, rubbing it.

I walked over to her and said, "Sit down, Clancy and let me massage your shoulder and neck."

"Happy to. *Ooh, ah, hmm,* you have magic fingers, missy. Hmm,"

I had her neck and shoulder pain worked out in about five minutes. "There you go," I said.

"Wow, what a difference, thanks," she said, moving her shoulder and neck around and around to see if the pain was really gone.

As she turned to leave I yelled after her, "See you Monday. Thanks for watching the kids."

She waved, "Any time."

I started breakfast. I placed bacon in the microwave and started mixing up scrambled eggs. I was waiting until I heard life moving around before pouring the eggs in the skillet. It was so quiet, and I started reliving Mike singing in my ear as we danced. About that time I felt hands going around my waist and a kiss on my neck. I shrieked, not expecting anyone there let alone a kiss on the neck.

"Sorry, I was trying to surprise you," Mike explained.

"I, I just wasn't expecting it," I answered, smiling. "Boy, you made a 1-80 the last couple of days."

"I hope I'm not moving too fast. But I felt the timing was right, Sara. I am crazy about you and have fought it long enough. Besides, I didn't want happy Zack messing up my chances."

"Mike, I was in denial, though I didn't know I was, when everyone kept saying you had feelings for me, I shrugged it off. I didn't know if you were ready to move on, or if you ever would be. I thought everyone was crazy. When we started talking about the Halloween party I felt a change in you, and you were more comfortable talking to me and showing a little feeling. You talked about Halloween being our first date and, well, naive or not, I got it and I knew our friends were right. After last night, all I can say is, *Wow!* For the record, *Happy Zack* never stood a chance. He's a great guy, a fun date, and

I enjoyed his company, but that's it."

"I am glad Zack's not in the picture, and, yes, I am so ready to move on," Mike pulled me close and kissed me gently. "Really ready."

"Mike, I'm crazy about you, too."

My cell rang. "Hello Mother Dora," I said as Mike and I parted from our embrace.

"Well," she went on. "Tell me, tell me," Dora demanded.

"Tell you what?" I teased.

"About you and Mike."

I smiled at Mike, who was now stirring the scrambled eggs.

"All is good."

"All is good. That's all you can tell me?" She practically screamed at me.

"For now," I smiled at Mike again. "I'll call you later."

"Oh, that's just BS," Dora said. "You better call me back soon."

"I will. Goodbye, Mother."

"Dora's dying to know what's going on between us," I said to Mike. "But first, I need to know myself before telling her anything. So, Mike, what can I tell Dora?" I asked.

"You can tell her that I am crazy about you, and I plan on having a future with you. You can tell her how we both enjoyed our kissing." He grinned from ear to ear, "What do you think, Sara? Do we have a future together?"

"Well, it looks promising," I teased.

The kids came in yelling, "We're hungry." Karen Anne yawned while she yelled and she started to choke. I raised her arm and pounded her back. *Always the nurse.*

"Well, you are in luck, breakfast is now ready," Mike's smile was still wide. Or maybe I should say he never stopped smiling and he smiled a lot lately.

After we finished breakfast the kids went to watch cartoons while Mike and I finished cleaning the kitchen. We sat down at the breakfast island for another cup of coffee and talked about Clancy and how we appreciate her. The more we talked, the more our whole demeanor changed. We were holding hands just drinking coffee. He brushed the hair off my face several times. There were a lot of sweet gestures off and on that, of course, weren't there the day before yesterday. We were very careful not to be too affectionate in front of the kids. That would remain more guarded. I didn't want to take anything away from them about their mother.

We were looking into each other's eyes when my cell rang again.

"Mike, I have to talk to Dora, now. She will not give up until I do."

He stood with his arms crossed and gently nodded his head up and down. "I know."

As I picked up the call, Mike kissed my forehead and he joined the kids.

"What took you so long? Why didn't call me back? Tell me everything!" She was full of anticipation.

I walked to the privacy of my bedroom and I told her every single detail including how Mike said good night after the passionate kiss and left me with my doodah about to explode.

"That dog, so now what?" She asked.

"I guess we'll figure it out as we go, and you'll be one of the first to know." I smirked.

"I better be the first." We hung up.

We were planning the day when Mike's cell rang. It was Katherine asking him a thousand questions about the two of us. Like me, he went off to another room. I heard him tell Katherine he was so in love with me. I fell backwards onto the kitchen chair in awe. There was something really real about hearing Mike tell his mother he was in love with me.

About fifteen minutes later, Mike came back into the kitchen where I was still sitting in awe.

"I guess you heard me tell my mother that I am in love with you, Sara. I am you know."

"Oh Mike, I love you, too." Tears started flowing.

My cell rang, again. This time it was Kate.

"Dora just filled me in. This is wonderful. You and Mike belong together, and I told you so way back when. This is great news."

"Tell the girls we will talk about it Monday," I replied. "You, Sherrie, Holly and Dora can come over for lunch. Mike must think we are a bunch of school girls. So, you call the girls and tell them to stop calling. See you Monday. Oh, and by the way, the party was great. Not to mention we made it through another holiday without incident."

"Well the incident turned out to be you and Mike, and we all think it is *great*," she purred.

I hung up just as Mike walked into the kitchen where I stood reaching for another cup of coffee and said, "Mother said she and Jax wanted to treat us to an early dinner at Casa Casa Mex."

"Us?" I asked.

"Well, yeah, us!" he reiterated. "It's going to be us from now on."

"I love Mexican food," I said, but I had a tiny reluctance about the, 'us,' from now on part. "Mike, I have a question about the 'us' part?"

"Did I forget to tell you that once I made my move, it was for a 100% which includes an 'us,'" he said.

"It all just happened so fast," I said.

"Nope, it didn't. We both had feelings we were holding on to. Yours was denial and mine was timing. And the timing is now. So, there is no denial that we are an 'us.'"

I knew he was right. It was all in the timing. Besides we were in love with each other and we both showed it, finally.

BEFORE WE LEFT FOR our dinner with Katherine and Jax, we played board games with Jeffey and Karen Anne. Chutes and Ladders was Jeffey's favorite. Karen Anne loved them all.

Just as we were leaving, Mike pulled me close and kissed me, but like a brotherly kiss.

The kids were watching, and Karen Anne said, "Oh, Daddy."

Mike and I smiled at her. I had a feeling the kids were going to see a lot more kissing.

We arrived at Casa Casa where Katherine and Jax were waiting. Katherine came to me first and put her arms around me, walking me back to the table.

"I am so happy for you two kids. It's about damn time my son stepped up. He's been in turmoil for a while now. But at last . . ." She said, giving me a squeeze.

"Thank you. I guess one way or the other we both were in a turmoil."

Mike pulled out my chair, and I turned to look at him confused. I thought, *I can pull out my own chair.* Then I realized this was part of the courting process.

We were all seated and had such a good time and probably overstayed our welcome. But it gave us a chance to get to know Jax better, as we hadn't really talked to him without a party or a bunch of people around.

I asked him what he did for a living, and Mike listened intently.

"I'm in the import, export business," Jax said, handing both Mike and me a business card that said, "Smithon Trade Company."

"What do you import and export?" I asked.

"It varies. I have to bid for business here in the states as well as other countries. That's why I'm out of the country so much."

"Have you always lived here?"

"No, I lived here for a short time and in Indianapolis, Nashville, Mobile and just left Chicago a short time ago before moving back here.

"What about family? Do you have family here in the states?" I asked.

"My wife died of cancer not long ago. My son dabbles in the stock market and works at Smithon." He took a deep sigh. "My daughter's very sick. She was traumatized when she was in college."

But he didn't elaborate. You could see him drift away in thought for a several seconds.

I changed the subject, and we started laughing at the different Halloween party activities and costumes and how much fun it had been.

We said our goodbyes at the restaurant door and watched Jax reach for Katherine's hand, holding it while they walked to their car.

I took Jeffey's hand and Mike took Karen Anne's. He reached for my free hand and we walked to Mike's SUV.

"Your mother looks happy, Mike." I said,

"Yes, she does, but you sure were interrogating Jax," he said, opening the car doors for the kids and me to get in.

I answered him, "He's mysterious. We don't know much about him and I thought it was time we did. As far as I can tell, he was the only tall, thin older man at the Fourth of July party and last night too. Several mentioned that when we were talking to neighbors and their guests."

"It was dark so it could have been anyone of the guests at the pool party," he said.

"Yes, you're right, and in the dark things and people can get distorted."

"Mother's tall and thin," he laughed.

"And home with us," I reminded him.

"I'm kidding, Mother wouldn't hurt a fly and she's the kindest woman I know."

"Yes, she is. But Mike, I really want to follow up on this," I continued.

We pulled into the driveway, and Mike came around to my door and opened it for me.

I giggled and held out my hand for him to take.

"Thank you, kind sir," I said, still smiling.

"The pleasure is all mine," as he helped me out of the car and pulled me into him.

"I could learn to like this chivalry," I said.

"I aim to please, and it is only the beginning," he said, beaming.

Gosh, new love is great . . .

Karen Anne, just waking up from the back seat with her brother, said, "Me too Daddy, help me up."

"My pleasure, princess."

CHAPTER 22

THE KIDS WERE TUCKED into their bed and sound asleep in no time. Mike got me Chianti and got himself a scotch and water then he sat down in his favorite

chair. In a few minutes he hopped up and came over to where I was sitting on the sofa. He sat down beside me and put his arm around me as we watched "The Specialist" with Sly Stallone and Sharon Stone.

Then, all of a sudden, there was the hottest sexiest sex scene I have ever seen. Sharon and Sly were having shower sex. I, we tensed up. *Oh, my god, hot, hot, hot.* I wasn't sure we should be watching this since we are in the beginning of a relationship. Too late. There it was. *hot*!

I found myself fanning myself, and Mike was laughing at me.

Needless to say, we had hot heavy foreplay without sex. That's right. No sex. I do not know how long I can do this. I really needed to get some *sex!*

But Mike wasn't going to go that fast. Though I could tell by the rise in his jeans he was wanting to. But no, not yet. I had to take a cold shower as I know Mike had to, too. We kissed good night. I went to my shower and he went to his.

I had just stepped into my shower when I heard my bedroom door open and footsteps to my shower. Mike dropped his robe and joined me. Again, *oh, my god*, Sly and Sharon didn't have *nothin'* on us. *Fireworks!* The shower water started steaming on its own.

I was in *ah!* I was a happy camper. I was thrilled. I was in lust. I was in love. Talking was not necessary. Actions said it all.

We just watched each other for a moment with glistening in our eyes. Smiling, he turned and left. I collapsed on to my bed still feeling Mike's touch. I tingled all over and fell asleep with a happy face.

The next morning, I could hardly walk. It had been so long since I had sex; the last time was the day Jerry didn't come back from an errand. I was, well, *sore*. But it was so worth it.

Mike was in the kitchen making breakfast humming a kid's song. "Zip-pity-doo-dah, zippity-ay, My, oh my, what a wonderful day. Hmm hmm."

He saw me and cracked up on how beat up I looked; he was still humming.

I looked at him and laughingly said, "It was so worth it even though I can't close my legs."

He said, "It sure was." He watched me walking and felt proud of himself for causing such an after-effect of the night before shower bliss.

The kids came running in causing us both to switch thoughts.

Karen Anne said, "I'm sure glad you're okay. I heard moaning like someone was hurt."

"Sara fell and hit her head. I had to help her get up," Mike quickly said.

Karen Anne said, "It must have been a bad fall."

Mike and I looked at each other and burst out laughing. I grabbed my head and said, "It sure was and hurt my leg too!" That would cover my look of just getting off a five-day horse-back ride."

Since it was Sunday, Mike said, "Everyone get ready for church."

After last night, we needed to repent, I thought smiling.

We ate our breakfast, and Mike thought we should go ice skating after church. The kids thought it was a great idea. Me, not so much. I was having a hard-enough time maneuvering my legs, let alone going ice skating. Besides I haven't been skating in years.

Mike said, "We're dating now."

"I thought the Halloween party was a date. Besides, don't guys ask girls out?"

He smiled and said "Yes, Halloween was our first date. But last night sealed the deal."

"So last night sealed the deal, and you don't have to ask me out now. Just assume?

"Sara, will you do me the honor of having an ice skating date with me and my children today?'

"Well, I don't know. Maybe, let me see. Do I want to go ice skating with you and your kids? I need crutches to walk, so how on earth am I to skate?"."

He pulled me to him and said, "Please go ice-skating with us."

"Okay, but I plan on watching and not participating!"

EVERYBODY AT CHURCH WAS greeting us more than normal with big smiles. But in all fairness, some of them were at the Halloween party so they knew about Mike and me. If they didn't before today they certainly do now.

We went by home and put layers of clothes on to dress warmly so we could better enjoy the outdoor rink at Crown Center.

It was located across from a shopping center, which was full of restaurants and a huge food court, as well as shopping.

After each of us took a fall more than once, we decided it was a good idea to go to the food court and have hot cocoa and shed some of our warm clothing. It was our first really cold day of the season.

Once we warmed up, we tried skating once again and finally gave up. Or, I should say the family tried to skate again. I was sitting at the side of the rink watching, due to the night before activities that had slowed me down. It started to snow the last few minutes of our ice skating. It was beautiful.

We stopped for a pizza that you bake yourself and went home and put the pizza in the oven.

It was another great day finished off with another Charlie Brown story that we had already seen five times this holiday season. Oh well, that's what kids like.

"Mike, I need to call Zack tomorrow and see if he made any progress on Harper's information I gave him. I have to stay on it."

"I understand. I don't have a problem with you seeing Zack. I know you need to keep in touch, and besides after last night, I am not worried about Happy Zack at all now. At all."

"Oh, you," I blushed. We hugged and went to our separate bedrooms.

I lay in bed reliving our shower scene over and over again. Being a woman, I wondered if it would be great every time. I just know it can't get any better than last night. I also know Mike was pretty proud of himself.

CHAPTER 23

IT WAS MONDAY, AND the girls all showed up as scheduled, waiting to hear all about Mike and me.

I put out the buffet lunch of Mexican casserole and drinks, which I paid for out of my own pocket. You know, my friends, my lunch, my money.

We sat the kids at a small kids' table and gave them their hotdogs, chips and Kool-Aid and they watched cartoons while they ate, which was bad for them but good for us.

As soon as we filled our plates and sat down, the girls started the questions coming from the left and the right. It was like a tennis match; my head going right then left and back right.

"Come on, give," my crazy redhead friend said. "And don't leave anything out."

"Come on Sara, spill; we are all married women and live vicariously through you," one of them said.

"The only thing I will tell you is to watch 'The Specialist' with Sharon

Stone and Silvester Stallone, especially the shower scene. You watch that, and then think ten times better. That was what it was like. That's all I am saying."

"Awe come, Sara, don't leave us hanging," Kate said.

"Girls, girls, girls, some things have to remain private. Just watch the movie," I said, playing with them.

Dora ran back to my bedroom and brought out my computer and pulled up the movie. She fast forward to the shower scene. The girls surrounded my computer, practically pushing each other away for a better view.

After the action really got heated, I heard, "*Oh, oh, oh yes*," Dora acted it out. "Only ten times better, oh, baby." Rubbing her hands up and down her body, turning her head in moans and groans.

"Really," I said, swatting at her. "Stop it."

They all looked at me and I said, "Yes" with a smile and a slow-up and down nod of my head. "Ten times better, and that's all I'm saying."

"But how did you get into the shower?" one of them asked.

"I opened the shower door and stepped in," I teased.

"Oh, for heaven's sake," Dora said. "Sara isn't answering anymore questions. Some things have to remain private. Tell me after they leave," she snorted.

"That would be a *no*!" I reiterated.

Not getting any more details out of me, the girls left and I am sure they were all going to be burning up Netflix trying to get *The Specialist* on tonight."

Dora stayed while I called Zack to get an update.

"Zack, any news on Harper?" I asked.

"I'm getting a warrant to go into Harper's garage tomorrow."

"Can I go along?"

"NO!" he yelled "But I will fill you in asap."

Then Zack asked me a personal question.

"Sara, do you think there is a chance that we could catch dinner and movie next weekend?"

"Oh, Zack. I can't. Uh, um, uh, Mike and I are together now, just since Halloween night." I stuttered, not wanting to hurt his feelings.

"Sara, don't feel uncomfortable. I knew you two were on the way of *being* together. It was just a matter of time. I could see the writing on the wall so

I am not surprised. Good luck to you both. Sure going to miss our dates though."

"We did have some good times. You've been a good friend. Maybe we can do lunch sometime. We are friends after all."

Pause. No response.

I continued, "Will you come over as soon as you leave Harper's?"

"I won't be able to. We have to take the evidence in and tow the car back to the police compound to go through it. I will call you or drop by as soon as we've gone over everything."

"Alright, it's just I am going nuts ever since Dora and I ran across the car and the boxes in Harper's garage."

"Please do not say that out loud again. You were never there."

"By the way, how did you get the warrant to get into Harper's garage?" I asked.

"I have my ways and the less you know the better. Just be glad I was able to get it. And tomorrow I will serve it. Now remember, mum's the word. You and Dora must never say anything, or it will blow the whole case. Not to your other friends or Mike, to no one. It will take a couple of days to go through the boxes and the car. So, hang in there. I will call you or come by in the next couple of days. Remember, *mum*." He hung up.

Holding my phone away from my face and staring at it, I said, "Zack said, 'mum's the word about Harper's garage, or it could blow the whole case' and we've come so close. You have to give me your word Dora, not to tell anyone, not even Richard or the girls, no one." Dora made the gesture to zip her mouth and throw away the key.

Good grief. I can always count on her to zip it.

Dora left when Mike came home. As she went past him, she hit him on his shoulder and said. "Nice going, Sly."

"Oh, my god! You told her." Mike acted upset, but he was only acting in front of her as she went out the door.

"Of course not. I just said watch *The Specialist*. I would say every one of those girls has Netflix going right now."

Mike smiled. "So, we're the talk of the town, but . . ."

"I hope you don't mind me telling the girls to watch *The Specialist.* I didn't give details nor would I ever. They really wanted the details, but I would never share our intimate times."

"I know how the girls are. I think you handled it just fine," he said.

Then I told Mike, "Zack said it would be a couple of days before he could pass anything on to me. Meantime, he said 'mum's the word, so we don't blow the case.' I am so anxious, Mike. We're so close."

"I know you are, Sweetheart. I know you want closure. Then it will be easier for us to move forward, and I want to move forward," Mike said, sympathetically.

Laying my head on his shoulder I said, "Me too."

CHAPTER 24

THE NEXT FEW DAYS went by *so* slowly. Zack had cleared out Harper's garage, and tons of evidence bags left Harper's house. I thought I would burst not knowing what Zack was finding out so I called him.

"Zack, this is Sara, what have you found out? Is it the car that killed Jerry, and what does it have to do with Harper?"

"Sara, be patient. I told you I would let you know what we found out, but we haven't found out much yet. We are just now picking up more bags of evidence. The CSI unit's working hard and going through everything. The work has just started. We're trying to get all the answers so there are *no* mistakes. I promise, Sara, I will let you know everything when I get all the answers. Hang in there, and I will let you know what I find out, one way or the other. But not for a few more days. Okay?"

"What do you mean, Zack, one way or the other?"

"As I said before, we have to make sure all the t's are crossed and i's dotted. It's just going slower than I wanted, but we are getting there."

"Another day or two? It's already been three days since you first cleared out Harper's place and today more?'"

"Sara, it may take longer. Some of these cases can take up to years."

"But Zack, it's already been years."

"I know, but thanks to you and Dora, we have evidence for the first time. I've been working with the detective who had your husband's case and we are on our way to solving Jerry's hit and run."

"Murder!" I shouted.

"Sorry, Sara, sorry," he said, as he lowered his voice. "Sorry."

We said our goodbyes, and I called Dora to give her the update, such as it was.

"Dora, I can't stand just waiting. How about lunch somewhere?"

"Yeah, that sounds good, how about the mall? Shopping sounds in order."

"Do you want to come by here or do you want Jeffey and me to pick you up?"

"I'll pick you guys up."

I called out to Jeffey to come into the kitchen. "Hey, lil' buddy, we have to get ready to go to lunch and shopping. Dora's on her way."

Jeffey looked up at me and said, "I don't like shoppin'." He was hanging his head and kicking the chair. I patted him lovingly on his hanging head then he looked up at me. "Okay."

We ate at the food court so we could each get what we wanted. That's what's fun about food courts.

We saw Kate, Sherry and the kids as they walked into the food court and were surprised to see us. The kids were happy about being together. Ben was toddling all over the place now and was fast. He's so darn cute trying to keep up with the big boys. Sherry could hardly keep up with him.

The kids got to play on the merry-go-round and a mini Ferris wheel. Needless to say, Jeffey was thrilled about going shopping now.

It's the first time we had all been together since their visit on the Monday after Halloween. Since they saw the police at Harpers, I filled them in on what Zack allowed me to say on Harpers case, which was close to nothing.

We went into a wig shop and tried on every wig. We were laughing so hard from the different looks we each were getting with a simple dark curly wig or long straight hair and then a red bouffant wig. I looked just like Dora's twin, except I didn't have her fake eyelashes and no such luck on matching her boobs. Kate snapped my and Dora's picture. It was incredible how much we looked alike *from the neck up*.

I put a long blonde wig on Jeffey and snapped his picture, then I showed him. He laughed so hard he fell over, which got Andy and Ben acting up. Finally, the sales lady told us to buy a wig or leave. She was trying to be nice, but we could tell she was fed up. Dora bought a dark blonde and a dark brown wig, but I knew she would return them as soon as she could. Kate decided to buy a hairpiece that matched her hair, which gave her an elegant look. Sherry and I did not buy anything, though Dora tried ever so hard to talk me into buying the red wig.

I declined.

We all decided that we had enough fun and parted for home. Dora dropped Jeffey and me off, and we immediately left to go pick up Karen Anne and her friends from school. I listened as they giggled in the high pitch, hurt your ears kind of giggle. I thought to myself they sound just like Dora and me when we were kids. No. Like we sound today.

Mike came in just in time for a pork chop dinner. He poured me wine, and I showed him Dora's and my picture.

"Wow, look at you! You and Dora could be twins. I like."

Hitting at him and missing, "What? You like?" I hit him and this time I didn't miss. "Oh Mike, we had so much fun," I said, as I pushed the pictures over one by one on my cell. "Here, look at Jeffey's picture."

Mike got a great big smile and said, "Hot doggity."

Clearly Mike didn't want to embarrass Jeffey about being a cute girl. But he did make a cute girl. Jeffey wanted to see himself again.

After dinner, we cleaned up the kitchen and poured a glass of wine and went to watch a little TV.

"Sara, Lizabeth's mother called today. They want to come see the kids. They thought it would be perfect for Thanksgiving. I told her they were welcome to.

"So, my mother, I assume Jax, and Lizabeth's mom and dad will be here."

"Well, I think that's wonderful. They should come. It's perfect timing for me as I called my mom already and told her that I was thinking of going to Denver to see her and dad Thanksgiving. My brother and sister will be there with their families, and I was kind of looking forward to seeing them. I haven't really decided yet. It would be perfect timing for me to go now," I told Mike.

Mike looked surprised. "That would be nice for your family, but Lizabeth's family wants to meet the woman they keep hearing about."

"Hearing about?"

"Mother and I have been updating them. They want to meet the woman that stole my heart."

"You told them? Wasn't that awkward?"

"No, not really. Mother or I talk to them every week. They like keeping track of their grandkids and, while talking to them, Karen Anne blurted out everything. So, no secrets in this family."

"Awkward!"

"Really, Sara, they are pleased for us that you are in our life. They also think it is time for me to move on."

"They don't think it is too soon? "I asked.

"Nope!"

"That does it. I will go to Denver for a few days and spend time with my family while you spend time with yours and Lizabeth's. Let them have one on one with their grandkids. I will be back before they leave and meet them. Doesn't that sound like a good plan, Mike?"

"I'll miss you. A lot."

"You know we have two weeks before I go," I sighed.

"Yeah, but I'm getting used to us." he said, reaching for me and pulling us together. "I'll miss this."

"We've been US for two weeks now, and we have two more weeks before I go to Denver,"

Later that night I called my mom. She was thrilled that I was even considering going to Denver to spend Thanksgiving with them, let alone actually coming. It was settled. I hung up and made my airline reservations. They would send me an e-ticket within the hour. Then I called Dora. She was more surprised than my mother, but glad I decided to go.

While I was in bed, trying to go to sleep, I started thinking of mine and Mike's shower sex. I finally climbed out of bed and headed for Mike's room. I wanted him . . . *bad!* I got to the end of bed and saw Jeffey in bed with his daddy. That was a game changer. I turned and stumbled over Jeffey's teddy bear. Jeffey stirred and Mike rolled over. I crept out of the bedroom and down the hallway back to my room.

Just as I got to my bedroom door I felt a hand on my shoulder.

"Whoa, Mike," I said, as I was slightly jumpy not realizing he was there. "I didn't mean to wake you."

"You didn't. I saw you standing at the end of the bed, and I heard you trip." He pulled me close and kissed me. "So, Sara, what can I do for you?" he asked as he pulled my pajama top off and cupped my breast and then leaned down and kissed it first. Then I started tucking at his pajama bottom and as I melted I kissed him back. Then looking up at him, I said, "Mike, I need to tell you that I wasn't on birth control the other night. So, I hope nothing unexpected happens."

"Would that be so bad?'

"Yes. I think a mistake would be bad. I wasn't thinking the other night. I just wanted you so much. And now we could have a mistake."

Nibbling my neck and moving his hands up and down my body he said, "It would never be a mistake. Never a mistake. Just a lot of love and lust. A lot of lust . . ."

I gave him a gentle shove.

"So, until you are sure, don't worry about something that might not happen. More than likely, nothing to worry about." He kissed me long and hard moving his hands down and down.

I pulled my head back and blurted out, "I am on birth control now."

"Good to know," he whispered, kissing me again as he laid me on the bed,

I gasped as he slowly moved his hand down my body caressing my breast and slowly down my body and his lips followed. I was lost in lust.

I woke up with Mike still lying next to me. He smiled.

"Best get back to my room. Wouldn't want to confuse Jeffey."

He hopped out of bed and hurried down the hall to his bedroom where Jeffey was still asleep. He never missed his dad.

Mike hopped into his shower and I hopped into mine.

I thought, *I didn't miss sex until it happened the other night when Mike kissed me for the first time.* I started humming "Love is a Many Splendored Thing." It dawned on me I had heard my mother singing it when I was a kid. I stopped humming it and switched to "Oh my love, I hunger for your touch," hmm mm.

THE NEXT MORNING, WE both got to the kitchen about the same time. Mike pulled me close to him and hugged me with a tiny kiss on my forehead. He just looked at me, smiling contentedly.

"Sara, you make me feel alive again. I'm so happy you are in my life."

"Ditto," I laughingly said.

"Ditto? What's this ditto crap?" he teased.

"It means, I feel the same way about you."

I started to pull away then I stopped looking into his beautiful eyes and said, "I love you Mike, madly."

"Ditto," he responded.

CHAPTER 25

A FEW DAYS LATER, ZACK finally called me with news.

"Sara, I didn't want you to think I would leave you hanging on this investigation. But we are still checking out a few things. As I told you, I don't want to mess this up. I know you're anxious. I know you want answers, and I will give them to you ASAP. Hang in there, kiddo."

"Oh, Zack, when I heard your voice, I was so excited. I just knew you had good news. What's taking so long? Thanksgiving is just around the corner, and I was so hoping you could nail Harper hook, line and sinker by then".

"It still could happen by then. We are getting closer."

"I know you are, and you probably need all kinds of time to do your job, but I want it done yesterday. Just keep me updated. I appreciate you calling," I said and hung up.

Mike and the kids dropped me off at the airport, and they watched me take off. I was excited about seeing my parents and the rest of the family. I hadn't been back there to see them since Jerry and I last went the spring before he died. It was long overdue.

I have a wonderful family. This Thanksgiving I was more relaxed around them than I had been in a very long time, mainly because my sister seemed nicer and easier to talk to. She has always had a way of ruining any holiday for my mother, which made it impossible for anyone to enjoy it. So, this was a first for her being nice. Though I was happy to see them and had a good time, I was glad to be back on the plane headed to Mike. However, I was a little afraid of meeting Lizabeth's family.

Mike picked me up at the airport. He laid one big kiss on me and hugged me tight. He opened the SUV door, put my luggage in, and helped me in the car and shut the door. He pulled away from the curb and asked me about my visit with my family. I told him it was long overdue and was so happy to spend a few days with them.

"My brother's kids are so cute and getting big. Seeing them in person was way better than weekly Facebook pictures. I do miss seeing them growing up and doing cute things. I do miss that. My brother Bill's getting better looking all the time. His business is doing well. My parents are healthy and doing great. Dad is thinking of retiring in a couple of years. Mother doesn't think she could stand him around her every day. Dad laughed and said he would be playing golf every day so *she* could handle it."

"I didn't hear you mention your sister," he said.

"Jean's another whole story. She was nice this time, and it confused me though I was grateful for my mother's sake. I'll just put it this way, she's no Dora."

"Well, I am glad you had a good time with your family. That's important," He smiled. "We're home? Wow." I was so wound up that I didn't realize we pulled into the driveway.

All of a sudden, I felt extremely nervous at the thought of meeting Lizabeth's family as I was going into the house

Katherine, Jax, Karen Anne and Jeffey all greeted me at the door.

"Welcome home, Sara," Katherine hugged me. Jax shook my hand. The kids hugged my legs, giggling.

They backed away from me and there stood a regal, but a little hefty, grandma and a grandpa who was also regal but thinner in appearance than grandma with two adorable children hanging on him.

Karen Anne grabbed the little girl's hand and led her toward me and said, "This is my cousin Lora Anne."

"Well, hello, Lora Anne." I said as I squatted down to her eye level and took her hand.

Jeffey pulled his cousin Jimmy toward me. "This is Jimmy."

I patted Jimmy on the head. "Nice to meet you, Jimmy and Lora Anne," I said, as I stood.

Mike took my hand and led me toward Lizabeth's parents.

"Louise and Morris, this is Sara. Sara, meet Louise and Morris, Lizabeth's parents."

I stuck my hand out, but Louise grabbed it and pulled me to her, and she gave me a big hug and Morris followed.

"We are so glad to meet you. Mike and all of these people standing here said so many

good things about you. We're so glad Mike's moving on." Then she whispered in my ear, "He's too young to mourn forever. We are so happy for him and you. He loves you, you know," Louise released me and smiled, as did Morris.

"These two messy kids are Lizabeth's sister Kim's, kids," Louise said, making a sweep with her hand towards them. "We had an opportunity to bring them with us when Kim was called out of town on business. Her husband had a chance to tag along with her. Sorta a work- getaway. So, we brought the kids to see their cousins."

"They're adorable. Sorry Kim had to work," I said.

"I don't think Kim minds. I know her husband doesn't. The kids behave mostly," Louise smiled, looking over at the four kids playing laser swords or something.

"Dinner's ready. We wanted to wait until you got here," Katherine stated.

She continued to say, while laughing. "And it's not leftover turkey either."

I smiled and said "Well, let's get to it."

The ladies had made a simple pot roast with all the pot roast fixins'. What made it especially tasty was the seasonings they put in.

After dinner, Katherine, Louise and I cleaned up the kitchen as we chatted about Mike and the kids.

"How long are you staying?" I asked.

"We came the day you left to go see your parents and we plan to leave day after tomorrow. We don't want to overstay our welcome," Louise smiled.

"No need to rush," I shared.

"No, No. That was our plan all along. We need to get Lora and Jimmy back to Kim. That is, if Kim will be home by then, and of course, if they want their children home then, too."

"What do you mean" if they want them home then?" Katherine asked.

"I talked to Kim Thanksgiving Day, and she acted like she and her hubby were enjoying their freedom. I think she referred to it as a second honeymoon."

Katherine chimed in, "Well, we missed her and Ken, and they both missed out on a good time. It has been a great visit."

Louise said, "I think they are making their own fun."

"I am very glad you're here," I said.

"Me too," Louise said.

We girls went into the family room where the guys and children were watching a great old favorite, *Mary Poppins*. The kids loved it, but the guys preferred football. I suggested the kids go to the hearth room to finish watching *Mary Poppins*, so Mike could turn on the game. A simple solution, which was a win-win.

While watching TV we visited and sipped Chianti as they reminisced about Lizabeth. I listened intently, learning all I could about her. She was an inspiring artist. That explains the paintings here and there, which were extraordinary. She loved to read which is why there is hundreds of books in the den. Katherine said Lizabeth started crocheting and knitting while she was trying to recover. It was admirable to see the throws on the back of the sofa and chairs that she had done, not to mention the doilies on all of the tables.

"I know I would have liked her. We probably could have been good friends. Oh wait, I forgot to call Dora."

I excused myself and went to my room and called her. She said she was just about to call me and, of course, gave me what for for not calling her before now. I joined the family again.

Louise asked me if I was all right. "How insensitive of us to go on and on about Lizabeth."

"No, no. I love hearing about Lizabeth. But it dawned on me that I hadn't checked in with Dora. I had to go call her before she sent out a search party looking for me."

"Dora's Sara's best friend," Karen Anne blurted out as she overheard me while running in and plopped down on my lap and up again.

"Yes, she is," I laughed. "More like a bossy mother."

Mike put his arm around me and pulled me close. "Dora's more like a protector of Sara than a mother."

"What do you think a mother is if not a protector?" Katherine said.

"Touché, Mother, touché," Mike smiled, hugging me tight. "Dora's got competition for being the protector."

"I guarantee you Dora would win," Katherine said.

"Well, she's been at it longer. Like all my life," I explained.

`Just then Jax walked back into the room. Where had he been? And why had I just missed him? I gave myself a mental note to ask Mike later.

WE ARRIVED AT THE airport and said our goodbyes to Morris and Louise. It was so cute to watch Karen Anne and Lora Anne hug and jump up and down over and over again. Jeffey and Jimmy said their goodbye by chasing each other, giggling.

Just before they were ready to board, Louise came back to me and hugged me and said how she felt comfort with me being in Mike's and the kid's live.

She was happy for us. Morris smiled trying to hold onto Kim's two children tightly, so they wouldn't get loose again. He threw up a hand in a goodbye when Louise relieved him of one of the kids.

We were on our way back home when Mike stopped by Jeffey's favorite park for the kids to run off some steam. Mike and I held hands watching the kids play. There weren't very many children at the park this time. No one Jeffey or Karen Anne knew anyway. I guess it was too cold.

"By the way, Karen Anne and Lora Anne? Why the Anne's? I asked.

"Oh that. Karen Anne is named after my mother Katherine Anne, and Lora Anne is named after Louise Anne. A coincidence. Cute though, huh?"

"Yup, cute," I repeated. About that time, I saw Harper and what looked like the same tall thin man I had seen before and in the same place.

"Wow, Mike. Help me chase the kids that way. I want to see who Harper's arguing with."

"What?' Mike asked.

I repeated myself, and he smiled, and we both started chasing the kids towards Harper. But, once again, the mystery man disappeared down the parking lot faster than we could get there. He was gone.

"Hi, Harper. Nice to see you, neighbor," Mike yelled.

"Well, aren't you the cute little family?" Harper said, being so smug.

"Who's your friend? I don't recognize him." I asked.

"No. You asked that the last time, and you still don't know him."

"Oh, well, he really looked familiar."

"He's not anyone you know," He snapped. "I gotta go. You cute lil' family have a good day." He climbed in pulling himself up on the seat of his big honkin' F350 Ford truck. He turned the key, and a rumbled poured out of the engine and exhaust pipe. He pressed the gas pedal.

"That reminds me," I said to Mike. I haven't heard from Zack since before I left to go see my family. Have you?"

"Nope, not a word."

We let the kids play for an hour then left for home, frozen. We were plenty cold.

We had leftovers for lunch with some of Mike's famous homemade hot chocolate that he mixes and stores in a big jar. All dry ingredients including dry powder milk that you just add to hot water. It is very good, and the kids always want seconds.

Mike couldn't quit kissing on me. "I can't wait until the kids go to bed. I just might have to put them to bed early. I mean we haven't been together since before you left for Denver."

He didn't put the kids to bed early, but when they did go to bed they went to sleep pretty quickly. Mike came to me a little later. Oh, what a night! As sensual as it can get. I didn't want it to end.

Mike was getting out of the bed, and I moaned, "Mike. Oh, Mike, I never want this to end."

He turned back toward me and stripped off his pajama bottoms then climbed back on top of me. "*Oh, Mike!*"

"Oh, Sara!"

Oh, sappy.

CHAPTER 26

THE NEXT MORNING, WE met in the kitchen. Mike had to go to work, though late. I had to get Karen Anne up for school and Jeffey just had to get up.

I called my neighbor friends and we shared how our Thanksgiving was, and I asked each if they had any information on Harper. No one did. "Sorry," they all said.

I called Momma Dora and asked her if she had heard anything and she hadn't. She did call Zack the other day but nothing. We made plans for lunch the next day.

I tried really hard not to call Zack. I walked the floor back and forth, pacing and chewing on my fingernails.

Jeffey asked "What's wrong, Sara?

"Oh baby, I am just waiting for Detective Zack to call with some good news."

"Okay, Sara, but I no baby." he was tearing up.

"Jeffey, I didn't mean *baby*. I called you baby like I do your dad 'cause I love you."

"Okay, Sara. I guess I a baby."

Talk about timing. The phone rang. It was Zack.

"Zack, thank goodness. I have been worried and wondering."

"Sara, I have exciting news. We have the evidence to get Harper. We have the proof and we will move on him tomorrow night, late. Then I will explain it all to you."

"Can I be there when you haul him out in handcuffs? I begged.

"Absolutely not! Oh, I saw you at the park yesterday. You and Mike looked happy. And though I got kicked to the curb, I am happy too. For you."

"Thanks, Zack, for everything. Really, for everything."

"Oh, and Sara, mum's still the word. You can't say anything to anyone. Not even the sleuth crew. Not one word. Not even Mike, and I know you are sharing everything these days. MUM! We can't take a chance on this one."

"Damn. I can hardly contain myself," I whined.

"You have to. I could have waited until it was all over to tell you, but I know how desperate you are for this to be over. It is almost over, Sara. Remember, mum."

We hung up. I could hardly stand not calling anyone. I was dying but Zack said, "*Mum*." Mum, it had to be.

It was already ten in the morning, and Clancy was just now getting here. I had a day and a half to wait for Harper's arrest. Mum, I kept reminding myself.

"Sorry, Missy, I had an early dental appointment. It was the only time I could get in. I had to get a filling replaced and it was an emergency. It was really hurting. All good now, thank goodness. I will work faster today."

"Oh Clancy, you're okay. No problem." I encouraged. "Heck, I can help. Jeffey and I don't have any plans today."

"Oh, missy, you don't have to. Appreciate the offer though."

"Clancy, I need to help."

"Suit yourself."

I cleaned hard and fast. I was so anxious, dying inside. I threw in another load of laundry.

Clancy said, "Missy, slow down."

"I can't help it, Clancy. I have all this energy. I have to keep busy."

"Well, you're wearing me out," Clancy said.

"Sorry, I guess I can iron." I set up the ironing board and turned on the iron. Problem was I had the ironing done in record time.

We got the house cleaned in half the time it usually takes, and Clancy went home early.

I changed my mind on dinner so Jeffey and I went to the store. About then it was time to pick up Karen Anne, and her friends Grace, and Vickie from school.

It was starting to snow. I didn't want it to snow until day after tomorrow, if then.

I didn't want anything to mess up Harper's arrest.

I just got the kids all home, and the snow was really coming down. I could only hope it would be okay.

MIKE AND I WERE making hot, mad, passionate love. And it was all me. I was a wild woman. He didn't know what the heck was going on, but he was loving every bit of it.

"I just have all this anxious energy. And I'm using it," I said.

"Whatever you're on, I want some," he laughed. "Bada-bing, bada-boom, baby. Where did that come from? I could hardly keep up. Whew!" But he was grinning from ear to ear. "I would go again but I can't. I'm exhausted." He rolled over on his back. "I'm done. Uncle!"

CHAPTER 27

IT HAD STOPPED SNOWING late last night, and the streets were pretty clear.

Dora came over, and we took Jeffey to lunch. She could tell something was up.

"You are getting a lot of sex," she whispered. A lot, by the way you are glowing."

Exasperated, I answered in my best Texas twang, "You bet your sweet tush. All I can get."

"You *diva!* Rub it in my face," she went on.

"*Sorry*, but the sex is unbelievable," I bragged.

"Oh well, you deserve it. I'm actually happy for you, but envious. We used to have monkey sex."

"It can't be all that bad. Can it?"

"No. Just not as often. We are an old married couple now," she mumbled. New sex is the best. Ours is old sex," she grimaced.

"Sounds like you need to step it up some."

"Nope, believe me, it is just fine the way it is. Did I mention we are an old married couple?"

"I'm just saying; watch 'The Specialist' again."

"Oh, we did and it was great. The most fun we've had in a while. Our shower will never be the same."

"Well, watch it again," I smirked.

Jeffey was playing in a time machine apparatus with some new-found' friends, as he put it. He didn't hear one word we were talking about. Thank goodness.

We got home in time for Karen Anne, and Mike came home a couple of hours later. It was snowing again, barely. I was hoping it didn't snow continuously. I was waiting with baited breath for late night to get here.

Mike could tell I was anxious, again.

"My place or yours?" he said and smiled.

"Rhetorically speaking, I would love to, but I am tired," I said, with a tear, as I didn't want to hold back from Mike what I was holding back.

"Oh, Babe, I am teasing. We don't have to have earth-shaking sex every night. Or every time, don't cry."

"I'm just tired," I explained.

"After last night I can see why," He was smiling from ear and ear again, remembering.

We got the kids in bed. Mike read a story to them and they drifted off to sleep. He carried Jeffey from Karen Anne's bed to his.

If I made one trip to the window to look out, I made a hundred. I kept looking outside. Mike asked why.

"Oh, I don't want it to snow again. The meteorologist called for more snow. I am just watching."

"Really?" he grimaced. "Watching for snow?"

10 P.M. came. I said goodnight to Mike, who was in the library looking for a book he needed for work. I kissed him good night. I thought it a great opportunity to sneak out.

I bundle up so I would be warm and grabbed a blanket then slipped out to get in my car. I let my car roll back onto the street where I could have a clear view of Harper's house. It worked. I cuddled up for the duration. I had my cell phone, just in case.

About 11:30 my cell rang. It was Mike. "What are you doing? I went into your room just to lay down by you and you weren't there. I looked out and saw your car on the street. What's going on, Sara?"

"Mike, I'll tell you later. But please, this is important. I promise I will tell you later." I said, softly.

"It's Harper, isn't it? You know something, don't you Sara?"

"I promise to tell you as soon as I know more. As soon as I know. I promise."

"Sara, I don't like for you to sit out there by yourself. I can't leave the kids or I would come out there with you."

"I know. I love you, I promise soon. Soon, Mike."

"I'll wait for you. I'll stay up."

"No Mike, it could go into morning. I'll wake you when I know something."

"God, Sara, I really feel bad. Maybe Mother can come over and I can sit with you."

"No, Mike, nothing can mess this up. Your mother's car lights will mess this up."

"Sara, tell me what is going on."

"I had to promise not to say anything to anyone. But I guess since it is close to happening, I can tell you, but you must stay put. Promise me."

"Tell me, Sara. What is it?"

"Stay put. Promise me, Mike."

"I see how much this means to you. I'll stay put and quiet."

"Zack called yesterday and told me they had enough on Harper to arrest him, and it is happening tonight. I just have to see it happen."

"Well, that explains a lot," Mike said, then added, "I will wait up for you and keep an eye on you through the windows."

"Okay but no lights"

"Deal."

It's 3 A.M. AND I am freezing. I see police pulling in ever so quietly. Lights off, guns drawn, moving very slowly, they surround Harper's house. I sat up and watched. About 15 minutes later Zack marched Harper out in handcuffs.

I got out of my car and with animosity I ran toward him yelling, "See you in 25 to life. Got ya, you repugnant jerk."

I gave Harper the bird. The one-finger salute. His IQ. And it felt *good.*

Zack smiled, looking over at me.

"*C'est la vie*, over and out," I yelled, with a few choice words.

Zack hauled Harper off to jail with his head hanging down.

I could go in the house now where Mike waited patiently. I was frozen, but seeing Harper get hauled off in handcuffs made me heat up. Mike had a heated blanket ready to wrap around me, and we cuddled. I lay my head back in Mike's arms and smiled with a magnitude of relief as I thought of Jerry.

CHAPTER 28

MIKE WORKED FROM HOME the next day. But since he was home, we had a nooner. Jeffey was napping and Karen Anne was at school.

We waited for Zack's call, and finally at 5:15 P.M. the phone rang. I ran to answer it on the 2nd ring.

"Hello," I said. Mike was standing with his arm around my waist.

"Sara, Zack here. I finally have good news for you. Harper confessed he was the one who did the hit and run. He killed your husband."

I gulped. I was hyperventilating. I couldn't breathe. Then anger crept in.

"Why?" I yelled. "*Why?*" Mike held me steady.

"Harper said he and Tom Solo were good friends. Tom wanted to surprise Mary for their 10th wedding anniversary with her dream car. Tom found the car that Mary had often said she would like to have someday. But it was a thousand miles away. Tom had no way to go get it without Mary being suspicious. Harper offered to go get it and drive it back. Tom flew Harper out to pick up the car and Harper drove it back.

"When Harper hit your husband, he had been driving all night trying to get home to Tom in time to surprise Mary that evening. Harper was so sleepy that he dropped off and ran the stop sign and didn't stop. It jarred him awake but he was scared. He said he had a few beers to boot. When he hit Jerry, it looked like no one saw him so he high-tailed it out of there not realizing he had hit so hard it killed someone. He ran and hid the car in his garage all those years ago. Mary never knew. Tom started blackmailing Harper instead of the other way around. Harper paid Tom every month. Harper felt bad, but he felt it too late to step forward. So, he parked the car and covered it with a tarp then piled boxes around it so no one could see it from the street or even walking up to the garage. He took the car to the repair shop after dark and had the front end replaced and brought it home after dark. He didn't want anyone to know.

"Harper told his wife Joyce that the car covered with a tarp was a project for him someday. Joyce never saw the car uncovered and assumed it was a junker. Just wasn't interested. Then she left Harper for good.

"On July Fourth, Harper was telling Tom he wasn't going to pay anymore. Tom got mad and, as you know, they were pushing each other around a little bit. The guilt already was killing Tom, but after all he wasn't the one who killed anyone. He had to pay for the car somehow without Mary ever finding out. Then Tom blackmailed Harper. The car was more than paid for so Harper didn't want to pay anymore. That's one of the reasons that Tom was drinking so heavily for so many years. He was feeling guilt, but not enough guilt to step up and turn Harper in.

"Since the car was bought a thousand miles away, it didn't make the news that far away since it was a local matter. Harper drove right home. He got bids for a paint job but never got it done. He just put a tarp on it, and it hasn't been started since. That's what you found. It wasn't a receipt for a paint job. It was a couple of bids to get a paint job.

"Harper said it was just a matter of time before he was arrested since Mike and Richard had gone over a couple of times asking questions. He didn't put two and two together then. He now knows Jerry was your husband. When I told him, he hung his head, and he's probably still crying.

"Harper said he knew it was too late to tell you he was sorry. But he always felt bad," Zack said.

"But not bad enough to come forward. That's not comforting. He killed my husband and took the coward's way out. *Not forgiven*," I yelled.

"Sara, it is finally over for you. Harper's not going to fight it. He signed and delivered a full confession without court time. He's going to jail for the maximum the judge is allowed to give him. He's done. Congrats on helping catch this dirt bag."

"But is he involved in Tom's killing? What about the blackmailing business he has?" I said. "I was investigating him because I felt he killed Tom. I never would have figured him for Jerry's death."

"The best we can find out, Harper didn't kill Tom. He said he's as confused about Tom's death as much as the next person," Zack said.

"But blackmailing?" I pursued.

"Okay, Sara, take a breath. Like I said before, Tom was blackmailing Harper not the other way around. However, Harper's been blackmailing several other schmucks, but we haven't found out any of their real names. They're all coded."

"So, you don't have the blackmailing victim's real names?" I interrupted.

"Harper's beginning to think it would be to his advantage to tell us," Zack said.

"So, if Harper didn't kill Tom, then who did?" I asked. "What about the tall thin guy at the park. Could he be a suspect?"

"No, the best we could tell he's just another poor schmuck getting blackmailed for having an affair. The guy didn't want his wife to find out. He was paying hush money to Harper who saw him a couple of years ago with another woman. He's one of the guys Harper's thinking about giving up his name. We'll find out anyway, but it would make it simpler for Harper just to give us all their names."

"You're kidding? So, this guy has paid Harper hush money for a couple of years. I hope she's worth it," I grimaced. "They're both scumbags."

"It's out of your hands now, Sara. Anything we find out about Harper, other than about your husband's death, is just icing on the cake. I can't really discuss it with you. Thank you again for your endless investigation. You took a heck of a risk," Zack said.

"Well, now we have to solve Tom's murder," I said. For example, the barrette, who did it belong to and whose hair was in it and who pointed their finger at me?"

"No, Sara. *Butt out*! I mean it. I will handle it. Don't make me arrest you for interfering," Zack said. But I could hear laughter in his voice.

"Tell me about the barrette, Zack. Tell me."

He knew I wouldn't stay out of Tom Solo's murder investigation. That's how I found out about Harper killing Jerry.

Before he said goodbye, he said, "It was Kate's daughter's barrette and hair, and we will probably never know how it was connected to Tom's murder, if anything." Then he drew in a big breath and said, "Donna who lives at the end of the block said the barrette belonged to you but she was just guessing. She wasn't setting you up but at that time we took everything everyone was saying for a possible lead. Grasping for straws."

"Thanks, Zack," I said, as I turned back into Mike, embrace and hung up.

Mike heard everything through the speaker phone. I put my arms around his neck and hugged him, then I called Dora and my other friends, as well as mine and Jerry's parents.

I wanted to go see Mary Solo, but Zack asked me to wait until he filled her in.

Poor, innocent Mary. She will be shocked that Tom kept the secret all these years.

A FEW DAYS LATER, after Zack filled Mary in and we got the 'all clear' to go see her, my friends and I walked over to Mary's. She was so happy to see us.

We sat down, and I took her hand. I told her the whole story about Jerry's death and that the police arrested Harper for it. I told her Harper was driving the car that Tom was going to surprise her with for their 10th anniversary.

"Oh Sara, I am so sorry. I didn't know until Detective Zanders told me," Mary started crying. "Tom said his surprise fell through. Now, I know why. The detective said Tom was blackmailing Harper. Do you think Harper killed Tom?"

"It's possible, but unlikely, so the case is still open. Zack will find the answers," I promised.

We shared coffeecake that one of the friends brought and drank fresh coffee that Mary had just brewed. We continued to visit for a while longer, which we could tell Mary needed.

Finally, we left Mary alone, crying.

CHAPTER 29

CHRISTMAS WAS JUST AROUND the corner. All the neighbors were taking advantage of the Indian summer and putting up Christmas decorations in their yards and on the outside of their homes. I thought it was starting to look a lot like Christmas. I couldn't get the tune out of my head as I continued to hum it all day. Now that Jerry's death was solved, it would be the first Christmas since his death that I knew I would enjoy.

Mike came in dragging more than carrying a beautiful Christmas tree. It was so big I thought it was going to be a Clark Griswold tree. He would cut the rope and the tree would take out the windows. I laughed out loud at the thought and Mike heard me. And he said, "*What?*"

I explained the *Christmas Vacation* scene and he remembered it. But once Mike set the tree up, it was beautiful. The kids couldn't wait to decorate it. They hadn't put a tree up in the last two years. Katherine had a small tree at her home with gifts for the kids. Santa Claus did visit Katherine's house. Mike just couldn't get into Christmas. It was too close to Lizabeth's illness and death. I totally got it.

But at last, it was a new life that we have embarked upon with the kids; Mike and I were looking forward to Christmas this year.

Mike hauled in box after box of decorations. We played Christmas music and sang along.

"We have started a new tradition," Mike announced.

We were singing and laughing while decorating the tree. Yes, a new tradition.

Mike asked if I had any decorations for the tree. I explained that I gave them all away to the young couple who bought my house. There was no room in my apartment I was living in; when I came to work for him.

"The kids and I will take you shopping for Christmas tree decorations so you can have your own to hang on the tree."

"Really, I don't need any decorations; I can enjoy yours," I told him.

"Nonsense, it's settled. We'll go this afternoon and you can to pick out some decorations. I'm think I'm going to need your help on Christmas shopping also, Sara. We can start that tomorrow," he said.

Christmas shopping was another first for me since Jerry's death.

"You know what, Mike; that sounds great. I would love to help you shop."

Before I knew it Mike dialed his mother. "Mother, can you watch the kids tomorrow while Sara and I start our Christmas shopping?"

He listened to her reply and then hung up.

"She said she would love to, but I need to take them to her house. Jax has already left for another trip to Hong Kong or whatever damn place he goes. She said they would need to bring their aprons cause they're baking Christmas cookies."

"Oh boy, fun." I said.

The kids heard what their father said and started jumping up and down about baking cookies.

After a few minutes of excitement, I stood back to look at the tree.

"Wow, it's beautiful. I don't think it needs any more decorations. Lizabeth had a lot of beautiful things," I said, noticing the group of decorations hung together at the bottom of the tree where Jeffey and Karen Anne hung their share of adornments.

"Yes, she did. She looked forward to Christmas every year. She started a couple of weeks before Thanksgiving so she would be done in time to turn on the lights on Thanksgiving night just like the Plaza. At least the outside lights. Now we can add yours."

Mike picked up a box marked "Christmas pictures." He opened it, looked in it and choked.

"These are pictures we added to every year. Lizabeth put them in frames and set them around the house, so we could remember each Christmas as far back as our first. I would like to put the ones with the kids out."

I looked at him and said, "Please Mike, put them all out. The kids would love it."

Mike pulled all of them out and started setting them around the house. They were of good times. Something I knew the kids would look at every time they went by. Sure enough Karen Anne went over to the end table and picked one up of her and her momma. Karen Anne was a couple of months old. She looked at it and smiled at her mother. She kissed the picture and set it back down and went to the next one and the next one. She picked up each one and looked at it and gently set each back down kissing the ones her mother was in including the last Christmas Lizabeth was here, with her head wrapped in a beautiful Christmas scarf. It was a professional photo of the family. She handed it to Jeffey, but he had a hard time remembering. Karen Anne watched him and went to him and explained each picture. Jeffey turned to Karen Anne and gave her a hug. It was so touching. I found tears starting to stream down my cheeks. I looked at Mike and he, also, had a couple of tears.

Then Mike told me that he had a guy coming by to decorate the outside of the house the next day. He wanted it to be special this year.

The next day after shopping, we went back by the house to hide the kids' presents before we picked them up from their grandmother's. They were all covered in flour. As was Katherine's kitchen.

"What the heck?" Mike asked, looking over at his mother and the kitchen.

"We had a contest," she said.

"To see who could throw flour the farthest?" he said.

"Watch it, buddy," she yelled, and she tossed a cup of flour all over him.

"That does it," he said, grabbing his mother and hugging her getting flour where she had none before. I just stood back in the shadows hoping not to be noticed. It didn't work. Mike, his mother and the kids wrapped themselves all around me covering me in flour. We laughed so hard at each other and the mess. We offered to help clean up, but Katherine wouldn't allow it. She said she started it and she could clean it up. Clearly a lady with too much time on her hands!

We stopped for a bite before heading home and when we took off our coats everyone looked at us. "We were baking Christmas cookies," Mike said. Everyone applauded.

We pulled up to the house and it was beautiful. It was breathtaking and elegant. Lights lined every nook and cranny.

"Oh, Mike, it's beautiful," I said.

"Yeah, Dad. Beau-ti-ful, Dad," Jeffey said.

Karen Anne couldn't say a word, only stared in awe.

My neighbor friends and I took turns babysitting so we could get the Christmas shopping done. Of course, Dora went shopping with me. We had so much fun.

"You know, Sara, I am so glad you are back into the Christmas thing. I really missed our shopping trips that started at nine A.M. and ended at nine P.M."

"Yes, it's good to be back to normal," I giggled. "I didn't know I missed it until now. I miss being loaded down with gifts and shopping until we dropped."

"You know my favorite thing is to shop. And I have missed Christmas with you." Dora gave me a quick pat on the shoulder and then stuck her arm through mine tugging me along. We shopped hard and long. We both got a lot done, including buying Clancy's gift. I checked my list of whom and what I had left to do.

One week went by so fast with two weeks to go. But I knew I would get it done. I needed to get my Colorado family gifts sent in the next couple of days. They were going to be surprised as I didn't even bother with Christmas cards in the past several years. I missed wrapping gifts, too. It was my favorite part of decorating, matching all the paper and ribbons to the decor of the house. Mike and his kids have turned me around, and I was so looking forward to it all now.

Mike and I hung my special ornaments he insisted I get. I also bought a nativity. Though Lizabeth had a beautiful one, I wanted one that Jeffey could pick up and look at. I wanted to explain the reason for the season to him. He was close to four now. He would understand about Jesus' birth better. Mike liked the idea.

Mike thought it was time we should make more of an effort to go to church. We attended with a hit and miss. But with the Christmas season on us, we would go every Sunday through the season. *What, three Sundays?* It was a start.

Mike came home almost every day loaded down with presents already wrapped. It looked like he bought the stores out. He, too, had missed Christmas.

CHRISTMAS WAS A HALF week away and the shopping was done. Katherine and I planned the menu.

Katherine had invited Jax. He didn't have any family here, and she thought he could join ours. "*Ours*" stuck in my head. It sounded good. "*Ours.*"

"Speaking of Jax, where did he disappear to Thanksgiving?" I asked Katherine.

"Well, I don't know. He just disappears a lot."

Mike came home so excited.

"What?" I asked him.

He just kept smiling from ear to ear.

Finally, he blurted out, "Sara, I have a surprise for you."

"What?"

"Well, neither you or I have felt like celebrating Christmas for a while. But, since we found each other, for whatever reason, the fact is, this is a special Christmas now. Okay, okay, I can't wait any longer." He paused almost like a fourteen-year old with his first girlfriend.

"Sara, I invited your parents, your sister, your brother, and their family here to spend Christmas." Mike was proud of his surprise. "Sorry your sister and her family can't make it, but your folks and brother will be here."

I started to cry, "Christmas with my family. It has been so long. Oh, Mike, thank you. Thank you so much. It means everything to me," I pulled him into me and gave him a deep passionate kiss. He reciprocated.

Katherine smiled, "We need to redo the menu and buy more food."

IT WAS THE WEEKEND before my family was to arrive. Mike decided that we should make cookies and candy. We made tons, or so it seemed. Anyway, we made plenty and without a flour mess.

Dora and I already exchanged gifts with Sherrie, Kate and Holly over lunch.

Of course, Dora and Ricard are invited to Christmas dinner with us. Their family lives so far away that they were only able to see them every other year. That was okay because they are my family any way.

It was December 23rd and the doorbell rang. My parents and family were here! I don't know who was more excited, me or the kids, or Katherine or Dora.

We took turns right down the line with hugs and kisses. After looking each other over, the kids took my brother Bill's little ones off to the family room to play.

Christmas was here. I hadn't been this happy since the last Christmas with Jerry. We made arrangements for my parents stay with Katherine while my brother and family stayed here.

Mike decided a week or so ago that we should have an open house Christmas Eve party. He was going all out for Christmas this year.

There are at least seventy friends and family here. Mike had it all catered with servers going around with wine refills, hor d'oeuvres of all kinds, even kid friendly snacks, and, of course, a bartender at the ready.

I saw my father over by the fireplace talking to Jax. It looked as though they were having a deep conversation. I wandered over close like I was tidying up, and I overheard Jax tell my father that the only family he had was his son who was in Europe and his daughter who was in a nursing home not far away. He had gone over to the nursing home to see her earlier today and would drop by to see her tomorrow, Christmas Day.

"It's heart breaking to see my daughter," Jax said, shaking his head.

My father asked, "Why is she in a nursing home so young? Was she in an accident?"

With my back to them I scooted closer pretending to straighten a Christmas stocking at the end of the fireplace. Jax didn't even notice me, thank goodness.

Jax said, "When she was in her second year of college, she had been gang raped by five students. They, of course, were drinking. They dragged her to a room and took turns at her all the while laughing and taking more turns at her. She was so traumatized she hasn't spoken or walked since."

My father put his hand on Jax's shoulder, and I heard him say he was so sorry.

Jax went on to say, "My daughter's serving a life sentence while three of the thugs only served three of the five years the court gave them, and the other two just got three years' probation. It just makes me nuts. It's the saddest and the angriest I've ever been."

"How long ago did it happened?" my father asked.

"Just over fifteen years ago," Jax said.

"That is a long time for your daughter to suffer, not to mention the sadness and anger connected with it."

About that time Katherine came over and said, "Excuse me," and took Jax by hand to lead him over to some friends of hers that she wanted him to meet.

I stepped closer to my father and said, "Whoa, I never heard Jax talk so much. You found out more about him in one evening than we could find out all these months."

"Oh, he had a lot to drink and just felt like talking. I was glad to listen. Though it was tragic what happen to his daughter."

Now my mother was dragging my father away, and I joined Dora and Richard. Mike walked over to us.

"Great party, don't you think?" Mike was beaming as he pulled me to him.

All of a sudden, Mike clinked his glass. "May I have everyone's attention?"

Everyone stopped talking and turned toward Mike to listen as he continued.

"As you all know, I lost Lizabeth, and I thought my life over. Then here comes along a nanny that was anything but a nanny. She saves lives, she brings down bad guys, and she helps the police solve crimes. The kids loved her right off the bat. Kids just know. Sara walked into my life still suffering the loss of her husband. We both had a lot to overcome. Each week that went by I felt something changing in me, but I fought it as I didn't think it right to do to Lizabeth. I did a lot of tossing and turning and soul searching. It was like Lizaberh heard me and relief came over me, and I started falling in love with the *nanny*. (*It got a big laugh*) We both started having feelings for each other . . ."

Mike called Jeffey and Karen Anne in and they stood by him.

"What Daddy?"

"Just stand here a minute, kids, like we rehearsed."

Both kids got the giggles and looked up at their dad for direction.

Mike got on one knee as did Jeffey and continued, "With that said, I would like to know if, in February, you will become my bride?" He held out a beautiful diamond engagement ring toward me as he took my hand. "Is February okay, Sara? Will you marry me?" Karen Anne jumped up and down and Jeffey did too, but I wasn't sure he understood.

Just like the kids, Dora started going nuts jumping up and down and yelled out, "Yes, she will."

I looked down at Mike who was busting with laughter at Dora's reaction.

I said. "What she said," pointing at Dora who was beaming. "I will, I will be delighted and honored to become your wife in February." I held out my hand for the ring to be placed on my finger. I bent down and put my arms around his neck, kissing him as he tried to get to his feet with me hanging all over him.

Dora said, "Okay already, enough with the kissing. It's time for a toast. It's time for a toast to Mike and Sara, forever, and it's about damn time," Dora raised her glass as did everyone; then they all cheered and applauded us.

Dora was beaming. Clancy came over and said, "I knew it, Missy. I knew it."

"Did you know Mike was proposing to you?" my best buddy asked me.

"I had no clue. Not one," I answered. I was taken by surprise, and now I know why Mike invited my parents and family here for Christmas.

Everyone took turns congratulating us and taking my hand to see my ring. *My ring.*

"Well, it looks like we'll be back here in February," my mother said. She hugged me then Mike, followed by my father. I noticed Jax stood back and said nothing while Katherine put her arms around us and said, "Congratulation you two."

It was an amazing Christmas Eve. I totally didn't know Mike was proposing, let alone was ready to get married in February or ever. Surprise! I fell asleep smiling.

CHAPTER 30

"Good morning, Mike. Wow, what a party!" I said as I reached up and kissed him, which was the first time I did so in front of anyone, let alone my brother. Mike kissed me back, but this was the first kiss I ever initiated.

"Good morning, Billy. I am so glad you were here for the special announcement," I said, giving him a happy hug. I'm just giddy and love this man so much."

"Mike told me his plans over the phone. It was perfect and the look on your face was a total surprise. Not to mention Dora. She hasn't changed."

Dora and Richard came waltzing in and she said, "Who hasn't changed?"

"That would be you, Dora," my brother Bill said, reaching for a hug from her and a fist bump from Richard.

Mike handed me a cup of coffee just as everyone started Richardling into the kitchen.

"Good morning, one and all," Bill's wife, Trisha smiled, giving me a sisterly hug.

Several of us pitched in to fix the enormous breakfast. Katherine, with my mom and dad, came in, and my mom immediately took over the kitchen. Dad loved to make biscuits so I pulled out the flour and other ingredients and set him up on his own work station.

"Hope we aren't late," Katherine said, trying to be upbeat though she would rather be back in bed.

I poured her a tall cup of black coffee in a Blue Socks World Series mug. "No," I pointed her to the table to sit and drink her coffee.

We were having an amazing Christmas morning. The kids tackled the Santa gifts and then we all tore into the rest of the gifts. The men cleaned up the wrappings and made room for the kids to play, while we women started preparing dinner, or the feast, as Mike like to call it.

My mother said, "Looks like we'll be back in February. Which day did you have in mind to get married, Mike?"

"I thought Valentine's Day, but now I'm thinking the last Saturday of February so we can have Valentine's Day and an anniversary separate. What do you think, Sara?" Mike was glancing my way.

"You're so thoughtful, Mike. The last Saturday sounds great," I said.

"I thought we could get married one year from the day you walked through my front door, but I don't want to wait another couple of months." Mike was looking for my approval.

Dora whipped her pocket calendar out of her designer bag, flipping forward to February.

We looked at the calendar making sure it was the correct year and the last Saturday in February was the 28th. She doubled checked her cell phone calendar.

'Oh, Mike, its perfect. The 28th is perfect." I started getting giddy again.

Immediately Dora started making suggestions. She was already making plans. Her mind was spinning.

Finally, I told her, "Let's get through Christmas first."

The announcement was made to everyone while eating the traditional turkey dinner.

We got through Christmas okay and said our goodbyes to everyone.

Since Sherri, Holly and Kate had gone in different directions for Christmas, they had no idea of the surprise proposal. Dora and I kept it from them until we met up with them for a luncheon after they all returned from their holiday trips. They weren't surprised at the engagement, only how soon the wedding was going to be.

Sticking my hand out for them to see my beautiful engagement ring, I told them, "It's out of my hands. Mike picked the date and she" I said, pointing toward Dora, "is planning everything else just like she did my first wedding. Sort of. This is right up her alley. I know this one will be beautiful too."

"Your first wedding I was afraid you would wear hiking boots down the aisle," Dora said, glancing around to all the girls. "Jerry and Sara went hiking and camping all the time. In fact, he proposed to her on the top of a hiking trail in a clearing with violins playing, duck under glass, and an arbor full of flowers. What did he say, Sara? Oh yeah, I remember he got down on one of his knees and said, 'You light of my life. Come Fly with Me,' Sara. Marry me."

"*Dora*," I tried to stop her so I could tell some of the story myself.

Dora leaned forward, looked at the girls one by one and said, "Do you know what Sara said? She said, 'Jerry you light up my life too, and I will fly anywhere you want to go. Yes, I will marry you.' Dora thought for a second, then popped out with, "But what I don't understand is... duck under glass? Yuck!"

"Well, that's the fast version. There was so much more than that," I squeezed in. "Jerry wanted elegance with our hiking boots so 'duck under glass' was what he got."

"The wedding was so great and, of course, it was because I planned it," my pushy friend said. "Instead of the wedding march, we had a look alike and sound alike young Frank Sinatra who sang 'Come Fly with Me.' My idea," she said. "All the guests were elated. They clapped their hands while a five-piece brass band swayed and played while young Frank sang. Sara and her dad danced down the aisle and, when they reached Jerry, her father twirled her into Jerry's arms. It was so darn cute," she said.

"And you cried," I reminded her. "Jerry and I wanted a different kind of wedding. We collaborated on what would be fun and a non-traditional wedding but with the traditional wedding apparel. And Dora followed through with the plan. The wedding cake was spectacular. Dora had a cake topper made of a couple in wedding attire holding hands, flying through the air."

"I couldn't find one, so I found someone to create it. It was a show stopper," she said. "Magical."

"Yes, magical," I agreed.

We had our friends, full attention, listening to every word.

"Jerry must have been creative himself," one of my friends said. "What an imagination."

"He was special in every way. He would've liked Mike. They are complete opposites and yet the same. I want a small traditional wedding this time," I said, waving my hands in front of Dora's face trying to get her attention. "Small wedding," I reiterated.

"Sure. Sure, small wedding," she blurted out, but I could see her wheels turning.

"Dora has tons of ideas, and I feel lucky she's actually going to let me choose colors and styles," I said, with a sing song. "Right Dora? It's going to be a beautiful wedding for sure."

"The first thing I did was book Mike's church for February 28th. But I have so much to do," she said.

"And WE will get it all done," I reminded her. "Shouldn't be too difficult since it's going to be a small wedding, right?"

"Right. We have an appointment to look at wedding dresses this afternoon," she reminded me. And since it was getting close to time for the appointment, we said our goodbyes.

This was the beginning of the wedding details.

Mike asked me to turn down the neighborhood New Year's Party. He wanted to take me out to the Crown Center party. He wanted to have a real date without friends or kids. He just wanted the two of us.

"Dora won't like it. We've celebrated every New Year's since we were kids. Even after Jerry was gone, Richard and Dora stayed with me in my living room to see the old year out and the New Year in," I said.

"I should have known, but maybe she won't mind if I promise her the rest of our life of New Year's."

It was a super romantic New Year's Eve, even with Richard and Dora celebrating with us. They were feeling a little bit romantic themselves and were giving us space. We danced and swayed to the music and celebrated the ringing in of the New Year before we headed to our luxurious hotel suite. And it was everything he wanted it to be for me and then some. We slept in and that was a luxury in itself. We met up with Richard and Dora for a wonderful brunch in the hotel restaurant before going home. Apparently, Dora's night went very well itself as she was beaming.

We got home where Katherine and the kids were starting the New Year's Day dinner. A little bit later Richard and Dora popped in for the good luck dinner of black-eyed pea soup with corn bread, pork chops, and salad. Dora brought brownies and ice cream, which the kids loved. It was all good. I already had the luck. But something kept gnawing at me. It was bothering me about Jax's conversation with my father. I felt I needed to find out more. Clearly Jax didn't want to talk to me about it when I asked him. I would have to let that boat float on by and find out on my own.

"Dora, go with me to the library tomorrow. The kids will love going there. I want to look up something on the hush, hush," I told her while we were in the kitchen by ourselves.

Of course, she kept on about what was so hush, hush until I told her I wanted to see what happened to Jax's daughter.

The next day the kiddos and I picked up Dora, and the four of us headed for the library.

I got them settled close to me with some children's books. We had just missed the kids' story time.

Dora and I started going through old newspaper articles. "What are we looking for?" Dora asked.

"It was something I overheard Jax tell my father about his daughter on Christmas Eve. I don't mean to be nosey, but I'm curious to know what happened," I told her.

"Oh boy, here we go again," she noted.

It took a couple of hours to find an article that was connected to Jax's daughter. But we had to stop short, because the kids were getting restless and started disturbing other people by running back and forth, so I told Dora we would have to come back when Karen Anne went back to school in a couple of days. I would ask Katherine to watch Jeffey. *Damn we were so close.*

"Are you going to tell her or anybody what you are looking for or why you want Katherine to sit with Jeffey?" Dora asked.

"For now, just you and I will know. Everyone else will think we are working on the wedding," I told her.

"Oh, right!" She replied.

A FEW DAYS LATER we were back at the library. I found where we left off. We started researching to find out what happened to Jax's daughter.

We ran across a Tara Smithon, a sophomore, who had been raped on campus by five students. They took turns raping her over and over again, all the while drinking shots of tequila, making them more determined to hurt the young college student even more. They left her unconscious from the beatings and the injuries to her vagina from repeated entry. Miss Smithon was rushed to the hospital with extensive injuries. No one was arrested.

Some students said it was the first big campus party, and everyone was drinking but didn't know anything had happened to anyone until the investigation. They heard rumors and finally the names came out. Only a couple of girls knew Tara. And not well. They said Tara studied all the time and wasn't into the social life on campus so it was a shock.

"Oh, my gosh, Dora, we have to keep searching. This can't be the end of the story. I need to get back home for now. We can finish researching from our own computers now, we know what we are looking for. I don't want to drop the ball. Jax said there was a trial."

"Sara, why are you so gung ho on this, anyway?" Dora asked. What's the interest?"

"It's just Jax was hurting so much when he told my father. And I have a really bad feeling about it. Why did the boys get off? Richard boy pay off that you hear about so often. Football scholarships or what? Something's ringing an alert in my head, and I can't put my figure on it. I just have to find out."

"Of course, you do," my best buddy said. "And you can't or won't let it go."

We found that we couldn't get enough info off our home computer. It wasn't because the information wasn't there. It was just that the library had the actual newspaper there, and the PC screens were larger. We were able to go back to the library several different days. The first we read about the trial, the newspaper said the police arrested the five guys.

At trial, three guys got five years. The first convicted was David Grayson, a junior on a football scholarship. Average family.

The second to be convicted was Tyler Woodward, a junior, on a football scholarship and a comfortable family income.

The third to be convicted was Skylar St. Patrick, a junior. Another football scholarship. Okay family.

Two other young men had reasonable doubt on the actual raping but did receive three years' probation for watching and not doing anything to stop it. They lost their football scholarships. One was only on a scholarship because he was that good, but from a dysfunctional family life. The last one was an okay student but better football player. Their names are Eric Salaman, Junior and Thomas Solo, Junior.

"Do you see the names, Dora? Do you see it? *Thomas Solo! Oh my God!*"

We continued to search ahead to see any updates on Tara's condition. Apparently, Tara spent months in the hospital before being released to a nursing home. She hasn't spoken or walked since that horrific day.

Thomas Solo and Eric Salaman both did not return to school. They moved out of state.

Forward three years. David Grayson, Tyler Woodward and Skylar St. Patrick were now out of prison. The newspaper says they are now serving their last two years on probation.

"That was years ago," Dora said. Then reading on, it said the father of Tara, Jax Smithon was waiting for them when they walked out of the prison gates. He charged the one closest to him, Tyler Woodward. He got a couple of good blows across Tyler's nose and broke it. Mr. Smithon was then arrested and spent the night in the county jail to cool off. He was warned to stay away from all five guys. Mr. Smithon had many sympathizers, and they didn't blame him for the way he felt. But, nonetheless, he had a restraining order to stay 200 yards away from them. Apparently, Thomas and Eric returned home.

"Dora, Jax was being punished; meanwhile they walked free to start a new life. Poor Tara has no life. She was the only daughter Jax and his wife had. I feel so bad for him. Wait, he does have a son in Europe. Why do I keep forgetting that?"

Scooting forward, the paper said that all five guys moved away to different parts of the country. Tyler Woodward was found dead. He had been bludgeoned to death and then a knife shoved into his heart. His billfold, laptop, watch and money had been taken. The billfold was found in a dumpster blocks away. The murder remains open.

"Dora, I want to dig up any information I can on the rest of these guys. I want to see if anyone else died."

"Of course, you do, but why?" she asked.

"I told you I had something that was gnawing at me. I want to see if my hunch is right. For some reason, I don't think this Tyler character is the only one of that group dead."

We kept looking until we found Eric Salamon in Seattle, Washington, married, two kids. He was found dead two years after Tyler. He was bludgeoned to death with a knife through his heart. Again, whoever killed him tried to make it look like robbery. Again, no leads, unsolved.

I looked at Dora. "Do you see a pattern? And why didn't the police put two and two together?"

"Well this guy was in Seattle and the Tyler guy was in Omaha. Why would the police think there was a connection? Apparently, all these guys lost contact with each other years ago," Dora said.

"The first thing they had in common was Tara," I mumbled. "The second thing is two are dead."

We looked up the next one. We researched David Grayson. There were several throughout the states. One was 80 and died of natural causes. One was 20-year-old boy who died in boating accident. Wrong age. Finally, one popped up in Fargo. He was the right age. He too was dead, the same as the other two guys. So, we knew it was the same David Grayson.

We started looking for Skylar St. Patrick. We looked all through the states and once again we got lucky.

"Here he is in Newark. He's the right age. He was killed just a year ago, and the same as the other guys. Dora, my gut's right. It's Jax taking revenge for his daughter. Not that I blame him. He had to be the tall thin guy Sherrie thought she saw that night Tom was found dead. Hit in the head and stabbed in the heart. And it's about fifteen years later. Tom was the

last one to die who took part in Tara's rape."

"What now? Where do we go from here?" Dora asked.

"I would like to talk with Jax. I would like to hear his explanation. It may be a coincidence, but I doubt it. It all adds up against him. A father's revenge," I added. "I have to think how I want this to go."

We copied all the articles we could and thought we could finish any further investigation on our home computer.

CHAPTER 31

WE WALKED IN THE house to see Katherine and Jeffey sitting on the floor playing with Legos. About that time his project of a tall tower tumbled down. They both were cracking up. Apparently, it wasn't the first time anything fell down.

"Katherine, I need to find a wedding dress. I tried on a dozen already, but I haven't found one I like yet. Dora and Jeffey are going with me tomorrow, want to come?" I asked.

"Well, I need to find a dress, too, and it sounds like fun. Thanks for including me. It means a lot," Katherine responded.

"Okay then. Later, we can pick up Karen Anne after school and shop for her a dress and then maybe we can meet Mike, Richard and Jax for dinner."

"Jax is out of the country again. Lord, I have no idea what that man does, but his business takes him out of the country too much as far as I am concerned," she complained.

I looked at Dora and back at Katherine and said, "Well, we can still go to dinner."

I thought to myself it was just as well, as I had a wedding to plan. No time to solve yet another murder, or in Jax's case, five. *Maybe*! Dora and I will figure it out later. Maybe that's wrong, but Jax s out of the country, and, as far as Katherine knows, he would barely be home in time for the wedding, if then. The wedding wouldn't wait but Jax can. It's waited this long so I'll figure out what to do later.

I know I will be in trouble with Detective Zack Zanders, #1 for getting involved yet again, and gamble his hanging around and asking the same questions over and over while I plan my wedding. Besides, Jax was out of the country anyway. But I knew I would have to tell him sooner or later, and I prefer later. Dora and I agreed not to mention our investigation to anyone just yet.

I carried the newspaper copies of Jax's alleged murders to my room and put them away.

THE NEXT DAY WE were in a bridal shop, one of many we had visited. Since it was my second wedding, it seemed harder to be appropriate in style and color. I just knew I didn't want white.

Dora and Katherine found their dresses. We got Jeffey outfitted and were still looking for me. I saw two dresses that had promise. I put one on, and I took the dress off as fast as it went on. Too foofoo. Then I tried the pale, pale pink on. It was beautiful, but I just wasn't sure. Since my tan had worn off over the winter, I thought my skin blended with the dress.

The consultant brought me an antique white dress that I felt had a bit of a green hue that was just enough to bring out the green in my eyes, yet it wasn't overly green. It was a drop waist and flared out to the floor so I was able to move my legs and dance. It had a lace overlay over the whole dress. Pearls were placed strategically to perfection over the bodice. It reminded me of something out of the 1950s, yet now. It had a tiny cap sleeve on the left shoulder and was strapless on the right. I walked out of the dressing room and Katherine and Dora both gasped.

Dora yelled, "That's the dress! Oh, Sara, that's the dress. It's perfect."

Katherine was smiling from side to side. "Yep, that's it."

Jeffey looked up and said, "You look beau- ti -ful, Sara." Then he went back playing with his cars on the floor.

I walked over to look in the curved mirror to see all angles. I turned and *whoa* boy, this was the dress, and not because I looked like a size two in a size eight dress, but because it was amazing.

Katherine came over with the perfect veil. She placed it over my fluffy ponytail and I smiled because I really looked like a bride.

Dora found the perfect shoes. It was complete. I would wear my mother's pearls. Dora said she had a blue brooch that was her mother's which would look perfect at my waist. I was ready to get married.

"You don't think the green is too green, do you?" I asked them.

"Heck no. You can barely tell its green except for the buttons with the lace overlay," Dora said.

The wedding consultant said, "We can change any buttons or any accent greens for a neutral color. It would match the lace overlay rather than the satin underneath." She walked away and came back with a couple of samples of how they would fit into the dress. We all agreed upon one without the green.

Now that I found *the* dress, Dora had to pick out a different bridesmaid dress which turned out to be better anyway. It went more with my dress, though, she would outshine me in the boob department, as usual. She looked so good. This was going to be fun.

Katherine hung her dress back on the rack. She said she didn't like it after staring at it awhile. She would look for another one, but meanwhile she found a mini bridesmaid dress for Karen Anne that matched Dora's dress a lot. We would bring Karen Anne back after school to try it on.

We left Dora's and my dresses for a nip and tuck. Mine needed a little hemming, and Dora's needed more fabric in the chest area, of course.

WE PICKED UP KAREN Anne and took her back to the bridal shop to try the dress on. She looked like an angel. More importantly, she loved it.

The consultant had been busy while we went to pick up Karen Anne. She brought out several dresses for Katherine that she hadn't seen before. She tried them on, and the third one was the one in fit and color. It was perfect for Katherine's tall regal frame. We left to meet the guys for dinner.

CHAPTER 32

We finished the wedding invitations and got them sent out just short of six weeks ahead, which was close to the appropriate time. Dora was doing almost everything. But as I said before, Dora was the woman in charge, a bossy, creative, take-charge planner. Thanks to her, everything was going smoothly. The church was booked, the reception hall was booked, and the food and booze were ordered with Mike's and my approval. The wedding singer was booked, and the photographer was hired, who was a friend of Richards. Richard would be on one side snapping pictures and taking videos, and his friend on the other side doing the same thing,

All we had left was cake tasting and ordering. Dora had already arranged the appointment. Mike would have to go with me to design and taste every kind of cake out there.

"Don't forget we have cake tasting day after tomorrow," I reminded him.

"Oh crap, I forgot to call Ray," he said. He got up to call his best friend, who now lives in Idaho. Now what did calling Ray have to do with cake tasting?

I heard Mike's side of the conversation.

"Hey Ray." Seconds go by as Ray was speaking.

"Yeah man. But what I called you about, I wondered if you would do the honor of being my best man?" There was a pause while Mike listened to Ray.

"Yeah, the nanny." They exchanged a few more words, laughing, then hung up.

"Ray and his family are coming. Ray said he wouldn't miss it for the world. He's excited about our upcoming nuptials. He said they just got the invitation."

Mike put his arms around my waist and lifted me up and swung me around and around singing, "Here comes the bride. La de da."

I started screaming, "Mike, stop. I am going to be dizzy."

He stopped, still hanging on to me tight. "God, I love you, Sara." He tipped my head up for a passionate open mouth, tongue swirling kiss.

"Oh Mike."

The kids walked in. So much for, "*Oh Mike.*"

TWO DAYS LATER, MIKE met Dora, Richard and me for cake tasting. First, we tried a raspberry chocolate.

"Nope, not crazy about the taste," I said.

"Me either," Mike agreed, turning up his nose and shaking his head, no.

"Hmm, I do." Dora sputtered out raspberry. "Oops!" she giggled.

Richard reached over with a napkin and dabbled her mouth, and then he said, "I kinda liked it."

I swear there is no accounting for some people's taste. I thought.

Dora was insistent on making it part of the five cakes that surround the wedding cake.

"No, Dora, I can't stand the taste. You can get one when you get married," I said, jokingly.

Richard, who doesn't say much, spoke up. "Dora, it isn't your cake, sweetheart. Sometimes she forgets it's not about her," he said, glancing at Mike, then me.

"No one knows that better than me," I agreed.

"Richard, you can tie your own damn shoes from now on," she blurted out at him.

Apparently, since he gained a little weight, he struggled to bend down to tie his shoes.

We continued to taste, and finally Mike and I chose just the right combination of the main cake and all the surrounding cakes including one raspberry chocolate for Dora.

We decided on a three-tier white cake and white icing, with five smaller cakes surrounding the bottom with different flavors, and a groom's cake of chocolate. The topper was a bride and groom and a little girl and a littler boy." It was going to be beautiful.

We were stuffed from all the cake tasting. But Dora asked if she could buy the rest of the raspberry chocolate to take home. The Better Cake Shop said, "Just take it. Dora was happy to accommodate, while Richard shook his head and said, "I give up."

As we walked out of the cake shop door, we ran smack dab into Mutt and Jeff, the bowery boys. Yep, it was Detectives Allen and Edwards. They looked at all of us and nodded their heads, "Hello," to everyone.

"I haven't seen you two in a couple of months," I smiled.

Edwards said, "Sure could have used your help a couple of times though," he snickered.

"He means it," Allen said, seriously. "It is much easier when we knew you had our six." He wasn't kidding either.

"We hear you're getting married soon," Edwards said, as he stuck his hand out to shake Mike's hand as did Allen.

Mike said, "February 28th.

"Congratulations," they both said, giving me a hug. "So, you will be out of the dating circuit," Allen said.

"Actually, Sara's off the market now," Mike said, squeezing my hand.

"Oh, my God, it's Detective Zanders as I live and breathe," Dora said, hardly containing herself.

Zack came waltzing up to Mike and stuck his hand out and said, "Congratulations. You're a lucky guy. Very lucky."

"Yes indeedy, I am." Mike said, with a double take on Detective Zack Zanders.

"May I?" Zack asked Mike. But before Mike could answer, Zack put his arms around me and gave me a more than a brotherly hug with a kiss on each cheek.

Dora looked at Mike. Mike just smiled, still staring Zack down.

We said our goodbyes.

Later Dora teased me. Putting her hand on her head she said, "Oh, Mike. Oh, Zack. Who will I ever choose?"

"Oh, shut up," I said swatting at her.

CHAPTER 33

FOUR WEEKS TO GO to our wedding. Jax was still out of the country. If he came back, Katherine didn't know it. Dora and I were waiting with baited breath. We wanted to talk to Detective Zanders, and we wallowed around about the idea but again decided to wait. I mean, what good would it do? Jax wasn't around.

It was late, the kids were down for the count, and Mike and I were alone. I decided to tell him about Jax.

"Mike, I think I should tell you what Dora and I found out about Jax."

"What about Jax, babe?"

"Christmas eve, I overheard Jax telling my dad about his daughter and what had happened to her. He told my dad a little bit about her attack in college. So, with curiosity, Dora and I went to the library and pulled up a bunch of stuff about Jax's daughter's case and basically how the five guys got by with it. Now they are all dead, and Tom Solo was the last one."

"Tom Solo?" Mike looked at me confused. "Who killed Tom Solo? You think Jax?"

"Exactly." I went into more detail and filled him in.

"So, we finished up with our computer and got all we need to know. The problem is, well, your mother. She is going to be crushed."

"Maybe. Did you talk to your favorite detective?" He smirked but was serious.

"Oh, you mean the "Bowery Boys" Allen and Edwards?" Then I smirked back at him.

"Seriously, Sara, you should talk to Zack. You should tell him everything and let him take over. After all its murder and it looks like you got Jax dead to rights. Call Zack."

"Trust me, I want to go to Zack, but I just don't know what to do at this point. Zack can't do anything until Jax comes back to town. Besides, we have the wedding and Katherine's so happy that I am not ready to blow that for her. I would like to wait until after the honeymoon. Give your mother that much time. That's if Jax ever gets back here. I have never been so unsure on how to handle anything in all my life."

"I guess there's no difference if you tell him now or next year, if Jax isn't in the country. You are the only one who has put two and two together. Whatever you do, I know it will be right," Mike said.

"Will it be right? I really don't know what to do. I almost called Zack several times. I am at a loss, and Dora's just as confused as I am, right or wrong."

CHAPTER 34

A COUPLE OF DAYS HAVE gone by since my conversation with Mike about Jax, and I still am not any closer to deciding on what to do.

"I don't feel right about not calling Zack. I reasoned that the time line doesn't matter. Jax is out of the country, and I need to get on with my wedding. It's right around the corner and things are running smoothly. Thanks to you, Dora."

I continued, "I also reasoned that Zack could investigate each of the murder victims. *If it was Jax who killed them.* Anyway, work the victims case by case. Zack can see if Jax was there or near there at the time of the murders. Not that they didn't deserve it."

Dora just sat and listened to me brainstorm.

"I want to go see Jax's daughter. I just feel the need to see her, Dora."

"Okay, I'll go with you," she said.

"Tomorrow, then?" I asked.

"Yep, tomorrow," she replied.

Just then Karen Anne came running through the door carrying a bunch of papers she had worked on and was excited to show us.

"Wow, Karen Anne. That's beautiful! And look at this one," I picked up another colored something.

Dora looked at me and mouthed, "What is it?"

I looked at her and said, "It is beautiful, that's what it is. Beautiful."

Kids just have a way of bringing joy into your life when you least expect it. We forgot about Jax for a while.

THE NEXT DAY WE left to go to the nursing home where Jax's daughter was staying. A Miss Finch greeted us when we got there. She showed us the way to Tara's room. As we were walking toward her room Miss Finch said, "You are the first one in years to come see her other than her mom and dad and brother. Now that her mom has passed, her dad's the only one who comes and not very often. Her brother only comes to visit a couple of times a year. He can't handle seeing her like this."

"Her brother lives in Europe, and her dad's out of the country a lot with work," I informed her. "So, a . . ." I tried to finish my statement but she interrupted.

"That's what he says when he finally shows up. But every time he's here you can see how he's hurting," Miss Finch continued.

We reached the door to Tara's room and Miss Finch walked over and gently put her hand on her shoulder. "Miss Tara, you have company. Sara and Dora are friends of your father."

Miss Finch stepped aside, and for the first time, we could see Tara.

Shock set in on both Dora and me.

Tara sat comatose, eyes half shut, and her head down. She didn't acknowledge us. She couldn't. I stepped back and grabbed Dora's arm. She knew what I was feeling as she was feeling the same.

Fifteen years later, and Tara still had scars on her face, her arms as well as her legs that we could see. They had to have been really deep knife wounds to be so prominent today. She had suffered and a lot. No wonder Jax went for revenge. That poor girl, now a woman, who could never know true love, who will never have children, never have a life outside the wheelchair. What kind of a judge could do so little to the guys who did so much to Tara?

I sat down in front of her and told her who I am. I introduced Dora. I talked to her about Mike's kids. I told her that I knew her father through Katherine, who is Mike's mother. I held her hand, and Dora took her other hand. I thought I felt her smile ever so slightly. She seemed to enjoy Dora's and my bantering back and forth, but it was a hopeful idea as she hadn't even flinched.

We told her goodbye and she made no motion. Both of us patted Tara's hand and left.

As we walked through the doors I said. "Oh, my God, Dora. That is, I just feel so bad."

"I know," she said. "Me too."

"I feel bad that we are going to turn her dad in for revenge killing five guys who did this to her." I felt a tear Dora put her arm around me and we both were melancholy after our visit.

Dora and I decided to call Zack to come over the next day, though we didn't know where to start or what to actually say to him. Karen Anne was in school, and Kate took Jeffey so we could talk without interruption.

Zack, Dora, and I walked back to the kitchen and sat at the curved bar. I had coffee and coffeecake waiting.

"So, this is how you treat your friends?" he teased, taking a bite of the coffeecake. "Well ladies, to what do I owe this pleasure? You were pretty vague on the phone," Zack said.

"First, let me tell you a story about Tara Smithon a college student," I explained.

I started talking and told him what had happened to Tara, the trial time and the sentencing of the five jerks who did this to her. Then I said, "Tom Solo was one of the jerks."

"What?"

"Yes, Tom Solo was one of the jerks," Dora repeated.

"But before I go any further, I want you to first see Tara Smithon. Promise me you'll see her before following up on anything," I asked. "Because when you see her, you'll understand better."

"But I don't understand," he said.

"You will," I said.

"Okay, I promise to see her first."

I went on to tell him what I had overheard Jax tell my father over Christmas about his daughter. How Jax broke down talking about her. Then he stopped talking and started drinking heavier. Dora and I went to the library to research Tara's rape and what we found out.

"We had to go to the library several times to work on this case before finishing up on our own computer," Dora said.

"We think he killed these guys to revenge his daughter. It tells you everything in these newspaper clippings. I made you a copy of everything we have. I heard Jax tell my dad that these five guys barely served time while Tara got life. No fairness at all," I told him.

"Well, that's interesting. So, you think Jax did all the killings?" Zack took a sip of coffee.

"Jax is out of the country, and NO one knows when he'll be back here. Katherine doesn't even know. She was hoping he'd be back in time to go with her to the wedding. And, since we don't know where he is or when he'll be back, you could check out our theory and see if Jax was there in all those cities, or near them, during the time they each were killed. Or am I crazy?"

Dora spoke up, "You're crazy, but not about this."

"Here are copies of everything we could find," I said, as I handed them to him. "I placed all the names and addresses of each of the jerks on top."

"I wish I could think of something to say. I know "Butt Out" won't work," he said. "But the truth is, I couldn't find out anything in my own investigation. But you overheard Jax say something to your dad and a theory was born. We may now know who killed Tom Solo."

"If you find our theory is correct, before you arrest him, I ask you again to go see his daughter. It will really make a difference in how you handle this. And I really want to talk to Jax one on one first."

"You want to talk to Jax one more time," he sing-songed.

"Oh, and Zack . . ." I bit my lip. "Katherine has no idea about all of this. She will be crushed. So, do not tell her anything. Deal?"

"I understand where you are coming from, but the law is the law," Zack said.

"I know but check out his daughter first. I'm just asking. Remember if I hadn't had a feeling about this, and Dora and I hadn't researched this, you would not have had a lead on Tom Solo's murder. Now would you? It's important that you see Tara. Promise me you'll see her. It will make a difference," I pleaded. Then I went on to say, "Guilty is guilty, but you will see why he is, if he is, when you read this stuff. Go see Tara."

"Deal," he reluctantly said. "I'll start right away checking this out. I am thinking you two need to join the police department with your investigating skills," he said. And he meant it.

Dora and I looked at each other then back to him and both said. "Hell No!"

"I would like for you to keep me updated," I asked.

"Even on your honeymoon?" he smirked.

Dora said, "You call me." Then she glared at Zack.

Zack got up, turned to me and gave me a hug goodbye. "In the words of Det. Edwards and Allen, glad you are on our side." And gave Dora a first ever hug. Then he left.

CHAPTER 35

TIME WAS CLICKING AWAY, and it was ten days to our wedding. Katherine was watching the kids so I could get the last-minute details tied up. Dora and I wanted to check the venue for the reception and the band that Mike decided he had to have.

We wanted to make sure the size would be accommodating for the growing guest list. We weren't going to have as big a wedding as I had had with Jerry, or Mike had with Lizabeth. But it was going to end up bigger than either of us had planned. Dora insisted on inviting more people. She just knew that everyone would be happy that I found love once again. How lucky am I? Twice in a life time. Twice! I tell you, twice!

We arrived at the venue and explained how Mike and I wanted it set up. It was going to be just right. The bar will be on one wall, the cake and other goodies near the back wall but where we could stand behind comfortably. The band that Mike had chosen would be across on a little stage. The buffet would be along the other wall closest to the cake. We decided on a buffet for a more relaxed atmosphere. We ordered so much food. No one would go hungry, and we would not run out of food. Mike said it wouldn't go to waste as we could donate to a shelter. Gee, I wish I had thought of that.

Looking everything over once again, I got tears in my eyes. It was going to be beautiful. Dora put her arms around me and hugged me long and hard and whispered, "You deserve it." We broke the hug and she said, "Let's go have a drink."

We ended up at this little bar and grill at happy hour margarita time. Dora got a frozen one and I got a Margarita on the rocks. It tasted so good and I slammed it down.

"Whoa, cowgirl. Slow down or you won't be able to walk out of here," Dora said, looking out for my welfare.

"Oh, I forgot how good these were," I said, as I held up my glass to order another. "Oh Garcon, one more round."

Dora called Richard and Mike, who were happy to join us.

The guys got there, and I grabbed Mike's hand and drug him to the tiny dance floor.

Dora looked at Richard and said, "Looks like we are the designated drivers."

"I don't mind; I haven't seen Sara this relaxed in years," Richard said.

I didn't remember much but I know I dragged Mike out on the dance floor on every song, and in between songs I took a shot of tequila.

I sang, "Lick your fist, pour salt on it, lick the salt off, drink the tequila and suck the lime. Repeat," as I slammed another.

Richard drove us home in Mike's car and Dora followed in hers. After delivering us home safe and sound, they went back to pick up Richard's car and, with a tear in his eyes, he said, "I love those guys."

"Me too, big boy."

The next morning Mike came into my room with a huge black coffee. "Here, Sunshine," he said, handing me the coffee.

"Whoa," I moaned. I barely could raise my head. "Why aren't you moaning?" I asked him.

"Number one, you had a head start on me. Number two, I did eat before meeting you. All you did was pick at the snacks we ordered. Number three, I can clearly hold my liquor better than you. Number four, I drank beer and you chugged down your margaritas. And number five, you started tequila shots and after a couple of them, you didn't bother to lick the salt or suck lime. Number six, I have been up and had several coffees already"

"Okay, okay, enough with the numbers. I got it. I am a bad drunk," I moaned.

Mike laughed and said, "You are not a bad drunk, but you sure are a fun one."

"I don't remember much." I took a sip of coffee. "My feet hurt."

"That's because you didn't sit down much. You made me dance for four hours."

"No wonder my feet hurt. I had three-inch heels on and I'm used to flats. What was I thinking?"

"You were concentrating on having fun and fun you had," Mike was clearly enjoying this.

"Did I miss anything? Did we have unbridled sex? Did we have monkey sex? Did we repeat The Specialist shower scene? Cause I wouldn't want to miss it."

"Oh Tiger, you wanted to, but I could not in good conscience take advantage of such a hopeless drunk. I knew you wouldn't remember and, Baby, when we make love, I want you to remember."

Clancy and the kids came running in. "Missy, I need to clean your room. You slept in long enough."

I looked at the clock. "Oh, my gosh, it's 10 A.M. I have to get a move on. I have to try on my dress again." I threw the covers off and realized I was naked. I grabbed the covers back and Mike laughed, Clancy turned her head, and the kids ran out just before I bared it all.

"Dora moved your appointment up to tomorrow. She called twice already."

"I didn't hear the phone or my cell."

"Babe, you were out. Passed out!"

I threw Clancy and Mike out of my room and jumped in the shower. I was starving, and I needed to hurry and get something to eat.

Mike had scrambled eggs, bacon and toast waiting for me. Love that man!

I pigged it down. *I said I was starving.* I called Dora, and all was good, though she was laughing her ass off about my actions last night.

I called Zack to see if he found out any more on Jax's daughter's rape and the five dead guys who took turns with her, almost killing her. I know she had to wish she was dead rather than the way she was, *if* she could think. I know I would.

Zack hadn't found out much more than I did. But, did say, after seeing Tara, he personally didn't blame Jax. He finished by saying, though he didn't blame Jax, he still had to pay for five murders, if he's guilty.

Which was still a possibility but it wasn't cut in stone that Jax committed the five murders, but who else?

I called Katherine to see if she had heard from Jax. The first thing she said was, "Sorry I ran out this morning and didn't get to see you, but Mike was okay to watch the kiddos when I left."

"What are you talking about?" I asked her. "Watching the kiddos."

"Mike called me to watch the kids while you guys were out last night. Good thing I brought an overnight bag," she said. "I had a feeling I'd need it."

"Katherine, I'm counting heads one more time for the wedding. Do you know if Jax will be back?

"No," she said.

Katherine was upset she hadn't heard from Jax, and, though he did this all the time to her, she was tired of waiting for him. I just wish I could tell her what we think is going on, but not yet.

I took the kids shopping for last minute shoes and accessories. Dora caught up with us and we had lunch, and then finished the shopping. It was countdown to the big day.

Mike planned the honeymoon, and it was a secret, but of course, he was counting on Dora to help set it up. And she wouldn't talk. I wouldn't know until we got to the airport, which wouldn't be until the next day after the wedding.

We got home, and Mike and Katherine were waiting for us. Dora went home after Katherine showed us the bird seed bags that she and a few of our friends made. The kids had said they wanted to throw rice. They had to settle for bird seed. *Check off the list.*

That made me think we had forgotten guest thank you gifts. I wanted something at each place setting. I called Dora. But of course, she had it taken care of. *Check.*

"Okay, what am I giving the guests?"

"Well, you and Mike are giving little crystal bells. They are about three inches tall, and they ring when shaken. Remember, we saw them in the department store a couple of weeks ago, and you said that would be a cute thank-you gift for the guests. So, the next day I ordered them. You wanted a bell theme. And the florist is getting big glass bells that look like crystal to hang here and there with ribbon going from one to the other hanging from the ceiling. Don't you remember?"

"Yes, but it was so brief that I'd forgotten, what with working on Jax's case and everything."

"Well, my big surprise for you is that I had 'Sara and Mike', with the date etched on each bell, and the store said they will put each in a light blue box with, a "For the Guest," written on each box."

"Dora, that is so thoughtful. I would hug you if you were here."

"Not so fast with the thanks, Toots. Mike paid for the bells. I just paid for the etching."

"Only you would have thought of it though. It's perfect. Does Mike know about the etching?" I asked.

"Actually, that's a surprise for him too."

FINALLY, IT WAS TIME to try my dress on for the last time before I walked down the aisle.

I couldn't believe it. It's the perfect dress. It was gorgeous, and I loved it. I was *really* happy.

They showed me Dora's maid of honor dress, and she had them put a piece of a matching lace across the bust. I asked the consultant, who was showing me Dora's dress, why Dora put the lace in. She said that Dora was so large they were hanging out and she didn't want to steal the show. The way they decided how the lace would go turned out to be perfect.

It was sexy but didn't show a bit of cleavage. It's a beautiful dress. I know, I know, bridesmaid dresses aren't supposed to be beautiful. This dress was.

I brought the dresses home, including Katherine and Karen Anne's too.

I hid mine and Karen Anne's. I didn't want Mike to see them. The wedding was less than a week away and our out-of-town guests would be arriving by the middle of the week. All of the tuxes also had to be fitted.

CHAPTER 36

MY CELL RANG, AND it was Sherri. She could barely speak. Finally, she gave up and gave the phone to Holly.

"Sara, Sherri lost her voice, and the doctor wants her to rest it for the next two weeks." Holly said, regretfully. "She won't be able to sing at your wedding!"

"But!" I sounded frantic and I was. "She has a beautiful voice and now— Well, it is what it is," I went on to say. "Sherry can't help it and should listen to the doctor."

Holly said, "Sherri wrote a message saying she's very, very sorry she can't sing at your wedding, but she will be attend the wedding with her mouth shut." Holly laughed then said, "That won't be easy."

I called Dora, the organizer, and, of course, she had the answer.

"Come with me tomorrow. I want to show you something. I think I can solve your singing problem."

The next day Dora picked me up, and we headed to a small theater that housed a theatrical group for small plays around town. We went in and sat down.

A little mousey four-foot nothing came in and with a munchkin voice, said, "Miss Dora, what are you doing in my neck of the woods? You want to do a dance number for us?"

Dora could in fact really dance.

Dora shook her head "no" to dancing but asked the munchkin to sing "Amazing Grace."

Munchkin started singing. She opened her mouth and all the munchkiness was gone.

She was even better than Sherry, who was more than really good.

"Wow, Dora! Where did you find her, and how long have you known her?" I was excited just listening to her.

"She's a neighbor kid from my old neighborhood. She grew up singing everything she could and can sing anything. I mean everything from blue grass to opera and all in between," Dora answered.

When the munchkin got through, Dora had her sing a country tune from a few years ago, "Breathe" by Faith Hill. She was just as good as Faith Hill.

The little thing's voice was much bigger than she was. Dora called her over.

"Sara, meet Anna Renee."

"Hello, Anna Renee. You have a beautiful and powerful voice for someone so small."

"I get that all the time," she replied in her munchkin voice.

We negotiated singing at Mike's and my wedding. And of course, Dora got a deal. Free.

Boy, Mike and everyone will be wowed as long as Anna Renee didn't ruin it by talking.

"Dora, why didn't you tell me about Anna Renee before?" I asked.

"You were dead set on Sherri and Sherri does a decent job on songs. I just thought it was set in stone. It's *your* wedding!"

"That's a first. You admitting it's my wedding," I gave her a nudge. "Actually, Sherri volunteered right off the bat, and I thought, well, okay then. Done! Check singer off the list." I explained.

"Funny how things work out," she said.

THE OUT-OF-TOWN HOUSE GUEST wedding party started arriving. It was going well so far. The house was going to be packed. What we couldn't handle, Katherine was happy to accommodate, as were Dora and Richard. We had it all covered.

Mike's best man, and best friend, Ray, and his family, arrived first. I never saw Mike so silly. Mike and Ray had to jump up and chest bump, but lost their balance and fell into the suitcases, which scattered all over the entry. They were laughing so hard that snot came snorting out of Mike's nose. And Ray was laughing so hard he cried. The kids were giggling and running around and around the two dads lying over suitcases spread-eagled. It was a funny sight. We girls didn't find it quite as funny as the guys did.

Then they got up and did the run-at-each-other tackle thing with Mike wrapping his arms around Ray's waist and heisting him up off his feet, and once again the two went down laughing.

"Okay you two, stop before you get hurt and end up in the hospital in a sling or worst." Ray's wife, Patrice, said.

Then Ray came at me, picking me up, swinging me around and said, "I never thought I would ever see Mike happy again. Thank you, thank you."

"Okay, Ray, put her down now. Sara, I am sorry," Patrice said, "Something happens when these two Neanderthals get together."

Ray unwrapped his arms from around me, and I was able to stand on my own again. Patrice gave me a greeting of a kiss on each cheek.

Dora and Richard showed up, and they hit it off with Ray and his wife. They were all telling childhood stories. Mike got out the beer and handed each of us one.. After all, it was Miller time, only it was Budweiser beer.

Mike kept pulling me towards him wrapping his arm around my waist. He was very attentive, which I loved about him. *Ah, new love.*

After a couple of hours of catching up, my parents arrived followed by my brother and his family, who had different flights. My sister and her family came dragging in next. We did all hugs and introductions each and every time.

Dora and my sister looked at each other but didn't speak. They clearly didn't get past the last time they met. Dora thought my sister could have treated me better and I have to agree. But again, it is what it is. Sometimes my sister is just plain hormonal. My mother said she was a cranky baby. Actually, I am surprised "Mean Jean" showed up for my wedding at all, and she brought her husband and two kids, too. Go figure! *Now, that is a surprise!*

My sister and I weren't good friends, but we are sisters. Dora on the other hand, is a best friend and a better sister.

Everyone was getting settled in their respective households. All but my sister, who insisted she and family stay at a nearby Comfort Inn. *Really!* Even though we made arrangements for her to stay at Katherine's with my parents.

The morning came and went. The guys all disappeared to try on their tuxes. Everyone but Ray's was perfect. Even Jeffey's. Ray had to have a little let out. A few pounds snuck up on him in the past years. Not bad, just enough that his pants were a bit snug around his waist and a button or two moved out on the jacket. His tux would be ready that afternoon. And it was.

ALL OF US WERE getting ready for the rehearsal and rehearsal dinner. Mike had picked out this great restaurant that could accommodate the wedding party, which, thanks to Dora, was larger now.

We went to the rehearsal and walked through the motions. Clancy and her two daughters took all the kids back to our house to care for them and feed them pizza. We in the bridal party went to the dinner, including my sister. Clancy should have been here, too. She insisted on sitting with the children. God bless that woman!

I saw Dora take my sister over to the side and say something to her. Dora was in my sister's face and shaking her finger at her. *I so wish I was a fly on the wall.* Whatever it was, my sister was behaving and treating me pretty darn good. Hmm. What did Dora say to Mean Jean? I suppose I will never know. But thank you, Dora.

There were many, many toasts to Mike and me with a lot of drinking. We were all having a great time. Then my sister stood up to do a toast of her own. *This should be interesting.*

"Well, I don't know Mike very well or even a little bit," she slurred. "But, I sure know my little sister, and I haven't been a very good big sister. I've always been so jealous of you," she said, pointing at me. "As your true Sister Friend Dora has pointed out to me more than once. I wish I could be her and be the sister I should have been. I'm actually jealous of her, too," she pointed at Dora. "Happy for you," and she passed out and fell back in her chair just as she was saying. "*Sorry.*" She hiccupped.

I sat with my jaw down to my feet. What the heck was that? Everyone, including my parents, were shocked. Maybe this was why Mean Jean didn't drink. She couldn't hold her liquor. She only had two glasses of merlot before she started to whine.

Her hubby said it was time to go as he picked her up and tossed her over his shoulder with half her butt showing. He headed out the door, then turned around and said, "You don't mind our kids staying at your house tonight, do ya?" and he packed my sister on out before any of us answered. Oh well, the kids were already at our house with Clancy.

Mother said, "Well, Sara, Jean's going have a headache tomorrow."

I smiled and Mike squeezed my hand. He said, "Nice speech though."

We all left about an hour later, feeling pretty good. Limousines were lined up to take us home.

THE MORNING OF OUR wedding Dora had made arrangements for the guys to go play nine holes of golf while she gave me a surprise bridal shower and she made it clear, No household" gifts, only personals for the bride. We were enjoying a champagne breakfast when my sister came in holding her head.

"Sara, I am so sorry about last night, but just know I love you and am very proud of you and here." She shoved her present at me and went to sit down with the other ladies still holding her head.

Dora winked at me.

"Wow, so many gifts and surprises for me! I'm truly grateful for my friends and family and a special thank you to my dearest wonderful Dora."

She blushed at my comment, which I can't remember ever seeing her blush before.

Mean Jean rolled her eyes but kept her mouth shut.

I opened present after present of lingerie. "I have more than a lifetime of lingerie providing I don't gain an ounce of weight. Some of these panties wouldn't cover a fly's butt, let alone a woman's butt," I said.

Everyone giggled.

"This is going to take some getting used to," I said, holding the G-string pair of thongs. I'm not into underwear that doesn't cover my whole butt. That's right, I like granny panties. Dora, on the other hand, the skimpier the better," I said teasingly. "Or, I could floss my teeth with them." Laughter broke out again.

"I feel your pain," Kate said out loud. "I like granny panties, too."

"But to be fair, I will wear these on special occasions," I winked. "I just hope they don't cause a hernia." *Another big laugh.*

"Give those to me," my crazy friend said, reaching for the thongs. "I'll wear them."

"We know," Mean Jean said, rolling her eyes.

Whoops! That meant Dora would have to have a talk with my sister, *again.*

Dora stared her down, and said, "At least I can tell the front from the back."

I ignored the two and opened a package that had a couple of pairs of men's sexy bikini briefs. And they were brief. There was a black pair and a red pair. Both pair looked like a tuxedo complete with the bow tie, what there was of them. I reread the card to make sure and yep, from Katherine. I blushed.

Dora said, "Wait ladies, I have one more present for Sara." She handed me a small suitcase and said, "I know I said only personals for presents but . . . Just open it." I did, and lo and behold, she had a whole sleuthing kit made up for me, even a lock-pick set.

"I bought myself a set too," she said. "I am sure we will need them."

"You're a riot, Dora," I hugged her.

With that thought, and with everyone visiting with each other, I looked at Katherine and asked her, "Is Jax making it back for the wedding?"

"You know, I haven't heard a word from him since Christmas. Oh wait, he was here New Year's Eve for one day to visit his daughter. Then he left the country, *again*. I just don't understand that man;" she sounded disappointed.

"I know you care a lot about him, Katherine, but I don't think he's on the up and up with you. I mean, disappearing for weeks at a time. No calls, not even a letter or e-mail."

"I haven't seen him more than a handful of times since we met." She paused, then said, "You know what, Sara, he's just a guy and though, at the beginning, I liked him a *lot*. I know there is more to him than I can fathom, but darn if he's not a tall drink of water," she smiled.

I was super relieved to hear she felt that way. That was music to my ears and would make it easier when the time came to tell her the truth about Jax. This was all good.

Dora stood up and, clapping her hands, and said, "Okay, ladies, we have a wedding to get ready for. We'll see you there. Scoot now. Hop, hop."

Everyone chattered with each other as they walked out the door.

"Next on the list," my buddy said, "is getting our nails, makeup and hair done. Come on, move it ladies. That means you too mea—" she stopped short of finishing "mean Jean" and gulped and finished saying, "Jean."

My sister, my mother, Mike's mother, Karen Anne, Dora and I made up the wedding party. And we giggled and chatted while getting made up.

The bridal party ladies were in transition from plain to beautiful when my cell phone rang. "It's a beautiful day to get married," Mike blurted into the phone. "I love you so much, Sara, and I can't wait to make you all mine." *The doofus.*

"Me too," I laughed into the phone.

"You too what?" he asked.

"I love you too, Mike, and I can't wait to make you all mine."

"Ooh ah," everyone cooed. Just as I was hanging up from my groom, my phone buzzed again.

"Sorry to bother you, Sara, especially today of all days," Zack was saying into my phone. "We think Jax has slipped into the country this morning. He may be trying to get to your wedding. I know it's out of the ordinary for me to ask you to keep an eye out, but just text me if he's there. I promise not to do anything until you give me the word. I promise you that much, but I want to keep an eye on him. I don't want him leaving the country again."

"Well, thank you for your congratulations, but I will already be busy and I don't think I'll have my cell on me," I told him and hung up. Number one, Katherine was sitting right there and number two, I had better things to do at this time, *like my wedding for heaven's sake.*

The time was drawing near. We were at the church and getting dressed. Katherine went to check on Jeffey, who was getting dressed and with Mike and Ray. I could hear the five-piece string band tuning up and Anna Renee doing her la la la la la la's.

I was getting excited and scared at the same time. I wondered how Mike was doing.

About that time Katherine slipped in and said, "Oh, Sara, my son is beaming from ear to ear. I did see the guys take a little nip or two. They were very happy in there. Clancy has Jeffey now and he's so darn cute. And Bill and your dad joined them."

I smiled with approval. "Mike, Ray, Bill and Dad are probably taking more than a nip or two. I'm pleased it is all going well."

"Dora," I called out. "How's Clancy doing with the kids?"

"Clancy and her two daughters have the children sitting down coloring and watching cartoons. They're still clean. Clancy's daughter Carol is bringing Karen Anne and Jeffey back any minute."

Oh. My. Gosh. I thought when I saw Karen Anne and Jeffey walk from behind the screen. How adorable they both looked. They were smiling big, and their little eyes were actually sparkling.

"You two don't look at all like the first time I saw you. You had dirt from head to toe. But now look how clean and cute you are," I said, remembering. I gave them each a hug and kiss.

"Okay, kiddos, go sit over there for a minute. It won't be long now.

Everyone was dressed and ready except me. All I had left was my dress to put on and something borrowed and something blue. Dora gave me her mother's favorite blue brooch, and Katherine insisted that I borrow her pearls with her diamond pendant and earrings. They were *gorgeous.* And because I was going to wear my mother's pearls before Katherine gave me hers, I decided to wear both. One nestled into the other and were so close in color that it was darn near perfect. I put Katherine's on the bottom so I could attach her diamond pendant and it hung down nicely.

I slipped behind the screen, and Dora helped me into my size eight dress that made me look like a size two. She pinned the blue brooch to the left side of my waist. *Perfect.*

I stepped out from behind the screen. Everyone turned and gasped when they saw me.

But I wasn't going to cry.

"Oh, Sara, you are *so* beautiful," both my mother and Mike's mother said in unison. Tears formed in both their eyes. *I am not going to cry. I am not going to cry.*

Both mothers together placed the wedding veil on my head. It was a special moment.

Dora opened the door and motioned for Richard and his photographer buddy to come in and start snapping me in my wedding dress. In fact, everyone was snapping pictures. The power of cell phones.

With the way cameras and cell phones are today, you can peek at what you just took and send them out all over the world in seconds. With that said, the photographer showed me one of Dora and me he had just taken. I asked him to make sure he made an enlargement for her and for me. It was so *good.*

"I want to frame this one," I said to him. "And surprise Dora."

My mother was so proud. Once again she had tears fill her eyes with a broad smile, "Oh Sara, you look so beautiful." *More pictures.*

"You look good for someone who has aged so much the last few years," Mean Jean said.

About that time Dora stepped in and said, "Jean, this is one of those times you shouldn't say your thoughts out loud. So think first before you speak." Then turning to me Dora said, "Don't worry, Sara, you haven't aged one bit. She's just jealous and striking out, the bit—um." She stopped short of saying it.

I turned to my sister and said, "No matter what, I still am and will always remain eight years younger than you." Then I looked into the mirror and smiled with pride. I'm sure the pictures being snapped now will be put in the trash once we see them, as no one else was smiling at the moment.

"Damn Mean Jean," Dora muttered under her breath.

"I should be used to it," I muttered back. With a deep sigh and a large smile retuning to my face, I said, "I'm ready to meet my groom."

I smiled bigger when Jeffey came running up to me and said, "Now can I call you Mommy?"

I was so surprised, and I did tear up. I knelt down to one knee and wrapped my arms around that precious boy. "Yes, Jeffey, you can call me Mommy."

"I think that is a great idea," Katherine said.

Jeffey smiled and said, "Yeah, Mommy."

Karen Anne smiled. I knew she was thinking of their mom. I also knew calling me Mommy would be a little harder for her. But then she smiled and said, ever so sweetly, "Mommy."

Everyone was choking up.

Helping me up and straightening my dress and brushing it off, Dora said, "Okay, everyone, this is a happy time, and we are ready to start this show." She opened the door and leaned out and gave Kate the thumbs up for the wedding singer to start.

It sounded so beautiful.

Everyone took their places. Clancy came back and said Ray, Richard and Bill got everyone seated including the moms. We were ready to start.

Dora went out and gave the high sign to the minister, and the band started playing "The Wedding March" music. *Whose idea was that?*

Ray elbowed Mike with a boyish smile. Karen Anne as the flower girl started placing rose petals down ever so softly as she walked down the aisle and everyone had a soft roar of laughter as she was really careful placing each petal just so.

Coming down the aisle, Little Jeffey followed his sister so proudly, carrying the rings as he beamed, the coos got louder.

Next, Dora, who looked so beautiful, started down the aisle and caught Richard's eye. As their eyes met, he lipped, *I love you.* She smiled broader.

My dad took my arm and said, "Ready, Babe?"

Deep breath. "I sure am."

"You are beautiful, daughter, and you are going to be so happy."

"Thanks Dad. I'm already happy."

Then the music switched, and Anna Renee stepped forward and starting singing,

"From This Moment On." (*Shania Twain*) It took everyone by surprise. It was so beautiful. It was outstanding. I noticed Sherrie's smile broaden. She had been outdone.

With that we started down the aisle. Everyone was standing and cameras were flashing.

I watched Mike, and I could see his smile. I read his lips saying "Wow."

This was the look and reaction every bride should see from her groom.

With Karen Anne standing next to me, and Jeffey standing by his dad, we said our vows with all our love to each other, and then the pastor asked Mike, "Do you Mike take Sara to be your lawfully wedded wife?"

"Yes, with all my heart," Slipping the ring on my finger.

Then we heard Jeffey say, "me too dad!" Again, he stole the show.

Then it's my turn. I answered "Ditto." Mike cracked up.

Then I said, "I sure do."

The minister then said, "Do you Karen Anne, Jeffery, Sara and Mike take this wedding to be one family?"

Karen Anne jumped the gun, and said smiling, "I do."

Mike and I looked at each other and said, "I do, too!" Then Jeffey yelled, "Yeah." which got a big laugh from the guests.

We turned, and the pastor announced Mr. and Mrs. Michael Farren and family to the guests. We marched back down the aisle with the kids as Dora and Ray followed a few feet behind.

Everyone was throwing bird seed and blowing bubbles as we went out the door.

We announced to everyone that we would see them at the reception after pictures of the wedding party were taken. Richard was pretty good at snapping pictures himself and as the other photographer got very creative. He had Mike throw the flowers to the guys and me the garter to the ladies.

"Get over here, Richard. I want you in the wedding photos."

The other photographer did a wonderful job.

CHAPTER 37

WE HEADED TO THE reception where everyone had already started the party. The music started playing as soon as we walked through the door. We danced in to a jazzy "You Belong to Me." The reaction of our arrival was uplifting as the applause rang out.

The music played softly while the wedding party got in the buffet line, followed by the guests. I have to say it was *really* good. The caterer was outstanding. I looked over and, standing by the entrance stood the hunky detective, Zack Zanders and his two side-kicks, Junior Detectives Edwards and Allen in suits fit for a wedding. *Mine.*

"What the heck?" Mike asked.

"Sorry, Mike. I think he thought Jax would show up here. He asked me to text him if Jax in fact did show up, and I said I wouldn't have my cell on me at my wedding. So, here he is in the flesh."

Mike said, "Go ahead, and see what he wants."

I walked over to where the detectives were standing and raised my hands in a *what is this?* gesture.

"Sorry, Sara, to interfere with your party, but we felt if Jax was here then we needed to know, and by the way, you are beautiful."

"Thanks, Zack, and I haven't seen Jax.

Mutt and Jeff were swaying to the music, and regretfully, I said, "You guys want to stay? Have a bite and maybe a drink?"

I barely got the sentence out when the young detectives were headed for the bar, "Thanks, we're off duty and just volunteering for this detail," spouted Edwards.

Det. Allen continued to say, "Zanders made us come."

Zack shrugged his shoulders and put his hands in his pockets.

"Come on, Zack, go have a good time. Who knows, Jax could show up."

Zack handed me a card. "I didn't know what to get you, so I put a gift card inside."

"Zack, you didn't need to do anything. But thank you so much," He handed me the card and an itsy-bitsy kiss on my cheek. I stuck the card into the card basket on my way back to Mike.

"Nothing can ever upset me now; 'he lost and I won. I have no fear', let him stay," Mike said, as he put his arm around my waist and headed to the dance floor.

Dora stood up and banged against the crystal glass to get everyone's attention.

The music stopped and we stopped in our tracks.

"I want to toast my best friend and her new hubby," Dora said, moving to our direction. "They both have overcome their tragedy of losing their first loves. But now they have found their last love in each other, and we celebrate them today. I would like to take the credit for this love by my forcing Sara to go to the interview with Mike." Everyone laughed. "And though neither one was ready to pursue any love connection, I could tell they had something special. It was just a matter of time. I knew sooner or later they would discover their love for one another. And here we are, raise your glasses to Sara and Mike. *Salute!*" We sipped our champagne that someone just handed us.

Then Ray stood up and raised his glass and said, "Not to be outdone by the maid of honor, and though I wasn't involved at the beginning, when I finally saw Mike with Sara, I too, knew it was a good match." He walked closer to us and continued. "May you be able to celebrate in fifty years from now with everyone who is here today. *Salute!*"

Mike and I held up our flutes and he said, "Thanks everyone, we're glad you are all here to celebrate our special day. Sara and I want to make a toast. Everyone raise your glasses."

"Here's to you, Jerry." I said, raising my glass high.

"And to you, Lizabeth," Mike said, looking to the heavens.

We tapped our glasses together and both said "We will always love you."

Everyone applauded and some cried, especially Lizabeth's parents, who were nice enough to share in this moment.

We had more pictures of cutting the beautiful cake and we kept it clean. No cake in the face.

Mike and I were on our fourth dance when Det. Allen asked Mike if he could cut in. Mike smiled and turned me over to him. It was a slow dance, and I thought we would be through when a faster piece of music started playing and Det. Allen twirled me around and turned me toward him and we did the two-step. Det. Edwards popped in and took over. I have to admit I was having a great time. Those two young men, *boys,* were so cute. Mike stood on the side-lines and kept time with the music. Then our neighborhood friend, Sherri, took Mike's hand and drug him onto the dance floor. Holly, Kate and Dora were waiting in the wings for their turn. Their husbands lined up for me. One after the other took turns dancing with us. We were all having so much fun. Everyone was up and dancing, even all the kids. Of course, the kids were.

I watched Det. Zanders walk over to Mike and say something to him and Mike smiled.

Both men walked over to me, and Mike took my hand and placed it into Zack's hand.

"Just for the dance," Mike said, and he walked away.

The music was a medium type waltz. Not too slow and not too fast. I can't remember the name of it, but it was beautiful.

Zack waltzed me around and around the dance floor. He could really waltz.

He said to me in a low voice. "I have always wanted to dance with you. I just didn't know it would be at your wedding." *Gulp.*

Zack gave me a hug and walked me back to Mike and said, "Thanks, Mike."

"I would say, any time, Zack, but that ain't going to happen." Then they both laughed.

The junior detectives were having a good time and really didn't want to leave, but they came over and said congrats and goodbye with brotherly kisses on my cheek and a handshake with Mike.

"Since Jax is a no show, we're cutting on out. But thanks for letting us stay at the reception," Zack said, as he hugged me and gave me a friendly kiss on the cheek.

Mike smiled as Zack turned and walked out.

"That was nice." Mike said.

'What was?" I asked.

"Zack used the excuse that Jax might be here to show up at our wedding."

"They had fun," I said, as nonchalantly as I could.

We made the rounds to personally thank everyone for coming and for sharing in our special day.

One more surprise to wind up a perfect time; Dora knows how I love the old Al Jolson song "Anniversary Song." As a kid I saw the *Al Jolson Story* on late, late nighttime movies and loved that song ever since. Now I pull it up on the computer ever so often just to hear it.

Two cellos, two violins, and two guitars started playing the "Anniversary Song." Mike, who was clearly in on the surprise, took my hand and we waltzed around and around. It was *so* wonderful. It was the Bride and Groom dance and the end to the perfect wedding.

CHAPTER 38

ALL OF THE OUT-OF-TOWN visitors had gone home on Sunday after Mike and I opened our tons of wedding presents. We spent time with the kids as we were leaving them in Katherine's care for two weeks.

Dora and Richard drove us to the airport, and Dora said, "Here. You're going to need to switch bags with me to fit the weather where you're going." She just smiled and forced the switch of bags.

Since I trusted her, I switched. We just got the mystery bags checked in when the intercom started crackling and I heard "boarding at Gate 27 for Fort Lauderdale." I looked at Mike as he led me toward Gate 27.

"Where are we going?" I asked him.

He just smiled placing his hand in the middle of my back pushing me down the ramp to board. When we were seated, he surprised me with a ten-day cruise to Barbados and back.

"That's why Dora repacked my things under the radar from winter to summer," I told Mike.

"Uh-huh! Your friend is always thinking ahead," he said. "She even got your passport." He said patting his inside jacket pocket.

We barely made it to Ft. Lauderdale, let alone boarding the Princess Cruise ship just before they pulled up the plank.

The purser showed us to our suite which consisted of a living

room with refrigerator, a bedroom with a king size bed, a walk-in closet with a dressing room and a bathroom with a shower and a tub. Wow, a shower and a tub. Then I discovered we had our own balcony.

"Mike, you went all out," I smiled and threw my arms around him.

"First class for my bride, all the way, first class." He picked me up and carried me to the bedroom for a little honeymoon. *Oh Baby.*

We woke up from our afternoon delight with the sound of the ship pulling away from the shore. We showered and got ready for our first formal dinner in the ship's dining room. It was delicious. Mike was amazed at how I forgot my manners at a formal dinner, and how I pigged down my food.

"What? I am starving after the afternoon delight and no lunch," I giggled with a slight blush.

"You had dessert." He laughed. "

"Hmm, yes I did." I replied, "I'm sure this won't be the only time you see me do unexpected things," I said, as I looked around the table at three other couples and our own officer. "We're newlyweds and still learning about each other, aren't we, honey?" as I took the dessert of strawberry swirl shortcake from the server.

We were walking hand-in-hand back to our suite when the swell of the waves was getting larger and we were swaying trying to keep our balance and not fall off the starboard side of the ship. We were off balance as the waves were getting more, making it very difficult to walk. But hanging on to a rail that someone thought ahead about just for this kind of weather, we managed to get inside the ship's interior. We took advantage of the sitting areas throughout. Other passengers were sitting in groups talking about how bad the weather was. And if it was going to be like this the whole time, then they were never going on a cruise again.

It was like that the first two days of sailing.

No one was able to keep their balance and walking in my stiletto shoes was impossible. My Mary Jane's didn't seem to have the same sex appeal, but at least I didn't fall off them. "*Thank you, Dora, for packing them,*" I actually said out loud.

The shows that had any movement in their act were cancelled. The actors couldn't stand and dance any better than the rest of us.

We decided to make the best of a bad situation and went to the onboard casino.

Mike went to play poker, and I started shooting craps, and apparently I was doing something wrong when a couple of mob-type guys said. "Hey, hey little lady, let us show you how it's done."

I came away with $1500, thanks the old wise guys. As I walked towards Mike, the little mob guys were yelling, "Come back." *I kept walking.* I waved the queen wave and walked on.

I was standing behind Mike, watching him win a hand and lose two. Finally, he stood up and said, "Done."

I counted my winnings out into his hands and he was amazed.

I yelled, "Thanks, fellows," to the mob guys.

Mike said, "Now I know how you won."

AFTER WE LEFT THE casino and since most of the shows were still cancelled due to the rock and rolling of the ocean, Mike and I spent most of the time in our suite, doing our own rocking and rolling. We are on our honeymoon, after all.

We went out on our private balcony and watched the sun set into the ocean and the stars start to peek out. It was so romantic and beautiful, though the water was still rough.

I told Mike I would be right back and left him standing on our balcony alone with the wind and the water blowing slightly over him.

I came out stark naked and put my arms around him and as he turned into me, he did a double take.

He didn't say a word, just pulled off his clothes and tossed them just inside the door and laid me down ever so gently on the balcony floor. Wave mist and wind were slightly rolling over our bodies. It was so sexual. So out of this world, so, so, *oh baby*. It was euphoric. Just when I thought I knew it all, I learned more. And I loved it. I love this man.

The next morning, we went back on the balcony and watched the sun come up. There is something to say about sunset and sunrise on the open ocean.

On the third day it was smooth sailing. Since the water in the pool wasn't splashing out on the deck, the pools were open. We were headed for an early swim in one of the ship's swimming pools. "Oh my," I gulped as I looked at all the nude bodies lying around the ship's balcony on the way to the pool. We couldn't help but look. I nudged Mike, "Eyes facing the bow, mister."

"Ditto," he smirked.

After we were through with our swim we went to an early breakfast of eggs benedict. I was sipping my coffee and heard a scream. A couple of tables over a fifty-something man had fallen off his chair and was lying spread eagle on the floor without movement.

Mike and I jumped up to see if we could help.

I started, "Staying alive," on his chest, but it didn't help. He was gone.

His wife was screaming, "No, no, no, not my Johnny. Oh, Johnny," holding his head in her lap.

I noticed a whole cookie and a partially-eaten cookie with crumbs all around his head. I gently took a napkin and collected all the cookies I could and slid them into my purse. I've watched enough Forensic Files to know to collect as much suspicious evidence as possible. And I am still a nurse who has been trained to get an extra vial of blood just in case. So, I picked up the cookies.

"Okay, Sara, I saw you pick up the cookies. Is your sleuthing kicking in?" Mike asked as we stepped away from the body.

"Something isn't right, Mike. That young wife wasn't crying real tears. She was just going through the motions and the emotion wasn't there. So, my interest and suspicion piqued. I think she just killed her husband."

We waited for the ship's gurney to arrive with their ME of sorts. I followed them to the ship's hospital, and I spoke to the ship's doctor, Dr. Johnson, while the Medical Emergency of sorts, examined him.

I told him who I was, *not that it mattered,* and introduced my new hubby. I told them that I would like them to run a poison test as I was sure that "Oh Johnny" didn't have a heart attack. They said they would do the best they could with what they had aboard ship but would put the deceased on ice. *On ice.* Poor Johnny.

I offered to draw the vials of blood for testing and I was surprised Doctor Johnson said go ahead.

I did two vials and marked them with John Manning and dated it. The doctor pointed toward the freezer.

The doctor and ME's of sorts were going to notify the next port authority. I told them that I was going to alert a detective I knew for him to follow up. They were not pleased.

Mike said, "You need to listen to her. She's good at what she does." He squeezed my hand.

They stared at me for a nano second. We left with the crew looking bewildered at what just happened. First a death and second a crazy blond, though be it a dark blond, telling them what to do.

Since sometimes Mike seems a little jealous of Zack and most of the time not, I asked if he minded if I called Zack for direction.

Of course, he was okay with it.

We were walking on the promenade and saw the lady who had just lost her husband walking arm in arm with another guy.

"Well, that didn't take long. She could at least wait a day or two," I smirked.

About that time another woman came running up to the couple and as they turned to go back the other way, I could see that the two women were mirror twins. Wow.

I told Mike, "That explains a lot."

The Mrs. Johnny was still pretending to cry while talking to her twin and walking toward the inside of the ship.

I called Zack. I explained what had happened and my suspicion.

"Something isn't right, Zack; I think she killed her husband. We witnessed the whole thing. I picked up the cookies for testing. The ship's doctor has Johnny on ice, and I got a couple of vials of blood for testing for poison. The ship's ME's were not qualified to perform the necessary measures to make sure Johnny didn't die of a heart attack, and, of course, I drew blood for testing before Johnny was put on ice.

Zack said, "Sara, it's amazing how murder just keeps happening around you. You're like a murder magnet. "

"I'm just lucky," I answered.

"I'll call the proper authorities. Do not do another thing until you have heard from me. I mean it, Sara. Nothing," Zack threatened. "Enjoy your honeymoon only." He hung up.

It was about one hour before the ship docked at St. Martens Island. We both were looking forward to planting our feet on solid ground, especially after two days in rough waters. I wondered if Zack had stopped the de-boarding of Johnny. I sure hope so.

Some passengers went on organized sightseeing bus tours, but we just walked the stores and decided to get a cabby with an attitude. We told her we wanted to go to the French side of the island. She took us but wasn't excited about it. Why? We never did find out.

The French side was actually prettier to us than the Dutch side where we docked. The French side was where famous people had their getaway homes.

We bought a few souvenirs from both sides of the Island for the kids, and then we boarded the ship and immediately got ready for the next formal dinner.

"Wow, I DIDN'T KNOW you owned a dress like that. I like. I like very much. You are the sexiest and most beautiful woman on this ship."

"I bought it just for the honeymoon. I was hoping you would like it."

"Oh, I like it very much. I am thinking of taking it off of you and making mad passionate love to you."

The dress came off as fast as I could pull it over my head and I didn't need Mike's help. Needless to say, we were late for dinner.

CHAPTER 39

As we were walking back to our room we decided to go to a bar that catered to our age crowd. We ordered a couple of drinks, and Mike found a table while I visited the little ladies room. Just as I rounded the corner to the restroom, I heard voices. I stopped to listen. *The sleuth in me made me do it.*

I heard Mrs. Johnny telling her twin, something that made me suspicious. Even more suspicious, something about poison and Johnny's favorite almond cookies. And something like, "I don't know why it took so long." I strained to hear the conversation.

I rounded the corner, went past them and into the restroom like I didn't hear anything.

When I got back to the table and told Mike what I overheard the twins saying.

"Dear old Johnny didn't have a heart attack but the little wife poisoned him with his favorite almond cookie. Something is going on as I suspected."

"Sara, do I have to remind you, we are on our honeymoon? No sleuthing."

"I can't help it. It keeps falling into my lap. I know something isn't right here.

But I put off my sleuthing for Mike's sake. *Tonight!.*

We had such a good time. We visited with some of the other passengers, exchanged addresses and cell phone numbers and swore we would keep in touch.

We snapped and texted a few pictures back and forth. *Memories.*

ON THE FOURTH DAY at sea we watched the sun come up again. It was beautiful. I was afraid that when we developed the pictures the way I like to do, that I would forget which it was sun up or sundown as they both were very, very similar. I decided to stick my thumb up for sun up and thumb down. Snap.

I asked Mike if he wanted to go for a walk before breakfast, and he said that he was going to call his mother and check on the kids. I told him to give them my love and I went out the door.

I ran into one of the crewmen and we exchanged pleasantries. I stopped and turned and said, "Say, that guy that died in the dining room. What did you guys do with the poor guy?"

"What guy?" he asked. "I didn't know anyone died."

Another crewman walked up where we were standing and he could tell his cohort had a confused look on his face.

"Hey, Todd, what's wrong?" he asked.

"Apparently some dude died in the main dining room, and she was asking what we did with him," Todd stated.

"Well, it sounds cold, no pun intended, but we do put them in a freezer until we make land."

"But, we were in St. Martens."

"Yes, but the mainland's what I meant to say. Got to take him home, I guess," he answered. "Some bureaucratic dude decided to take him to the shores of the U.S.A.

Interesting, I thought. So, there can be an autopsy American style. Hmm! I like that very much. *Thanks Zack!*

I walked on and watched the private island of Mayrue off in the distance.

Mayrue is a private-Island where the passengers would spend the day on the beach swimming with a big cook out that lasted all day. A shuttle took a load of passengers after load of passengers off the cruise ship and dropped them off on the island. As everyone stepped off the shuttle onto land, the natives were there wanting to braid your hair or sell you a sea shell that anyone could bend over and pick up off the ground. But it was the way they made money. The Island had no businesses on it. This is the only means of making a living. That and I understand tons of marijuana crops were inland. Some of the ladies got their hair braided, even a couple of the guys. And some folks got suckered into buying a seashell. The steel drums played from the time we landed until we left, and I loved it. I loved the sound.

We had such a good time swimming and playing, going in and out of the water. Some of the crew was videotaping me flopping around in the water close to the shore. Every time a wave came towards the beach the wave tossed me around like a big white whale that was beached. The crew was filming me and I yelled, "*Cut!*" Mike had been swimming but heard me tell the crew to cut and swam to me.

"Come here, my bride," then sat beside me and started clowning around making it impossible to cut. The crew kept recording.

I yelled, "Stop! Enough!" They just laughed and kept recording so Mike and I started kissing and holding each other, falling over on the sand letting waves bounce off us as we teased the camera. I jumped up and wrapped my legs around Mike's waist, and he walked out of the water with me snuggled close to him. Later, I found out they put some of the video in their next advertising video. *Hmph, think maybe we should get paid?*

The one thing about cruise ship lines, people from all over the world were aboard.

One couple from some other country came out of the water, pulling down their suits to get the sand out, which left them stark naked.

Nudging Mike I said, "Oh my goodness, do people of other countries still not care about nakedness? I know the body is supposed to beautiful but— Theirs are not."

"Wonder what country they're from? I don't understand their language," Mike said, while watching the couple in amazement and listening to their jibber jabber.

They dusted the sand off, put on a clean dry suit and repeated it all over again. Back in the water, sand in their suits, pull them off, swipe at the sand, put clean suits on and start all over. I bet they had ten suits in reserve. We saw more bare breast and booties as well as frontal views that day than the rest of the cruise or the rest of our life. Some pretty good to look at and some not so much. The only ones guarded were Americans. *Viva, USA.*

We watched Mrs. Johnny with her twin and the twin's main squeeze, clearly a *sleaze-ball,* walk across in front of us. It didn't look like Mrs. Johnny was mourning anymore. She appeared to be making the move on the next poor unsuspecting victim without any trouble.

Mike was watching my wheels turn in my head and said, "You aren't going to be happy unless you are involved. You are working on it in your head now, aren't you?"

"Honestly, Mike, I tried not to care, but something smelled rotten and I just have to find out what is going on. I am sorry."

"Well, that is one of the many reasons I love you. Just don't forget we're still on a honeymoon here."

"I promise."

Later I called the kids and also spoke with Katherine.

"All is well," she said. "They are having a good time and can't wait for you to come home. Where are you? I hear steel drums."

I explained, "Cruise lines either buy an island or rent an island to spend the day on the beach and have a huge cook out. It's a passenger favorite. You know what the most unusual thing for me is?" I asked her. "It's the servers in little tiny motorized boats with all kinds of cold beverages driving right up to you while you swim. They had all kinds of drinks. But in the sun all day, I think alcohol could be deadly. It still didn't stop people from ordering their favorite alcoholic beverage and charging it to their cabin. Mike and I tried it once or twice only to see if the server had what we wanted on his little boat." I rattled on. "What's going on there? Jax back?"

"Nothing new on the home front. No Jax either. Enjoy your alone time together. I hear the steel drums again," she said. "Oh, your buddy Dora dropped by a couple of times to see if I needed a break from the kids. That's so nice of her. I have her number if I want to take her up on her offer."

"Yeah, she is a special friend. Believe it or not, I miss the crazy redhead. It's dinner time. Mike's already in the line to fill his plate. Talk you later. Love and kisses. Bye for now." I said.

After we had a bite I wandered to the edge of the beach where it was virtually empty of people and called Dora. I told her what was up. I asked her to call Zack and fill him in and see if he was working with any police personnel in the port of call. I felt sure I would be able to solve this or at least have enough information to give the police to solve by the time we returned to the states.

Fifteen minutes later Zack called.

"Dora called," he said. "Okay, okay, since you can't stay out of anything this is what I need you to do."

I listened. "Uh-huh . . . Uh-huh. Will do."

"Oh, and Sara, be careful. You tend to be the best investigator I seem to have. You stumble on more by accident than the investigators do on purpose. Be careful. Let me know what you find out. His name's John Madden."

"John Madden?" I repeated. "Yes, that's what the doctor said. Oh, John Madden."

"Not the same. Later." He hung up.

It was time for me to follow-up with the mirror twins. I decided the next time Mike and I ran into them, I would introduce myself, as well as Mike and start asking questions.

Luck was with us. Mike and I were running late and grabbing a bite of lunch on the deck when we saw the twins off in the distance with the one twin companion walking towards us.

"Okay, Mike, I am going to stop them and introduce you and me."

Mike smiled as he knew there was no stopping me now. I was on a mission. And now he was a part of it.

It's like we were thinking alike as they reached us rather quickly.

"Hi," I said, as I stuck out my hand to one of the twins, the one I thought killed her husband. *Oops, I hope I didn't think that out loud!*

"I'm Sara Farren." *I was still getting used to that.* "This is my husband Mike." *And I was still getting used to that.*

We shook everyone's hand and they introduced themselves to us.

"Nice to meet you," the dead man's wife said. "You're the one who tried to save my Johnny. I am Brooke Madden and this is my twin, Sheila McRoy, and her husband Dennis."

"Brooke, I am so sorry about the passing of your husband. Mike and I tried to help him, but he was gone so quickly. How are you coping?" *Like she actually was.*

"Oh, it is so hard to be only married two years and lose Johnny so soon," Brooke said.

Oh brother, you *hardly got the sheets changed.*

"Two years." I repeated to Brooke. "The honeymoon was barely over," I said, "Poor, poor thing." I patted her hand. *Murderer,* I thought.

Mike and Dennis were exchanging pleasantries. Then I heard Mike ask Dennis what John did for a living. Mike seemed very interested. I could tell he was pumping Dennis as much he could without being too obvious. I couldn't wait to hear Mike tell me what he found out.

Meantime, I was nicely pumping what I could out of the mirror twins. *Liars!*

Later when Mike and I were alone and no one was within hearing distance, I asked Mike what he found out.

"Sara, I'm not too bad at this sleuthing thing, myself." Mike said.

"Come on, Mike, spill."

Teasing me by stuttering as he knew I couldn't stand not knowing he finally said, "Dennis said that he was the new partner in John's business, Madden Industries.

"The Madden Industries. Wow, John was worth a lot of moola. Looks like Brook won the jackpot," I commented.

Mike went on, "The thing is, John was twenty years older than Brooke and he has adult children who would stand to get a great share of the fortune and 51% of the business.

Brooke would," he was trying to say, before I interrupted him.

"*Wait* a damn minute, beginner sleuth. You could not begin to find all that out from Dennis just now. What gives?" I said, astonished at my man.

"Well, I got a little from Dennis, but, while you were in the shower, I did get on the internet and found tons of stuff on this cast of characters. And as I was saying, Brooke would get $5.5 million for just being married to him for two years. She would get an additional million every two years she was married to him. She would get no other assets per the prenuptial. She will not get the house, no household things, no per cent in Tom's business, nothing, zero, just the $5.5 million. Apparently his first wife will fair pretty well. She has 10% in Tom's business that she helped him build over the years. She needs for not."

"So, I don't know what Brooke would gain by killing him," I said. Glancing at Mike, who I must say was very impressive.

I continued, "So his kids get 51% and his ex gets 10% and that leaves 39% for the rest of the partners to work with. So, what would they gain? What about Dennis? What would he gain? What is the deal with Brooke and Sheila? I've got to figure this out. A man died in front of us and it wasn't a heart attack."

"Slow down, Sherlock," he said. "Honeymoon reminder!"

And so, I did. Just like that I went in to reverse and slowed down.

We had a mid-afternoon honeymoon, you know, night things in the middle of the afternoon things, and then went to one of the early shows before another formal dinner. While we were at the show we sat next to a geriatric couple. They were Frederick Foxley and his girlfriend Mandi Stewart.

Both worked for the Brooklyn police department in their heyday. Foxie, as he liked to be called, or just Freddy, said he was a retired detective, and Mandi worked as a medium who helped solve or helped find clues to assist the police to solve crimes, plus she was a civilian police secretary as they were called back then. Both were in their early eighties and had been together for forty years. They wouldn't marry. They both said they been there and done that marriage thing. Foxie lost his wife after just ten years of marriage when they were young. They had a son and daughter who are both in their fifties now. Mandi 's divorced and has one daughter who is also in her fifties.

Mandi said, "Foxie and I love each other and feel this arrangement works for us. So, we worked together for fifty years and lived together for forty years."

Living in sin. I laughed at the thought. Mike caught me counting the fifty years and forty equaling ninety

"The years over-lap, Sara," Mike teased me, as he could tell my calculator was going off.

"So?" Mandi was saying. "What do you think about the dude who died in the dining room the other day? I met the widow. She's a piece of work. She was way too young for him."

"Aren't they always?" I smirked.

"I haven't yet got a handle on it. I must be losing my touch. The mind's not as sharp as it once was," she said, pointing to her head. "Foxie and I noticed we weren't the only ones snooping around. You come up with anything?"

I just looked at her.

"Ah, come on, toots, I know you're checking it out. Foxie and I are investigating also" She said, "We never stop working. We just don't get paid now. But it's still fun to think we make a difference."

I was trying not to be opinionated, as was Mike. After all, we had our own investigating going on. We should just listen to the geriatrics talk. Maybe pick up some vibes of our own. So, we shrugged our shoulders.

The show was over, and the old couple stayed close to us and, oddly enough, were keeping up.

I hugged Mike tightly as we walked to our late dinner. I looked around and whispered, "Are they still there?"

Mike giggled, "Looks like we have partners, whether we like it or not."

We turned to go to our table where we had Officer Kearan Overlander, one of the engineer officers, who had joined us again. Before we were seated we ran smack dab into, who else, but the mirror twins and the evil Dennis. *Well, I think he's evil.*

I put my hand on Brooke's shoulder, "Brooke, how are you feeling?" *Like I cared.*

"Oh, I am going to live on. It will be hard," she explained. "But I will."

Right, it would be hard to move on with only 5.5 million dollars. How will she ever do it? I thought.

I must have smirked with my thought as Mike nudged me in my side, though gently. But I knew what he meant.

I went, "*What?" with my eyes and raised my eye brows.*

I looked at Brooke and asked, "Is there anything I could do for you?" I lied.

She shook her head, "No." *Thank goodness.*

We walked on over to our table and sat down with our officer and a couple who were from Chicago, who bickered with each other about barbecue, cruise lines, airlines, department stores and any other thing they could think of. She was nice enough, but he was a control freak and kept adjusting his toupee. The other couple, sisters from London, were very proper and funny with it.

We covered world affairs and how wonderful the cruise was. We really won them over and got their attention when Mike talked about Kansas City barbecue. Hilda and Priscilla from London were intrigued. But mostly Hilda was intrigued with Mike. She sat with her head in her hands just staring at my good-looking husband of about one week in two more days.

Like the Chicago couple, Joan and Ben, the London ladies were in their fifties. You're never too old to admire the opposite sex. And Hilda was really admiring Mike. I smiled with pride.

We said our goodnights to our table partners, but Hilda wanted to give Mike a big hug. Just one, but it was longer than it should have been. Mike gently pulled her arms away and reached for me.

"Ready, my little bride?"

Meantime, the geriatric couple was dogging us.

"What do you think, Mike, should we find out what all they know?"

Mike said, "Might as well."

So, we let them catch up with us. We went to a quiet place on the deck and sat down at a table with over-stuffed chairs around it. *Comfy.*

The stars were shining down on us, and it was hard to concentrate with the sky so beautiful. But I tried.

We ordered a round of drinks, and while waiting on them, we talked small talk. When the drinks arrived, that's when Mandi started talking.

"You know, I knew you guys were on to something. I could feel it," Mandi said.

"She means, she really feels it," Foxie gleamed. "She just knows."

I thought it would be better to get what they knew before I came forth with the little Mike and I knew.

"Mandi, what do you think is going on with the twins and the evil Dennis?"

"You do feel the same about that trio as we do. I think that that one twin killed her poor unsuspecting husband. And the other two helped her," Mandi spouted. "We saw you pick up the cookies."

"I'm a nurse, and it didn't appear right to me. Brooke's the twin that we suspect killed her husband. Sheila's married to the evil Dennis," I explained.

"Yeah, yeah we got that much." Foxie said.

We shared each other's knowledge we had gathered off the internet so far, and, of course, our theories that we had come up with.

After talking and sharing what we thought, we decided to be friendlier with the trio and stay close to them. But since it was late, we decided to restart our sleuthing first thing in the morning. We would see where the trio was and have breakfast close to them.

"Good night Foxie and Mandi. See you in the morning," I said, as I put my arm into my man's and strolled towards our cabin.

"Good nigh, honeymooners," they giggled. "I bet I know what they're going to be doing."

Mike and I smiled and he said, "Yeah, I know what they'll be doing."

We sat on the own private veranda for a nightcap and decided to talk about us and not the mid-evil trio.

I sat there with my eyes closed, and I felt Mike watching me. I stayed quiet. Out on the ocean you could hear the waves build and crash in the pitch black of the night. Not a cloud in the sky, just bright stars. I opened my eyes and it looked like you could actually reach up and grab one. *Geez, that sounded like a song title.* The ship was gently curving into another direction, and the moon appeared on our side of the ship. It was so large. I turned to Mike who was still watching me. Just as we turned our eyes back to the ocean, we could see a dolphin silhouette jumping out and back into the water over and over again with the moon behind him. Not far behind were three more following the one dolphin's lead.

"Oh Mike, this is beautiful, all of it. We can't see this back home," I cuddled close to him.

"It is beautiful and so are you," Then he kissed me deeply and wantonly.

"Hmmm," and he melted into me.

CHAPTER 40

I LOVE TO WATCH THE sun come up as much as the sunset. So early in the morning Mike and I climbed out of our honeymoon bed and slipped into t-shirts and shorts. We stepped out on the veranda to watch the sun come up. As it slipped up over the water we could see clouds forming

"Is it supposed to rain today?" I asked Mike.

"I'll go and get the ship's weather channel for the forecast," he said.

Sure enough, the weather report said a storm was brewing to our left and would be moving in about 10 A.M.

We did feel lucky as the weather had been perfect after the first two days of rough waters. Perfect. So, if in fact it did rain, it would change our game plan with the geriatric detectives. But then it would move everything and everyone onto the inside promenade. That is where all the restaurants, diners, fast food, jewelry stores, t-shirts stores, crystal stores or anything-you could-want stores were located. It was like an indoor mall. *Sorta.* With higher prices.

Being stuck inside could make for a nice change. We had spent most of our time outside on the decks in and around swimming pools. Not to mention the tours of islands we enjoyed. Later this morning we would reach Barbados. We hoped it wouldn't be raining then.

But for now, we would meet the geriatric detectives for breakfast as planned in the little diner up top and on the deck before the rain came.

We had just been seated when Mandi and Foxie come leading the evil trio towards us.

"Hi, Sara and Mike. You remember Brooke, Sheila and, of course, Dennis. I asked them to join us. Won't that be fun?" Mandi beamed.

No!

We shook hands with everyone and moved to a larger table. *I guess you couldn't get closer to the trio than this.*

Mandi, Sheila, Brooke and I huddled together and the guys did their huddle.

We ordered breakfast and shared cruise stories.

Mandi and I were biting at the bit to ask questions.

Finally, I asked Brooke how long she and Johnny had been married. *Like I didn't know the answer.* I was trying small talk.

"We met two and half years ago and had been married just over two. I never thought anyone of his status would even give me the time of day. But he loved me. We were not a match in age or education or social skills, nothing. Yet he married me. Who knew?" Brooke almost blushed.

You did, you dweeb It's not who you know, it's who you oops. I stopped my thought.

"You moved pretty fast," I suggested.

"Yeah, Johnny didn't want to wait. And now he's, he's dead." She acted like she was choking up. *And you killed him.*

"So what kind of business was he in? Did he leave you okay, financially?" I probed.

"Oh, Brooke will make out just find," Sheila interrupted. "And so will Dennis and me."

"How's that?" I was inquisitive and straightened up in my chair acting interested.

Brooke spoke up, "Johnny just made Dennis a partner with his company a month ago. I thought that was so nice, since he's married to my twin."

"You know Johnny was worth a lot of money. His kids and his ex-old lady will really be rolling in the dough when they read the will," Evil Dennis chimed in, pleased with himself as he was ease dropping in our conversation.

"I just wished Johnny had fallen overboard rather than die in the dining room. And now he's in a freezer, poor guy," Brooke said.

Hmmm! I thought then said, "Brooke why would you say that about falling overboard?"

"Oh, I just would rather not be frozen is all," she blurted out.

As opposed to sinking to the bottom of the ocean! I thought.

She bounced up and put her arm through her sister's when the announcement came over the intercom that we would be in Barbados in one hour, and apparently, we ran out of the rain. It had gone north of us. So, we would have a rain-free day after all.

As they walked away, I yelled after the trio, "See you later."

They just kept walking.

"Well," I stood up and motioned to Mike, "That went well. We better go get ready."

We all parted and went our separate ways. If the senior citizen detectives had more questions, we would have to get the answers later.

CHAPTER 41

Mike and I walked down the plank and headed for the tour bus that was on our agenda.

Barbados Island was an English colony island. Queen Elizabeth had ruled here also. The police, known as bobbies, were directing traffic with their black and white checkered Sillitoe Tartan headgear, blowing their whistles and swinging their arms for the traffic to move or stay put.

After waiting for our turn to advance, our tour bus headed through Barbados to the other side of the Island and visited the 1600s Gun Hill Signal Station up on top of a hill overlooking the ocean and shore. This is one of the places they manned the guns against piracy and other enemies that tried to overtake the Island. It was high enough to warn friend or foe.

"Mike, look, there is the huge white lion that had been hand carved by a soldier out of a single rock. Look how regal it looks still standing guard."

Mike squeezed my hand to acknowledge the excitement I was showing.

Reading the plaque, I said, "It says here that the lion has been standing guard since 1868. A Captain Henry Wilkerson of the 9th Foot Regiment carved the lion out of one huge rock with the help of four laborers."

Mike was looking out over the crystal clear-aqua-colored water and said, "Can you imagine pirates coming ashore and climbing up here?"

"I think of Johnny Depp when I think of pirates. So, no," I snorted.

About that time, it was time to board the tour bus.

THE BUS PULLED IN front of The Sunburg Sugar Plantation, which is famous for their rum for over 300 years. They were handing out samples of rum to everyone and, of course Mike loved it. We toured the mansion sipping the rum. The guide said the mansion had fallen into disrepair twenty years ago, and they had closed it down for a few years. A young lady from the States came and restored it and is now living there. There were sugar cane fields that extended further than the eye could see. The thirty-five-year-old lady had restored the old planation to its original glory. The rum was so good that Mike asked the guide for more.

The guide said, "No. We only have just enough samples for the tourists each day."

Mike said, "Well then, can I buy a bottle? You sell it, don't you?"

The guide said, "I don't think they have any extra. I'll have to check with the owner."

Mike said "Then let's ask her."

The guide said, "She isn't here and she's the only one to make that decision."

I'm thinking, *No extra. What on earth? Can't make a decision, hmph!*

About that time, riding up on this huge white stallion, *right out of the movies,* was the lady who owned the sugar plantation. She was beautiful. She came right up to the group. She got off her horse and led him around going towards the back of her mansion.

Mike graciously yelled, "Madam, this rum is so good, I was wondering if I could buy a bottle."

She turned and smiled, "I'll go check and see if we have any extra. Wait here."

In a few minutes she came back to Mike and said, "$20.00."

"Thanks," Mike said as he exchanged the $20.00 for the jug of rum.

I put my arm around my handsome husband, and the Sunburg Lady smiled and said. "Enjoy."

We got back on the tour bus and now everyone was our best friend, but Mike would not pop the top.

Mike had other plans for the rum so he refused to open it as he teased the bus group.

We headed back to the city. Mike and I walked to an outdoor café, sat down and got a light lunch. Mike noticed the evil trio was close by, but they didn't see us. He nudged me to look toward them.

I told Mike, "I think I will try to get close and eavesdrop."

I went in and around a clothing store next to a straw market that was right there. So far, so good. They didn't see me. I slid in right behind them and heard them arguing.

"Brooke, they are not going to release John's body. You are stuck. We are stuck. All you had to do was slip the poison cookie in after his dinner while he was drinking his coffee, so while you were doing your stroll on the deck, the poison would hit him and with a little shove, he would accidently fall overboard. *But no*. You gave him the poison too early and now he's in a freezer. You blew it."

"You know how Johnny loved his almond cookies. He just had to have one. He couldn't wait. He ate it while waiting for dinner to be served. He said he was hungry. I couldn't very well say, '*Stop!* that's for after dinner so I can kill you,'" Brooke was physically upset.

Dennis spoke up and said, "We got to think of something because I am not going to burn for this. Brooke, all you had to do was stick to the plan. You did blow it."

"Anyway, how did I know it would kick in so fast? He could have died in our cabin. I didn't know the time line," She started crying.

Then I heard Dennis ask Brooke, "Did Johnny change his will, or are you going to get stuck with a measly 5.5 million? Are his brats going to get it all?"

Brooke said," Johnny agreed that he would sign the new will. I have to get it out of the safe and double check."

"You should have already checked the safe, you dumb ass," evil Dennis scolded.

"Stop it, Dennis," Sheila yelled at him.

I heard all I needed to know. Brooke confessed and so did the rest of the trio.

I snuck back around to Mike and told him what I just heard.

"I have to get in their cabin to search for the poison and those cookies. I did keep part of the partial cookie and broke off part of the whole cookie, and I gave the rest to the ME to run test on, though his testing is so limited because of being on the ship. And he isn't certified for forensics. Or barely is."

Mike and I decided to stroll by the trio and make nice. We didn't want them to jump ship as it were.

"Hi, you guys. Are you enjoying Barbados? We just left the Sunburg Sugar Planation. They are famous for their rum," Mike held up his jug.

"We just went shopping," Dennis said, holding up numerous designer bags.

"Sweet," I said.

Sheila said they got a lot of nice things. *Apparently, price didn't matter.* Brooke looked like she was crying.

"Are you okay, Brooke?" as I placed my hand on her arm like I was concerned. *Not!*

"She's just fine," evil Dennis smirked.

"Mike and I are going to head back to the ship. See you later," I acted innocent. "Feel better, Brooke."

"I think we'll walk with you. It's time to get back," Sheila smiled.

We all walked slowly pointing at one thing or another of interest. If I didn't know they were killers, I might have enjoyed the walk back.

We got on board and went for a drink and guess what? Our new best friends, the trio, joined us for drinks too. We looked up and Mandi and Foxie came strolling over from their table. I swear we didn't see them sitting over there.

"Hi, you two, come join us," Mike suggested. *Like fat chance you could keep them away.*

"We didn't see you off ship, Foxie. Where did you and Mandi go?" Mike said.

"We've been to Barbados a couple of times before. We just stayed on board and played Bingo. No big deal," Mandi said. "Besides I had to call home and check a few things out."

"I hope everything is okay there," I said.

"Yes, indeedy, it is," Mandi smiled.

Apparently, she did more checking on the evil trio.

We sat there about thirty minutes, then Mike and I excused ourselves, and when we stood up everyone stood to go.

The evil trio walked one direction, and Foxie and Mandi walked with us.

"I'm anxious to get into Brooke's cabin. I need you two to occupy the evil trio." *Well, they are evil.*

Mandi said, "No problem, we'll keep them busy."

"Damn," I said, out loud.

"What's wrong, dearie?" Mandi asked me.

"My best sister friend, Dora, gave me a beginner sleuthing kit for a bridal gift, and I wish I had it with me. Who knew I would need it?"

I went on to explain that Dora and I just started sleuthing since Tom Solo's death and how it carried over to Jerry's death. Now we are hooked on sleuthing.

"Oh, dearie, you can borrow mine. I don't leave home without it," Mandi beamed.

So, I borrowed Mandi's *break-in* kit. We made arrangements for her and Foxie to entertain the Trio on our layover on St. Thomas Island. Mike and I would go off on our own and then slip back on ship. Mandi and Foxie would make a tour arrangement with the trio. She would explain that Mike and I needed some alone time, being newlyweds and all.

Meantime, we all hung out together. Again, if I hadn't known that they were cold- blooded killers, I might have liked them. Though it would be a stretch, and I would not have included them on my Christmas card list.

CHAPTER 42

THE DAY WAS PLANNED out. The trio, with Mandi and Foxie, walked off the plank one way and Mike and I walked off the opposite direction. They climbed aboard a tour bus, and Mike and I made a U-turn back to the ship as soon as the bus was out of sight.

We went directly to Brooke's cabin. I wiggled the lock picks this way and that. I got frustrated and had to take a breath and start over. Again, I failed.

Mike put his arms around me in just the right time as a group of people were hurrying by to debark before it was too late. Mike just held me a few minutes and kissed me. I melted.

The coast was clear. I squatted back down and started picking the lock again with success.

Mike and I had latex gloves on and were careful not to disturb anything. We picked up and set it back down just like it was. I opened up a drawer by the bed and looked for a vial or something that cyanide was contained in. Mike found a small bottle, but it turned out to be a perfume sample. We kept searching.

I found the package of almond nut cookies. Brooke had them in a plastic bag but still in the original torn bag, as well.

Boy, they smelled good.

I carefully place, a couple of cookies and crumbs in my own plastic bag. I looked at Mike and said, "Bingo."

We didn't know how Brooke had poisoned the cookies. Did she pull one out and put a few drops of cyanide on it, or did she poison the whole package? I didn't know but was hoping the cookie and crumbs I have in my possession were part of the cyanide.

"Did you know that cyanide smells like almonds and was really easy to disguise in almond cookies." I asked my man in a whisper.

"Why, yes I did," he whispered back.

We kept looking throughout Brooke's cabin but came up empty. We moved on to Dennis and Sheila's room and the lock picking was easier.

We again carefully picked things up and set them back just where we found them. We went through the drawers, the closet and suitcases under their bed. Everywhere we could think of, and everyplace there was any space of any kind. No luck. No incriminating evidence.

We locked up and slipped back off the ship and went sightseeing with the cookies in my bag.

We took the cookie and mailed it overnight to Dora.

I tried calling her to tell her it was coming. No answer, so I had to do something I really hated to do. *Text!*

I simply said.

`Pkg coming, don't eat. Poison. Call me PDQ.`

We met up with the trio and the geriatrics just before we boarded again. Clearly Brooke was not mourning. But you could tell the evil trio had something on their mind.

Mandi and Foxie were having a ball.

"Boy, those two are hard to keep up with," Brooke said, pointing to Mandi and Foxie.

"Yep, I notice they don't let any grass grow under their feet," Mike smiled.

I was thinking time was ticking. We only have two days left to snoop for evidence.

Dora, the texting queen, didn't text me but instead used her one finger to push the #3 on her speed dial and immediately called me. She knows I hate texting. I like the old-fashioned way. I believe in voices.

I explained to Dora what we found out. I told her when she got the cookies to give them to Zack to get analyzed. ASAP.

Three hours later Zack called me, "Sara, what are you up to *now*? What is going on?

You can't just use me for your sleuthing projects, your private lab. Your private anything," he yelled. "Didn't I tell you to butt out?"

Mike was smiling as he heard Zack yelling into my phone as I held it away from my ear. Mike listened to my side of the conversation, and he cracked up on my explanation on why, where, what and who.

"Zack, you gave me instruction as to what you needed from me and you said I was the best investigator you have. You did Zack. I was just following orders.

"Zack, the body's still in the freezer, still fresh or it will be when it thaws. The authority must be here to take the body off the ship or this trio will get by with murder. I sent the cookies and crumbs as I suspect they are laced with cyanide throughout them. I could be wrong, and Brooke could have just put drops on the cookies she gave John."

"Why did he have cookies at dinner from a package and no one else did?" he asked.

"According to Brooke, the almond cookies are, were, his favorite and Brooke knew they probably wouldn't have almond cookies on board. And think about it, what a better cover than cyanide that smells like almond in almond cookies? She brought the cookies to surprise John. And she sure did. Brooke isn't as dumb as she sounds, and her sister and brother- in- law helped devise this murder.

"So, Zack, I need your help," I begged. "Oh, and thanks for convincing the powers that be for not taking the body off the ship yet."

I felt like I was repeating myself from our last conversation. But I was trying to drive home the importance of this murder.

I told him of mine and Mike's new partners, Mandi and Foxie.

Zack said, "I'll check out your new partners, Mandi and Foxie, and their police precinct 407 where they said they worked out of. See if they are legit."

"Zack, they're in their 80s, and you would be hard pressed to find anyone who still knew them who was still at the 407. You best check their personnel records in Human Resources as I feel sure it was way before computers."

He said, "Don't worry about it. I know how to get the information across state lines. Five states away to be exact," he reminded me.

"I don't know why I should help you, but I have to admit that your amateur sleuthing always pays off. You have good instincts, and now you have Mike sleuthing. I'll get on this and apparently I have to work fast." With that he hung up with a grunt.

Mike and I decided to stay in and call for room service for dinner. We thought there wasn't anything more we could do right then and, after all, we were on our honeymoon.

We enjoyed the quiet of no one talking and no rattling of dishes. We had our lobster, champagne and chocolate, covered strawberries, *My favorite of all, chocolate things.*

We were just starting to get in the honey-moony thing with long passionate kisses and foreplay when someone loudly called our names and pounded on our door insisting we answer.

Trying to find our clothes that we had tossed earlier, we both yelled, "Just a minute."

They responded, "Hurry."

Mike and I looked at each other like, what the heck?

It was Mandi and Foxie.

"What are you two doing?" I asked, as Mike and I grabbed some clothes from the floor and opened the door with me still pulling down my t-shirt over my bare breast and Mike pulling sweats up over his bare posterior and just in the nick of time.

Foxie said, "Move over and let us in, hurry," he said, as he squeezed by us pulling Mandi behind him. "You won't believe the luck we've just *had!*"

We waited. Finally, Mandi pulled out of her bag a small 6" bottle in a plastic bag.

She stood there smiling and holding it out.

"Look what just fell into our hands."

I reached out and took the plastic bag and, with a tissue around it, held it up for Mike to see.

"Is this what I think it is?" I asked, with enthusiasm.

"It sure is, dearie, and none too soon. We were out on the deck just now when we ran across Brooke. She was sitting by herself and relaxing with her eyes closed. We startled her and when she jumped, she hit her bag, and it went flying. Foxie helped her pick her stuff up, as I can hardly get back up once I'm down, you know, my knees and all."

Mike and I looked at her wanting her to hurry up and tell us about the bottle.

"Anyway, while Foxie was down on all fours, the bottle came rolling out from her lounge chair. Brooke didn't seem to notice. Foxie picked it up with a tissue lying there and set it aside and picked up a couple of things and gave them back to Brooke. As I distracted her, Foxie reached over and picked up this bottle with the tissue and slipped it into his pocket. See, it fell into our hands. How lucky is that?" Mandi beamed.

"Very lucky," Mike said.

I pulled on a pair of latex gloves and unscrewed the lid to smell the bitter aroma of almond.

"Wow, that's it," I yelled. "That smells like bitter almonds, and it isn't almond extract," I was so excited.

"Okay," Foxie said. "We want you to hold onto this. Brooke knows I helped her pick up her belongings, and when she finds out the bottle's missing, we will be the first ones she will ask. I want to say, 'sorry I don't have it',"

"Me too," Mandi added.

"I will put it in our safe until we reach stateside day after tomorrow," I said.

"Meanwhile, I think we got them. All has fallen in place. So, let's enjoy the rest of the cruise," Mike said.

We all agreed and the octogenarians left.

Mike and I went back to our honeymoon with more excitement and with a lot more gusto. Our soft romantic start before the interruption went to mad passionate sexy love making. There was so much sweat coming out of every pore of our bodies that we would have to change the sheets, again.

"Shoo-woooe, babe." Mike tried to catch his breath as he rolled over. "Baby, that was—*Ah, fantastic!*Just what was that?" He was smiling with great satisfaction.

I sat up and I was feeling pretty satisfied myself. "My libido's on over-drive. Wow. I don't know, but I hope someday we can do *that* again. Oh baby," as I tried to get my breath.

After laying there reliving our bridal bliss, we giggled and raced to the shower.

CHAPTER 43

THE NEXT MORNING, BEAMING with reliving the night before and what solving a murder could do for our mood, we took a stroll hand in hand on deck before going to breakfast.

"We missed our first sunrise this morning," I said.

"Yeah, but it was worth missing. You wore me out, and it was nice to be able to sleep in," he said, "You know, that was a first?"

"What, sleeping in?" I asked.

"Well, that, too," he laughed.

We rounded the end of the ship heading toward the dining room for a hearty breakfast. *We earned it.* We saw the evil trio down on their hand and knees. We walked up on them and stopped.

"Lose something?" I asked.

"Oh, I spilled my purse last night and I can't find my favorite lipstick. I can't go without my favorite lipstick," Brooke whined.

"Wow, it must have been special. Could it have rolled overboard?" I suggested.

"It was the perfect color and brand new," She sighed. "I really hope it didn't roll overboard," Brooke kept whining.

"It wouldn't be a bad idea if it had rolled overboard," Dennis said. "You can always get more,"

"It wasn't that easy to find. I'm not sure if I can find another tube," she started sniffling.

"Well, that's too bad," I tried not to smile as I looked up at Mike.

We started walking away leaving the trio hysterically looking for the missing tube of "lipstick!"

Brooke looked up yelling after us, "If you see Mandi and Foxie, tell them I would like to talk to them."

"Will do," We both said. *Dum de dum, dum.*

We sat with our assigned couples, The Millers and the Hollinsworths. Kearan, the engineer came strolling up and sat down with us.

We all exchanged our exciting cruise stories, minus the sleuthing.

After having yet another delicious meal we stayed around in the dining room and shared our shopping experience and what we bought. Other passengers we had gotten acquainted with started walking up to us and joined in the conversation.

One of the guys said, "The only thing missing is getting to play golf."

Puh—leese!

Mike said, "There is a driving range up top, but some say it just wasn't the same as playing 18 holes of glorious golf. But I guess it could scratch the itch if you really have to play."

"See you, hon," one of the guys said. But his wife wrapped her arm through his and said he wasn't going anywhere.

An announcement came over the intercom that we were approaching Nassau, the straw basket capital of the Islands.

Mike and I excused ourselves as we wanted to see if we could find our favorite geriatrics. And I wanted to call Zack to tell him we got the tube, and it's safe and sound.

We saw Mandi and Foxie just a little way down and motioned for them to stay put and I held my hand up like I was going to make a phone call before meeting them. They nodded they understood.

Mike joined me while I called Zack.

"Good morning, Zack."

"Good morning, Sara, Mike," knowing Mike was listening on the speaker phone.

Mike smiled but didn't say anything.

"You told me it wasn't that John Madden, the football guru. You didn't tell me about John Madden of Madden Industries, billionaire. And that shit would hit the fan on his death. We had to read about him on the internet. He's always on the news for some creation that will save the world or fighting lawsuits," I explained.

"Sorry, Sara, I didn't know his importance either when I first talked to you, but it piqued my interest when you said his wife killed him."

"Zack, we're headed for Nassau which is the last port of call before arriving stateside."

"That changes everything, Sara. I will have the proper authorities waiting for you tomorrow. I have to check a few things out. I want to have all the ducks in a row. I'll call you back in an hour or two."

"Zack," I tried to catch him before he hung up. "Zack."

'Yes Sara?"

"Nassau is today and then we'll be heading home tomorrow and, Zack, we found the vial of cyanide and it's in safe keeping."

"Great job, that's a sure conviction. Hang tight, Sara," he said, hanging up.

While waiting for Zack's call back, Mike and I decided to hang out on the deck and watch our approach to Nassau with Foxie and Mandi. I told them Zack was working on a strategy. The experienced senior citizens excused themselves to find a restroom. As we watched them walk away we noticed a young couple waggling toward us. She was holding her hands under her huge belly and he was trying to get her someplace to sit.

He yelled, "Help, my wife's in labor."

Everyone around just looked.

My RN snapped to, and I jumped into action. Mike followed.

We helped the young father sit his wife down on a reclining lounge chair close by.

"Hi, I'm Sara and I am an RN. This is my husband Mike," I said, touching Mike's arm.

"Thanks for helping. This is Emma and I'm Eric. She's about 5 weeks early."

We got Emma reclining and legs up. Mike handed me a beach towel that the staff had just put out for the guests on all the lounge chairs. I placed one under Emma. Mike and Eric turned the chair around so Emma's bottom wouldn't be exposed to the world.

Mike held one beach towel open and up and so did Eric for privacy. Emma had water pouring out of her and she clearly had dilated. I watched as the baby's head crowned.

"Eric, your baby's coming," I told him as I noticed his legs started to buckle. "Eric?" I yelled.

"Okay," he said, sucking it up.

"Push, Emma! Thata girl, push! Looking good," I coached.

"Yeah baby! Lookin' good! *Push!*" The excited husband said, but he couldn't look.

The ship's doctor appeared just in time, and I helped him deliver a seven-and-a-half-pound baby boy!

The new born just wailed as I wrapped him in a clean towel Mike handed me, and then I showed the infant to Emma and handed him to his daddy.

Emma was crying, so happily. Eric was over the moon with pride.

Eric turned and thanked Mike and me for helping them. He went on to say that he asked for help all the way down the side of the ship. We were the first people that actually cared.

"The one person who helped is an RN. We are so lucky," Eric said.

"We were at the right spot at the right time," Mike said proudly. "She's amazing," pointing to me.

We found the sanitizing ports that were strategically placed all over the ship and I pushed an application on my hands. "Great invention," I told Mike, rubbing into my hands.

About that time the ship's doctor rolled the new mom and her son to the infirmary.

Eric turned back around from some distance away and yelled, "Thanks again, Mike and Sara."

We waved back, okay.

We went back to the rail, and we could see Nassau still in the distance. It actually seemed further away. But how could that be?

"Do you think we will ever have one of those?" Mike asked.

"What? An island? I suppose, it's possible," I answered, teasing him.

"No silly, a baby." He turned me around and looked me in the eyes.

"I suppose, it's possible," I giggled.

My cell rang.

"Sara, Zack."

"Hi there, what did you work out?"

"Since Madden was killed in international waters, we want Interpol involved. Since Madden is the Madden billionaire, the FBI has been invited to join the party. Not to mention the U.S. Marshalls, and me and a few locals."

"You?"

"You don't think I would let my favorite sleuth and her husband, take down a killer without being there, do ya?"

"From the Midwest?" I asked.

"I took some vacation time. You did call me to help. And helping is what I am doing," Zack said. "Furthermore, a handful of authorities in a heli is going to land on your ship just before you get in U.S. waters. We want to search The Evil Trio, as you call them, their cabins and their property."

"We?"

"Yep, I will be one of the ones to land." I could hear laughter in his comment.

"See you then." We hung up.

Mike said, "You looked shocked."

I explained what Zack just said.

"Really?" Mike rolled his eyes. "He still cares about you. Funny thing, it doesn't bother me." *Hmmm. Okay maybe a little.* Mike thought to himself.

"Nothing to be bothered about," I said. "I think he just wants to be involved in a huge takedown. It is a high-profile case involving a billionaire, you know. He'll get recognition and all that stuff. A feather in his hat sort of. It sure wouldn't hurt his career. Besides, it's you I want to have a baby with." I hugged him.

"A baby, hmmm?" Mike looked down at me and kissed me gently.

We looked up and could see Mandi and Foxie heading for us in a bit of a hurry.

"Going to the bathroom again?" I asked them.

"Funny, ha, ha!" Mandi said. "Just went."

We filled them in on the big take down and planned from this point on to stay clear of the evil trio who was going down and soon.

We arrived at Nassau later that day. We walked around the straw market for a while, then took a horse-drawn carriage ride around the market to sightsee. A lot of young people on the street yelled they wanted to braid my hair, but I turned them all down. However, we saw Mandi getting her natural curly, mostly salt and little pepper hair braided.

We rode by and gave her the thumbs up. Foxie, who wasn't far from her, was getting conned into buying a sea shell that he could have easily picked up off the beach, himself.

The carriage slowed, and we stopped at a little outside café, the Little Café. We ordered the favorite drink of the island. We couldn't pronounce the name of it, didn't know what was in it, but it was great. We had a second then we thought we would try some of the island cuisine. The server, a true native of Nassau, made the decision on the menu for us. We couldn't pronounce the meal, either, but it was delicious, though we thought it was something they had an abundance of and were pushing on all us patrons. Perhaps the "Special" of the day. We had a hard time understanding the server's heavy accent. I just hope it was something we had before.

When the food came, it was just okay. We certainly have had better cuisine.

It was getting late so we headed back to the ship.

The evil trio was headed back, too. They spotted us and asked what happened to us. "Hey, are you ignoring us?"

I explained, "The cruise is almost over, and so is our honeymoon. We just needed some alone time."

They nodded that they understood, smiled and walked on giving us our space. If they only knew what awaited them.

We checked in with our geriatric friends and went to our last night of formal dining.

We enjoyed our last dinner with the Williams and Hollinsworths and our very own Officer, Kearan Overlander. We took more pictures of each other. I asked one of the bus boys if he would take a picture of our table so we scooted closer to each other and he snapped the picture.

When we looked at the picture, sure enough, he took a picture of our table. Hot rolls, half-filled wine glasses and half-filled water glasses, wadded-up napkins. It was hysterical. That explains why the bus boy looked at us strangely when we asked him to take a picture of the table. We kept the picture. And we sent it to the William's and Hollinsworth's I-phones.

We heard music and watched while all the servers marched in line carrying, "Baked Alaskas," which were on fire. It was very impressive. The servers delivered one to each table fanning the flames out then slicing the cake. All I could think of was, "*Chocolate.*" I had seconds. *After all I didn't have to fit in my wedding dress anymore.*

We said our goodbyes to our dinner buddies. We swore we would keep in touch. But we all knew it was a long shot, and it probably wouldn't happen.

Mike and I headed to a little dance club. We were enjoying our alone time, drinking, and dancing and just enjoying the reggae music. We thought we had it made. But, no! The Evil Trio came walking in and spotted us. Mike nudged me so we turned and looked into each other's eyes with tiny kisses here and there on our lips, cheeks, neck and eyes, hoping the trio would get the hint. They didn't.

"So, it's our last night on the cruise," Dennis said, sounding disappointed as he pulled in beside me and left the girls standing. Finally, they pulled up chairs and sat down.

Mike and I didn't want to seem rude *to killers*, but we continued to hang all over each other hoping they would take the hint.

After a time of small talk Mike and I were still trying to throw out hints of wanting to be alone, Sheila finally said, "Oh, how insensitive of us. We're interfering with the last night of your honeymoon."

We just smiled.

"Come on guys, give them our numbers and leave them alone. Here give me your phone."

I handed Sheila my cell, and she put in her and Brooke's cell numbers into my cell. "There, now we can keep in touch." And they turned and found another table.

Mike and I decided we had enough music, dancing and drinking. We left and gave a finger wave to the trio.

Brooke held up her hand like a phone to her ear and yelled to us, "Call me."

I looked at Mike and said, "When hell freezes over!"

Since it was our last night aboard, we stopped off at the mid-night buffet where Mandi and Foxie had just finished snacking. We exchanged a few words and said we'd see them in the morning. I had already filled them in on the upcoming events.

Mike and I ate so much. I had more chocolate which, in my opinion, is the best invention *ever* next *to sanitizer ports, jet planes, fax machines, okay cell phones.*

We headed up to our suite to have the last night of mad passionate sex on the open seas rocking and rolling.

CHAPTER 44

It was our last morning on board of what could have been a great cruise. The Honeymoon making was exceptional, but the unexpected murder was a complete surprise and wasn't in our plans.

The baby delivery was great, and I was pleased I could be there to help.

Meeting our new geriatric detective side-kicks was a hoot. Zack had checked them out and they were legit. They were everything they said they were.

Eating breakfast with Mandi and Foxie, he said, "We're going to stay a couple of days in Ft. Lauderdale before going home. We got nothing better to do," Foxie said. "Do we Mandi?"

"That's what retirement is about," she chimed in.

We just finished breakfast and got back to our suite to pack, when Mike and I heard a horrific noise. We stepped out onto our private balcony as we heard the twirling of the helicopter propellers buzzing overhead, trying to land in the exceptionally windy weather. We hung on tight to the rail for the heli wind to slow.

We looked at each other, and Mike said, "It's time to take a stroll out on deck and act like we are curious about what's going on."

Mike held on to his hat, and I tried to hold on to my hair when we stepped out onto the promenade. We got out there and joined the numerous sightseers already out on deck, looking up.

Foxie and Mandi were holding on to the rail as they walked up to us.

"Looks like we're just in time to see this go down," Foxie said, with an elbow in my kidneys.

The heli blades slowed down enough for four important looking gentlemen dressed in black suits, white shirts with black ties, aviator sun glasses, and FBI haircuts to step off onto the deck.

"Holly smoke," I said out loud. "Is that Zack?"

Sure enough, dressed the same as his cohorts, Zack came waltzing over to us while the others stayed back.

"Where are the suspects?" he asked.

I said, "Where's the President?"

"Ha ha ha a hhhaaa," he smirked. "Funny!"

We looked around, and I saw Brooke standing by the rail wondering what was going on. Sheila and Dennis just walked up to her.

I walked over to them to make small talk while Mike explained to Zack who they were and introduced Mandi and Foxie to him.

The evil trio and I turned our back to them to chit chat, still holding onto our hair and hats as the heli blades slowed down to a near stop even though the wind was still strong.

Zack brought the other three suits over and surrounded the trio, and I stepped back.

The FBI agent spoke up and explained what was going on, and the detective read them their Miranda rights while he and the other suits put handcuffs on each of the trio.

Brooke dropped her head and would not look around. Her mirror twin and Dennis were doing the *What Did I Do* act.

The trio had been arrested just inside international waters, but now we could ease into the USA right away. We watched as the U.S. shore got closer and closer.

We could see the rest of the acting authority figures waiting on the dock.

Finally, we were docking and the trio was lead down the plank to waiting patrol cars with Zack leading the way. They kept them separated from each other and in their own patrol car. He talked to the FBI and the U.S. Marshalls, and they followed him back onto the ship where he directed them to me and introduced me, with Mike, Foxie and Mandi as my investigator team who witnessed the murder and then proved it. The forensic guys came aboard with their equipment and went directly to the trios, rooms.

Zack stayed behind with us as we held on to our hair while the helicopter took off to return to land.

After the heli noise had lessened and you could hear again, Mike turned to Zack and said, "Well, Zack, you just couldn't stay away?" Mike smiled and put his arm around my waist pulling tight against him.

Zack smiled, "How could I when you two got me involved? How could I not be here for the takedown?"

Mike thought with a little green eye, *exactly* how could you not, with Sara here? He gave himself a mental head slap, smiled and thought after all, Sara chose me. Get past it. He had to remind himself ever so often. Then it dawned on him. I have to get over it or I chance losing Sara. Just then his jealously was gone. Almost.

More authorities joined the crime scene investigators and started searching the trio's cabins and were able to find evidence that the plot to kill John Madden was apparent. They found a copy of the real will and a fake one not yet signed. Apparently they were going to perform forgery.

I handed over the bagged cookies and the vial of cyanide to Zack, who in turn handed it to the lead detective, Joe Gerrea.

They hauled off tons of bags of evidence or what could be evidence. We weren't allowed in the cabins, so who knew?

We watched the ME's roll the poor dead frozen body to an awaiting "meat wagon" as I heard one of the heartless ME's say out loud.

The John Madden children and his ex were waiting while the ME rolled him by.

I could see the ME trying to tell them something by using his arms, swinging them around explaining. Probably saying "You don't want to see your dad frozen."

Finally, all the interrogation of all the passengers was over. The only ones left to interrogate were the crew.

We were all allowed to leave one by one pulling our bags down the plank and to dry land. Only it was starting to rain.

The police asked all of us who were in the dining room and witnessed John Madden's demise to stay for a few days until they got this all sorted out. I imagine some people didn't own up to being around the suspect so they could go home immediately. Mike called Katherine, and I called Dora to let them know that we were staying and why. Katherine was fine and Dora wanted to hop the next plane to Ft. Lauderdale to help investigate but I told her no! *Ah, the wonder of cell phones. The next best thing to being there.* I reminded her the investigating was over.

We stayed at the hotels closest to each other and were interrogated in one hotel which happened to be the one we stayed in. Out of the twenty-five hundred on board, only a couple of hundred of us either witnessed the death of Johnny Madden or were in the dining room during his death. But some of the guests were on the other side of the dining room and didn't know there was a death, let alone a murder. The passenger cabins closest to the trio one way or the other were questioned as well. The ship's staff, who served the food or whatever their connection to the suspects was, also was interrogated.

As each witness was interviewed, the interrogator asked for them to come back to testify when it went to trial or they would be subpoenaed. This was going to take a while.

Mike, being a super nice guy, asked Zack if he wanted to join us for dinner, along with Foxie and Mandi. He did and so did the senior citizens, Foxie and Mandi. We had a great time talking about the whole experience of the crime and how we got involved in the sleuthing and sharing information. How we were on the same page from the get go.

Zack was amazed, "So, Mike and Sara, you're a sleuthing team now?"

"Yeah, she has that effect on people, as you well know. But, I have to say, she is good and it's a blast." Mike gave me a quick kiss and squeezed my hand. He went on to say "Ever since Sara walked into my life, it has been nothing but exciting. She's a bright star. I am so lucky to have her. So, Zack, if I haven't said this to you before, I'm saying it now. Thanks for waking me up."

"Yes, so you told me more than once. You are lucky, that's for sure," Zack said, smiling at my man.

Meantime, Foxie and Mandi sat quietly looking at Zack and then Mike and back again, while listening to the conversation and watching my reaction to all of this. I just smiled.

Eric, the new father, came strolling by our table and stopped. He smiled great big and said, "I was hoping to see you two and thank you again for helping deliver my son. We wanted you to know we named him Michael S. S for Sara but since he's a boy, S was it. Cool uh?"

"Wow, that is cool," I said, as we both smiled up at him. Mike took Eric's hand and shook it.

I went on to ask, "How's mama doing?"

"Emma and Mikey are doing great and resting in our room. We'll be heading out for home in the morning. Since we only live 150 miles away, our family will be picking us up. The grandparents can't wait to get their hands on him," he said, proudly.

We exchanged addresses and phone numbers and promised each other to keep in touch.

Zack smiled and just shook his head.

"What?" I asked.

"You're just so busy," he said.

"Just at the right place at the right time, Zack," I replied proudly.

"And lucky," my groom chimed in.

Zack looked at one then the other of us and once again reminded us that the police would need additional information so we needed to hang out for a couple of days, since we were witnesses to the Madden death and Mike and I did have the vial and cookies. We wanted to see what was going to happen to the *Evil Trio* anyway.

I understood the police needed to speak to us over and over, but I honestly didn't know what else we could add. We already repeated what we witnessed and heard several times.

I was glad Zack stayed. After all, without him, we couldn't get the updates on the evil trio. I also wanted to know about the autopsy on John Madden. I was 99% sure I was right about him being murdered. I just wanted to know the other 1%, too.

We said good night and called it an early evening after we checked into our hotel room. The same hotel that Zack and the geriatrics checked into.

We were looking forward to time alone.

The only beach time Mike and I had on the cruise was the day on the Island of Mayrue. We were looking forward to going to the beach here at Ft. Lauderdale while we waited for the information. We weren't in a hurry to get back home, though we missed the kids.

We had an early breakfast and went sightseeing before hitting the beach. I bought a new floral one-piece swim suit in one of the many stores aboard ship. It had cut outs in all the right places making it pretty sexy. I decided to go ahead and wear it.

After we set up our chairs under the umbrella, I dropped my cover-up and Mike went, "Holy cow, you look, wel, sexy. Wow."

I smiled, as the suit did what I wanted it to do.

We were in and out of the ocean for a couple of hours and decided we had enough sun.

We went back to our hotel and ordered lunch in, and while waiting for our lunch, I scribbled in my new diary that I bought to start my new life. It had a lot in it already.

We cuddled for a while then ended up in the shower together just like "The Specialist." Once again it was awesome.

While drying my hair, my cell-phone rang. I asked Mike to get it.

It was Mandi.

Mike lipped who it was. Oh, what the heck, I thought. I turned my hair dryer off while Mike held the phone out to where both of us could hear.

"We just won four tickets to, "Hair," the musical at the amphitheater. You two think you could get out of the bed long enough to enjoy the show?" she giggled.

Mike and I shrugged our shoulders to an okay, why not? "It will be tough, but sure," Mike said.

We got the time and the where to meet up with them. Mike and I didn't have much time to grab a bite before meeting them in the lobby. We got a few bites of cheese and crackers out of our hotel fridge.

"Whew," I took a deep breath as we met the geriatrics, who were dressed in a god-awful floral. Foxie's shirt matched Mandi's strapless maxi dress. *Yes, I said strapless.*

"That was fast," I said to Mike, as I checked out Mandi to see what was holding up her strapless dress. If anyone stepped on it, *well hello*, all of Mandi would be exposed. I mean *all.*

"We just won the tickets right before we called you," Foxey said. "We bought a raffle ticket to help out the animal shelter here in town, and they immediately had the drawing. Voila, here we are!"

We got a shuttle to the amphitheater, which was beautiful the way it was laid out. We got some popcorn and soda, *the rest of our dinner,* then we found our seats. Not bad seats either, twenty rows up, center.

It was a great production and was really good. It wasn't Mike's type of a show, but he enjoyed it anyway. It was fun. We were glad Mandi and Foxie thought of us.

We got back to the hotel where we ran into Zack in the lobby, and we joined him for a drink in the hotel bar. But I didn't want a drink. I wanted a cheeseburger with fries. Everyone ordered burgers.

"I know you are anxious to know what is going on. It will be a couple more days before the autopsy is done. The body has to thaw first, and they don't want to rush it, as you can imagine. But they were able to confirm that the almond cookies were indeed poisoned. And the vial was indeed cyanide. You were right," Zack said and glanced around at all of us, shaking his head in approval.

He went on to say that the trio's goose was cooked.

"We have them dead to rights. They will all stand trial. The Madden family are grateful that we, I mean, you took the initiative to find out the truth. The will wasn't broken or yet falsified. The fortune was still intact and was still in the Madden kids' hands. Oh, and Dennis got demoted," Zack chuckled.

"The police will interview you one more time and then you can go back home. However, they will have you come back to testify when the trial starts. I think it will be a slam dunk," Zack continued.

"So the evil twins and their sidekick will have their comeuppance. Their just due! I love this country," Mandi said, as she tugged up her strapless dress and tucked her boobs in.

"Darn dress! I told Foxie I needed a breast implant." *Tug, tug.* We just watched her struggle in amazement. "Foxie said it was *too* late. Why heck, he won't let me buy my favorite body wash by the case anymore. He says I wouldn't be able to use it all up at my age. So, I buy two at a time now. Ain't that funny?" she said without a blink.

"Uh-huh," I said, for a lack of anything better to say, watching her tug at her dress. Then I turned to Zack.

"You know we've been told the same thing several times now," I said.

"I know, but it's routine to be on the same page with other interrogators who are building an unbreakable case. We must make sure the witnesses understand how this works," Zack said. "The authorities here are letting me in on the investigation only because I brought it to their attention, and I helped with the protocol of getting the ship in and, of course, my connection to you, who I said worked for me. Not such a white lie. We have worked on a couple of cases together," he said.

"Three, and all you worked on with me, was telling me to butt out."

"Thank goodness you didn't listen," he said.

"So, the trial will be here in Ft. Lauderdale for sure? I thought since the murder happened in international waters, between the islands, that perhaps the trial would possibly be held oh, I don't know. Perhaps St. Thomas or Barbados?"

Zack came back with, "You wish, but no. It boiled down to Americans killing an American. The final decision was to try the trio here."

Mike knew what I was thinking. He knew I would rather visit the islands again.

He smiled and said, "I will take you on the same cruise for our first anniversary."

I hugged him and kissed him with a quick thank you kiss.

Zack turned his head and smiled.

Mandi and Foxey were looking at us then at Zack, Zack, then us.

I thought I should get Mandi alone and explain the history between Zack, Mike and me.

After a brief explanation of the past year, Mandi understood the connection.

CHAPTER 45

We flew back to Kansas City the next day where the children and Katherine waited, along with Dora and Richard, for us to come up the ramp and through the airport gate.

The kids came running toward us. Karen Anne jumped into Mike's arms and Jeffey into mine. As soon as I put Jeffey down, my voluptuous friend Dora grabbed me for a great big welcome home, while Richard shook Mike's hand and finally Katherine hugged us both.

Dora put her arm through mine as we walked to get the luggage while Jeffey hung on to my other hand. The little guy was pulling a bag almost as big as he was, but he managed still to hold onto my hand.

"Well, trouble just follows you, doesn't it? Tell me all about it," my best friend said.

I laughed and told her, "Whoa, Girl. I will tell you all about it when we get settled at home, maybe tomorrow. Besides, since I called you for help, you know most of it."

"You're right," she said grabbing one of my suitcases. Loaded down with our luggage, we headed to our respective cars and caravanned home. When we opened the door, we were greeted by a huge surprise party waiting for us. *A welcome home party*, thanks to Dora's leadership, with the help of Kate.

"*Dora*," I said.

She shrugged and had a big smile on her face as did Kate, who was now walking up to me.

"*Surprise!*" Kate yelled. "Let the party begin!"

I looked at Mike and he said, "Let the party begin!" He held up a glass of God knows what that someone handed him.

After a couple of hours of celebration of our return home, finally everyone left and we were alone with the kids, one big happy family. We looked at each other then we both looked up to thank Lizabeth and Jerry, again.

CHAPTER 46

MIKE TOOK THE REST of the week off. He didn't have a new project going so he could afford to stay home. He said, "it's a vacation after a vacation."

Kerplunk. Clancy was coming through the door. *Swoosh, swish.* She shuffled into the kitchen. She slammed her supplies down on the counter, not realizing it.

"Welcome home Mr. Mike, Missy," she sneezed.

She gave each of us a hug. "*Ca-choo.*"

Putting my hands on her arms, I gently pushed her away from me where I could see her face so I could analyze the sneeze action better.

"Are you alright, Clancy?" I asked. "You sound and look like you are coming down with a cold or something. Your eyes are glassy and droopy."

"Oh, I'm alright, Missy. Well, time's a wasting," she said. "Got to get to it. *Aaa . . . choo.*"

For someone not that much older than me, she sure sounds like she's pretty folksy like some of my gram's friends.

She headed for the laundry room and I followed her.

"*A . . . choo . . . a.*"

"Okay, Clancy, you are coming down with something," I felt her head and it was slightly warm. Suddenly her eyes were running and nose was dripping. It was coming on fast. I handed her a tissue just as she let out a big a-c h o o and filled the tissue. I handed her another tissue.

I walked to my room—what used to be my room—to get my nurses' bag. Okay, it's more of a shoe box that I put drug store supplies in.

Clancy was reluctant to let me take her temperature. But I gave her no choice.

"Open," I demanded sticking the thermometer in her mouth. After a few minutes the little *bing* went off and I checked it.

"Clancy, you have a low-grade temp. You need to go home and rest," I suggested.

"No, no Missy. I haven't missed a day of work in five years."

"Well, there's a first time for everything," I said. "If push comes to shove, you didn't miss today either."

Clancy started sneezing one right after the other. She couldn't stop the snot running. She was getting sicker by the minute.

I yelled for Mike, "We 're taking Clancy home."

I drove Clancy in her car and Mike followed with Jeffey. Thank goodness Karen Anne was still in school.

Clancy gave me turn by turn as she sneezed and blew her brains out. She was getting worse by the moment.

We pulled into her neighborhood and, looking around, I raised my eye brows with amazement.

She lived in a gated neighborhood. A million dollar and up neighborhood and as we pulled into her driveway, hers is several millions up.

"Home, sweet home." She sneezed.

I helped her in with her cleaning supplies she always carries.

Whoa. I said to myself. This is *beautiful.*

"Clancy? This is so beautiful. Why on earth would you clean houses owning something like this?"

She sniffled and said, "*A-choo. A-choo. A-choo.* Good money in house cleaning," she teased. "My husband and I have done quite well all these years, but I love cleaning. It is self-satisfying for me to look back and see what I accomplished. *A-choo.* Some people like to garden, play golf, tennis, et cetera. Cleaning's my euphoria." *A-choo.* "I really enjoy it."

Clancy was speaking differently now. She no longer sounded folksy and I nicely pointed it out to her.

"You don't sound so downhome folksy now. You walked into this beautiful home and you changed."

"Well, it is embarrassing to clean people's homes and some are less than mine. I just don't want them to know. *A-choo.*" She blew her nose again, "I guess I'm hooked on cleaning."

"So how did you get hooked on cleaning?"

"*A-choo.* My daughter was cleaning to get herself a breast augmentation. She didn't want me to know. *A-choo.* She got enough money to get her breast enlarged and decided to move to California with her sister. She asked me if I would take over her little business until her customers could find someone else. *A-choo.* I liked it and stayed with it. Mike was one of her first customers. *A-choo.* "I only have three homes now."

"Hmph, do tell. Come on; let me help you get to bed. I'll run to the drug store and get what you need to battle this cold and be back in a jiffy."

Mike overheard some of what Clancy said. And when I looked at him with bewilderment, he simply said, "Who knew? That explains the really nice birthday and Christmas gifts, not to mention our very expensive crystal set of glassware she gave us for our wedding."

I dropped Mike and Jeffey off at home and went to the drugstore and got what I thought Clancy would need. I had already asked her if she had a thermometer and she didn't. She told me to pick up one, so I did.

I got back to Clancy, who now had a full blown cold. I took her temp and it was currently 102.3. It was higher and creeping up.

"I think you will be down a few days. You need to rest so stay in bed. I'll bring some soup when I come back."

"I'm so cold. Will you turn on the electric blanket for me?" she asked.

I doctored her and tucked her in, making sure she was okay for me to go. Though I hated to leave her feeling so bad, I told her I would drop by in a couple of hours to check on her.

When I came back about 4 P.M., her husband answered the door as I was about to put the key in the lock that Clancy gave me.

"Oh," I said, startled. "I wasn't expecting anyone to be home with Clancy."

"Sorry, I startled you. I'm Donald Clancy. Come on in." he opened the door wider. Anita's expecting you."

Anita? Hmmm. I knew her as Clancy. It never dawned on me she had any other name.

"Thanks, I'm Sara Carlton, I mean Farren. I just got married." I smiled with a little giggle. "I'm still getting used to the name change."

"I know; Anita and our daughters were there helping out at the wedding and I came too."

"I don't remember meeting you," I said.

"You were a bit busy, and your friend Dora recruited me to work the bar. Apparently, she was one bartender short."

"No way," I said, "I had no idea she badgered you into working my wedding."

"Oh, trust me. It was fun. Since Anita was so involved helping Dora with the wedding, I didn't know anyone. So, tending bar was a great way to talk with people and I really enjoyed it."

"Well, it is nice to know you had our back and you had fun," I said patting his arm.

"The food was delicious too," he smiled.

"Again, it was Dora and she did outdo herself."

I excused myself and took the chicken soup to the kitchen. Donald followed to help me find the things I needed to serve the hot soup.

Donald carried the tray of soup and crackers to Clancy, and I followed. to check on her.

She was a mess.

She tried to introduce us to each other, always being the good hostess.

But she could hardly speak. Her throat was now raspy.

I helped her sit up to sip some chicken noodle, more broth than noodle.

My nursing skill had kicked in yet again. I gave Clancy cold meds that I bought over the counter. My favorite is Zicam. But I usually use Zicam when I first start getting a cold and it zaps the cold right now. I'm not sure about when the cold has gone as far as Clancy's. We will see. I also started her chewing vitamin C to help build her immune system.

Donald told me that he would keep an eye on Anita and would keep putting liquid down her, along with more broth. He promised to call me if she didn't get any better by morning.

CHAPTER 47

"How's Clancy?" Mike asked me as soon as I walked through the door.

"She's really got it bad. I don't think we caught it in time. I'm afraid it will turn into pneumonia. Donald said he would call me if she's not better by morning."

"What are you doing?" Mike asked me as I rattled a bag with cold medicine in it.

"We are going to stop a cold before it starts so chew my groom, chew." I handed the four chewable vitamin C immune builder pills to him.

"I guess if I refuse, it wouldn't be a good idea," he said. "Jeffey, come in here."

Jeffey came running in, looked up at his dad and said, "Am I in trouble, Dad?"

Mike laughed and said, "No son, you are not in trouble. Sara has something for you,"

Jeffey did a semi- circle and faced me. "Am I in trouble, Mommy?"

Oh, my, gosh, I melted. He called me Mommy. At the wedding he asked if he could, but this was the first time he just came out and said it.

"Here you go, son," I said, as I handed him his orange flavored chewable.

I smiled and glanced at Mike, who had tears in his eyes as he just witnessed a special moment between Jeffey and me.

Jeffey had his hand out and said, "More please."

The box instruction said two a day and since I just gave him one, I said, "Okay, but only one more, for now."

"Thank you," and he ran off.

I sat down on Mike's lap and said, "Clancy's home is beyond elegant. I never thought she would live in a gated neighborhood or in a three or four-million-dollar home. And she likes cleaning and cleaning other people's houses. I guess home cleaning does pay well," I smiled as I got off Mike's lap to go put laundry in the dryer. He pulled me back and said, "Thank you."

"For what?" I asked him as I kissed his forehead. "For what?" *but I knew* and he knew I did. I got off his lap again and went to put the laundry in the dryer and decided to call Dora's number.

Dora, who looked like she belonged in a multimillion dollar home, came up from sleeping on a dirt floor. Her mother died when she was five years old. Her dad, who had nothing and barely scraped by, had no way to take care of her so he basically gave Dora to her oldest sister who was old enough to be her mother. She wasn't much of a mother though. Dora had two hand- me- down little dresses to switch off, a few pairs of undies and a pair of shoes and literally slept on a pile of blankets on the dirt floor in a shed out back of the house. Her sister had a daughter Dora's age, who was Dora's niece. She felt bad for Dora and would sneak her extra food and clothing out to her and begged her mother to let Dora move into the house. Finally, Dora's sister became her mother and Dora called her 'Mom,' and Dora's niece became her sister and she was allowed to stay in the house. Dora was treated so badly while growing up that she couldn't wait to leave. Talk about a Cinderella story. Cinderella had it made compared to Dora.

Finally, Dora was in high school and got her own paying job at the drug store soda fountain and as a stocker for the K-Mart store. She worked through high school and graduated with honors and met Richard. Richard, who came from a middle class all-American family treated Dora like a queen. Which is why every hair is in place and she's always made up like a movie star and why she drips in jewels. Richard said she deserved it. So, to sum up, Dora came from a crappy background and went into adult life where she was confident, organized and knowledgeable. She's creative and can do anything she sets her mind to. I am the luckiest person in the world to have found her. Yup, proud she's in my life. As far as her sister mother and niece sister are concerned, well, both are dead. But let me tell you, Dora never treated them as badly as she was treated. Dora did better by them than they did her.

She gave them money; always nice birthday gifts and Christmas presents. Dora never missed a Mother's Day. She's just special and considerate that way, but very bossy.

To hear Richard tell it, he saw Dora's big red hair and fell in "like." Dora turned around and Richard fell in love . . . with Dora's enormous boobs. Finally, he noticed her eyes. That's a man's view, or at that time, a boy's view. Was there any difference?

Richard and Dora have a great business in "Century Management Cleaning," where they clean tons of businesses and corporate offices. They have 75 employees and they all work 40 hours plus a week. Dora pitched in when needed, being careful of her nails. And like Clancy, Dora likes it. But, meantime, she helps me sleuth and we really like that.

"Whatcha doing?" she asked me, as she could tell that I had drifted off in thought.

"I was thinking how you came up from childhood to now, and how grateful I am you have been my best friend since kindergarten. I just remembered what you have overcome."

"Good grief, what brought that on?" she asked.

"Just glad you're in my life," then I changed the subject.

I told her how sick Clancy was and how nice her home is. "I'll probably be looking after Clancy for next few days," I said.

"I'll help out," Dora offered.

"Thanks. It's nice to have a back-up plan."

"Did Katherine see Jax while you guys were honeymooning?" she asked. "Or at least hear from him?"

"No, she said she never heard a word from him. She's going to be really hurt when she finds out his history. I wonder if I should fill her in on what we found out. I'll ask Mike what he thinks."

"I'll be glad to get this Tom Solo mess put to bed now that we know it's Jax who killed him," Dora said.

"Well, we're 99% sure he's the killer."

We chatted a few more minutes and hung up.

I decided to talk to Mike about telling his mother about Jax.

Mike came in with the kids from a fast food place and as he was setting it all out for us to chow down on, I said, "Mike, what would you think about finally telling your mother about Jax?"

"Yeah, she should know. It's time. She's coming over for breakfast Saturday," he said. "We can tell her then."

Relieved, I said, "I know she'll be hurt. She really liked this guy."

"He certainly hasn't treated her right by going so much and coming back just long enough to dangle a carrot in front of her nose. He acts like he's interested, but I don't think she cares as much about him now as she did at the beginning. She can handle it. She's been through a lot worse," he said.

"I think I'll check in on Clancy," I said, as I left the room to call so I wouldn't interrupt the Knicks vs Golden State Warriors game that was just starting.

Donald answered and said he didn't think Anita was any better. He said he was taking her to the hospital in the morning if she didn't show any improvement by then. He promised to call me one way or the other.

I finished the tons of laundry and put it away. Mike and I put the kiddos to bed. He and I took turns reading a Harry Potter story that clearly would not get done tonight if ever. We tucked each into their bed, turned off their lights and said good night.

Mike and I walked down the hall hand in hand to *our* brand-new bedroom that he had had done with Katherine's supervision while we were honeymooning.

I noticed Mike had taken Lizabeth's portrait down.

"Mike, what happened to Lizabeth's portrait? You took her down."

"No, I had Mother move her," he said. He took my hand and led me to the den and flipped on the lights.

Looking around I was amazed.

"I had Mother put up all the pictures I had around the house of Lizabeth and display them in the den, including the portrait. She looked around and also displayed all the pictures of Jerry she could find. I hope you don't mind Mother going through your things to get Jerry's pictures. She went down in the basement and went through your furniture drawers and trunks to see if she could find more. Now, we can all visit Lizabeth and Jerry all we want to."

"Wow, Mike. This is beautiful."

I looked around at all of Jerry's pictures and there were pictures that Katherine had enlarged to 8x10 that she found in my trunk that I had forgotten about. It was amazing.

We were both pleased of the great job Katherine had done. It was a shrine and yet it wasn't. I had tears in my eye just looking around.

We went to bed and I found out the honeymoon wasn't quite over. Was there a *ménage a trois* for two? *Whoa!*I can't catch my breath.

THE PHONE RANG JUST as we were going to sleep. I answered as I sat up. I looked at Mike and lipped, "It's Donald."

"Okay, Donald, I'll meet you there," I said getting out of bed.

"Clancy is unresponsive. Donald said the ambulance just left with her and he's on his way out the door behind them."

"Go. Go." Mike said.

Thank goodness I took a shower after the va-va-va-do. I threw on my clothes and hurried out the door to the hospital. I met up with Donald who was pacing, worried sick.

"What did they say?" I asked. "Did they tell you anything?"

"Nothing, yet," he said, looking at his watch. "They're checking her out."

We had chatted about fifteen minutes when the ER doctor came out.

"Mr. Clancy," The doctor said, looking around.

"Here," Donald said, raising his hand and rising up from his chair. We walked closer to the doctor.

"Your wife's going to be alright, but she does have pneumonia. We have her on a liquid drip and antibiotics. Thank goodness she isn't allergic to anything. And Mr. Clancy, I'm relieved you got your wife here now rather than in the morning. She was going downhill fast."

Donald dropped his head and started to tear up. He thanked the doctor and shook his hand and asked, "Can I see her now?"

Donald took my hand and said, "Come on, Sara." I started to hesitate, but he seemed to be more secure with me there beside him.

We walked into Clancy's room. Donald took a step back and teetered a little.

"I wasn't ready to see Anita with tubes sticking out everywhere. I don't think she has ever been the hospital except to have our girls."

"Oh, the girls, do they know?" I asked.

"Yes, yes, I called them on the way here. I think they are coming together."

He moved slowly over to his wife. Donald took Clancy's hand and gently held it, then leaned down and kissed her forehead which was about the only place there weren't any tubes.

She opened her eyes and blinked trying to adjust her sight. But she looked past Donald to me. "Sara?" Her eyes were in my direction when she opened them.

"Hi Clancy. You gave us quite a scare." I edged to stand closer to Donald.

Clancy's eyes followed and stopped on Donald.

"Donald. I didn't see you but I felt your touch." She drifted off to sleep holding on to her husband's hand.

"This was exactly what Clancy needed. Rest. She's going to be alright and she'll be going home in a couple of days," I told him. "I think I will head on home and check on Clancy tomorrow." *Which it was already tomorrow.*

"And Sara, thank you."

As I was leaving, I saw Clancy's daughters walking towards me, and I updated them before they stepped into their mother's hospital room.

CHAPTER 48

I WALKED INTO THE HOUSE where Mike and the kids were eating breakfast. Mike got up and poured me a cup of coffee. He handed me pancakes and bacon that he kept warm for me.

"Yum, this hits the spot. I am famished," I smiled, with saggy eyes. "I think I want an egg to put on the top of the pancake for more protein." I started to walk to the stove.

"Whoa Babe. Let me do that before you fall over," Mike said, "Over easy or medium?"

"Just so the yoke is runny and the white is done. I want to burst the yoke and let it run down the pancakes with just a little maple syrup."

They all looked at me. "What? It's good. You should try it sometime."

When I finished eating, I kissed Karen Anne goodbye as she got on the school bus, then I went back in the house and headed to bed for a nap.

I slept for four hours when Jeffey jumped on the bed.

"Come on, Mom," he said. "We're going to lunch."

I smiled, "Give me thirty more minutes."

"Nope, Mom, get up," he said, jumping up and down on the bed.

"Okay, I give," I said, as I headed for the shower.

MIKE TOOK US TO "Wanda's," a little mom and pop restaurant that has down home cooking and have the best biscuits and gravy in town. Only they quit serving biscuits and gravy two hours ago. We walked in, and to my surprise, there sat my best buddy and side-kick Dora with her side-kick hubby, Richard.

Mike grinned. "I know you haven't spent much time with her since we got back. Surprise!"

Jeffey ran and jumped onto Dora's lap. She tickled him so much he snorted out snot.

The new mom sprang into action. I whipped out the tissue and started wiping away.

Lunch was great and so was the company.

Katherine called Mike's cell. "Hi Mother," he said and then listened to what she said.

"I need to, want to see you. PDQ," she said.

"On our way, see you in a few," he replied.

"Wonder what that's all about." Mike shrugged as he hung up.

We arrived at Katherine's and rang the doorbell then opened the door and ran smack dab into Jax.

"Come on in," Katherine said, looking enamored. "Jax and I have news to share with you."

We followed them into the living room. Katherine sat Jeffey in front of his own private cartoon channel with cookies and milk. Katherine brought in scones and hot chamomile tea and set them in front of us.

Mike and I looked at each other like, *What the?*

I picked up a scone and took a bite but set it down as I was full from lunch.

Katherine blurted out, "Jax asked me to marry him." She held out her hand to show us the ring.

I spit out the half-chewed scone almost on Jax. "What?"

Always the gentleman, Mike stood up and went over to shake Jax's hand and kiss his mother in congratulations. "I need a drink. Uh, to toast the happy couple," he said.

I choked and sputtered more scone. I wiped off the crumbs and sipped a little chamomile tea, put on a fake smile and gave both of them a hug. "Well, that's a surprise," trying to keep my composure.

I kept hacking. "I guess I must be catching Clancey's cold."

Mike put his arms around me. The whole time he knew what I was thinking.

Oh, my god! I kept screaming in my mind.

"We know this was sudden, but we won't tie the knot until fall. Maybe, in October," Katherine said in her little southern twang,

"Meantime, Jax is leaving in a week and won't be back for a couple of months. So, we can plan the wedding while he's gone. Jax said the sky's the limit. Didn't ya, Honey?"

Jax stood up by Katherine and put his arms around her. "That's right, Baby, whatever you want, the sky's the limit.

I was smiling but dying inside to wise Katherine up.

"Well, then we can start planning Saturday," I exclaimed.

"Jax has a meeting Saturday so he won't be joining us then," Katherine acted disappointed.

"Well, that's a shame," Mike acted disappointed too.

I just stood there and kept thinking, *Oh, my god!*

Then Jax said. "Ah you don't need me to decide anything. Just tell me where and when."

We all gave a little giggle.

Oh, my god!

We couldn't wait to get Katherine alone.

We visited a while longer and left.

In the car I said, "*Oh, my god!* Mik, what are we going to do?"

"I still plan on telling her about Jax on Saturday," he said.

"Good, though I don't want to hurt her. But we have to stop her before it's too late."

Meantime, Mike and I wanted to drop by the hospital to see Clancy while Katherine watched Jeffey for a couple of hours. Wondered how Jax liked that?

CHAPTER 49

On Saturday we were sitting down to one of Mike's famous breakfasts and, of course the kids were giggling, snorting like little pigs. They were seeing who could show off the most in front of their grandmother. And they wanted to try the soft egg yolk on the pancakes with a little syrup.

Piercing the egg yolk and watching it run down the sides of the pancakes, Karen Anne took her first bite. "Hmmm, this is good," she said.

"Yeah," Jeffey joined in, "Good Mom." *I still get a smile on my face when Jeffey calls me 'Mom.'*

Surprise, surprise the kids loved the taste of the yolk on the pancakes. They went to watch Saturday morning cartoons, and we started clearing up the dishes.

Finally, Katherine said, "You two sure have been quiet. What's on your mind?"

"Come sit down, Mother," Mike said. "Sara has something to tell you." I gave him the *look.*

I got the coffee pot and filled our cups with more coffee. You can't have enough coffee in times like this. I stuttered a few seconds for the right words to start while still giving Mike the *look* for putting me on the spot.

"Okay, Sara spit it out," Katherine said.

"You can't marry Jax.

"I know," she said softly.

Mike and I looked at each other and at the same time we said, "What?"

"I know I can't marry Jax."

"Then what is this all about?" Mike asked.

"I know Sara and her buddy Dora have been working on Tom Solo's murder. I found notes on your computer, Sara. Forgive me for reading them, but you left them there unprotected, and I couldn't help myself. I know I shouldn't have been nosey, but I saw Jax's name and I was drawn to it."

"How long have you known?" I asked.

"Right after Christmas," she said, "I was babysitting while you were shopping for your wedding and there it was. I started to say something numerous times, but I didn't think it appropriate to bring it up and spoil your wedding."

"Wow!" I expressed. "Wow."

"So, Michael, can you elaborate on *Wow*?"

"I thought we were catching you off guard but instead, you caught us off guard. We had planned on telling you today when you dropped the bombshell about marrying Jax the other day. Then we weren't sure how to handle it." Mike looked relieved.

"We didn't want to hurt you. We didn't think it was going to be a big deal since Jax is in and out of the country so much. He's gone more than he is here. We just weren't sure how you actually felt about him, then you said you were marrying him in October."

"October smotober. I fell out of like with that guy about his third trip leaving me. It was fun while he was here, but frankly, I got tired of him being gone so long. What kinda life's that?"

"But."

"But nothing. I figured something was up when you kept asking me if I'd heard from Jax. When is Jax coming back? I didn't just fall off the turnip truck from Minnesota, you know. I had my own suspicions. Then your information on your computer confirmed it.

So, tell me what you know and update me so we can set up a sting."

"Wow!"

"I do wish you could say something other than, 'wow,' Sara."

"Wow."

"Enough with the "Wows" you two." She said, using her fingers for a quote sign.

"Sting," I finally spit out.

I told her play by play everything Dora and I found out. I told her how it all came about. Who all the players were and what happened to Jax's poor daughter and how Jax finally got revenge. Tom Solo was the last attacker.

"Det. Zanders was just waiting for Jax to come back"

"My sleuthing daughter-in-law. You never cease to amaze me," Katherine was ecstatic.

"And you amaze me," I told her.

"Okay, ladies, I think I am going to vomit with all this sugar," Mike said.

"So, what's the sting?" Katherine asked again.

"First, I wonder if you would stick around and watch the kids while Mike and I go see Clancy. I have only been to the hospital a couple of times this week, and she's home now. I would like to take her this casserole I have in the slow cooker," I said.

"I'll be happy to stay with my grandkiddos."

"I'll call Dora and Det. Zanders this morning to meet us for pizza about five. We would plan out "The Sting," and we'll need you Katherine to pull it off. Only it's not going to be an elaborate sting. More like a setup and gotcha.

"I'm on board and will do what it takes to get Jax," Katherine said.

"Don't be too hard on Jax. He was revenging his daughter and the lack of that judge's sentencing of those five guys, horrendous act. Often these judges just slap a hand and allow these athletes to get by with murder. Money talks so they walked. I realize before you say anything it's not just athletes who walk. But in this case, it was."

"I hear you, Sara, but he shouldn't have taken the law in to his own hands," she said.

"True, but looking at the end result after all these years of what it's done to his daughter, I can understand his reasoning, "I said. "Dora and I were shocked and wanted to kill these guys ourselves after seeing Jax's daughter Tara like that."

"Let me know what you need from me, I'll be around to do it," she said, with mixed emotions.

Mike and I took Clancy and Donald the tuna casserole and tossed salad I made for them. Donald was thankful for the food. Clancy herself was doing a lot better. She said she hated leaving us high and dry. The doctor said she could go back to her cleaning jobs in a couple of weeks. The doctor just shook his head in disbelief, knowing she didn't have to clean houses but did. I assured her I was handling the Farren household just fine. But the main thing was, Anita Clancy was going to be just fine.

We left there to meet up with Dora, Richard and Zack at the Pizza Shack to work out a plan of action.

"Okay, we'll have a barbecue tomorrow. Mike will grill for the first time this spring. It is a bit early to barbecue, but the weather's supposed to be decent and it won't be too cold. Mike's the only one who has to stand out in the cold anyway," I teased.

"I thought you could help me turn the steaks," he teased back.

I turned to Zack and said, "We'll call you when it's time to pick up Jax."

Winking, Zack said, "What no steak?"

"But Jax will know something is up uh, uh," I stuttered.

'Relax, I'm just teasing, he said. "Just text me when you're ready."

So, the plans were being laid out. We'll be preparing Jax's last meal as it were. Everyone would come to the dinner and boom, we'd confront him. Then Zack will pick him up.

While waiting for a cheese pizza to go for the kids, Mike called Katherine to fill her in. Jax was standing right there so she only listened then replied,

"That will be great, and I'll have the kids ready to go."

When we picked up the kids, Katherine and Jax had their coats on to leave. Later we found out that Jax was taking Katherine to meet his daughter.

KATE WAS OUT OF town for the weekend and would be disappointed to miss out on the take down. Since we didn't want the kids to be here throughout the process, our neighbor Sherrie graciously took them. The kids were thrilled.

Dora and Richard arrived, followed by Katherine and Jax for the barbecue.

"Wow, everything smells and looks so good." Katherine said acting like it wasn't Jax's last home-cooked meal.

While we were enjoying dessert that Dora brought I stepped into the other room and texted Zack. "Ready."

We were chit chatting having after dinner drinks when the doorbell rang. I answered and brought in Detective Zack Zanders, followed by Det. Edwards and Allen and a few uniforms.

We walked in and everyone immediately turned and looked at Jax.

He knew what was up. He collapsed into the chair and immediately said, "I felt the law failed my daughter. Tara's still in a mental prison and physically ruined and always will be. Most of the time she doesn't even know her own name while three scum bags did only three years of a five-year sentence, and the other two got a "get out of jail" free card. Then the cowards scattered across the country putting as much distance from each other as they could. Well, I found them one by one. Grayson, Woodward, St. Pat Richard and Salaman finally got theirs. And lastly, Solo. Oh yeah, I killed them all and I feel justified. I revenged my daughter's injustice."

No one said a word. We just let Jax say what he needed to say for a very long time.

Jax looked at Katherine. "On July 4th I was just looking forward to spending a good time with you and your family. But then I saw Tom Solo making an ass out of himself, falling all over Sara. When I put two and two together, I knew I had to finish the sentence he never got. I hated him. I hated them all so much. I had to get Tara her justice.

"I am glad it's over. I knew it was coming. I kept so busy that the law couldn't keep up, but then I met you, Katherine, and I slowed down.

"Katherine, I know that I wasn't around as much as I should have been. Trust me, I wanted to be. I will say in front of God and your family, I really do love you. I really wanted to be with you. And from the bottom of my heart, I am so, so sorry. I guess there won't be an October wedding." He had tears in his eyes when he went into the whole story of what actually happened. Then he broke down. Katherine went to him putting her arms around the man who was in so much pain.

I asked Zack to step out of the room. "I just hate this," I said, rubbing my temples. "He's in so much pain. What's going happen to Jax?"

"Jax confessed to all the murders. That's a plus. He just said he doesn't want a trial. I know he'll serve time, but I don't know what the judge will do. Maybe he'll get lucky and get a slap on the hand like Tom Solo did and walk. I just don't know how much time he'll serve but serve he will." Zack explained. "Murder's murder no matter how justified it seems, and no one can take the law into their own hands. Though, I don't blame him, and that's off the record."

We went back to where everyone was still waiting and two officers were standing on either side of Jax.

"Sara, I know you and Dora have visited my daughter a few times. Will you please check in on her for me? She needs someone to care," Jax said.

"Yes, I promise," I replied.

Zack nodded, and Det. Allen and Edwards stood Jax up, handcuffed him and started walking him to the door while reading him his rights. Jax was headed to prison. No doubt.

Katherine did something that no one expected. She ran over to Jax and kissed him.

We all looked at Katherine in surprise. Later she said she just felt so bad for him that she wanted to give him something as nice as she could, a kiss goodbye.

CHAPTER 50

A COUPLE OF MONTHS LATER we sat in court watching, listening and testifying.

Jax stood in front of Judge Morrison to accept his punishment.

"In light of all you have confessed to, and your filling in so many blanks of all the cold cases of a David Grayson, Tyler Woodward, Skylar St. Patrick as well as an Eric Salamann, then finally, Tom Solo. I know you feel justified.

"With that said, after researching your daughter's case I know as a father I would want to seek revenge and want justice as well. It is also against the law to take the law into your own hands.

"I hereby sentence you to fifteen years in the state prison. With good behavior, you could be out in ten years."

The Prosecuting Attorney stood up. "Your honor, he killed—"

Judge Morrison banged his gravel. "The ruling stands. Court dismissed."

Jax turned and looked at me and lipped, "Thank you."

He gave a finger wave and air kiss to Katherine and lipped "sorry."

She smiled and finger waved back to him.

"Darn, another time and another place," Katherine said, as if she meant it.

We all turned and left the courtroom.

CHAPTER 51

THE PHONE WAS RINGING when we unlocked the door and walked in. It was the DA in Ft. Lauderdale. They were ready for Mike and me to testify against the evil twins and their side-kick. Everything had come together. It would be great to see Foxey and Mandi.

Katherine once again would care for the kids while we were gone.

Later we put the kids to bed and, of course, had our family reading story time. Mike and I went for a nightcap and a snack. We went to bed and it was fantastic love making. I hope the honeymoon never ends. There is something that feels so right when our naked bodies are wrapped around each other and touching as we fall asleep. Hmmm! I could lay here like this forever.

The next morning, we were on our way to Ft. Lauderdale. We each testified. First Foxie testified, second Mandi testified, then Mike and finally me.

We could stick around a couple of days before the cross examination, or we could go back home and return in time for the cross. (We had to testify three different times since each Brooke, Sheila and Dennis were tried separately.)

We went home and were glad we did, as it was longer than a few days. It was two weeks. We returned and did our duty. It took almost a year on all three trials of going back and forth. It wasn't a slam dunk. But in the end the Evil Trio got theirs.

Sheila and Dennis got twenty years to life with a chance to go in front of the parole board in fifteen years. The John Madden family vowed they would be there to ask the board not to grant parole each and every time.

Dear sweet Brooke will never see daylight outside of prison. She will die there. She went out of court screaming "It's not fair. It's not fair; they're guiltier than me."

WE WENT OUT FOR dinner with Foxie and Mandi one last time. *Probably.* Though they said they were going to come see us and maybe we could sleuth together again. They offered to help if and when we have to solve another crime. Just call.

The next morning, we said our goodbyes to them and them to us. After they were out of sight Mike and I made a big U-turn and headed for the beach. Life is good.

AUTHOR NOTE

THIS STORY WAS BASED on a reoccurring dream from when I was a young mother. It gnawed at me until I wrote it out in long hand (before computers). After I retired, I ran across the story and started working on it until the finished story today. It is my first book that turned into my second book. *The Key Club Murders* turned out to be my first book.

I enjoyed writing them and wished I had started writing at an earlier age. It's never too late.

MY THANKS TO

Julie Andersen, Carol Anne Schneider, and The Woodneath Library Critique Group, who said I couldn't end *Who Killed Tom Solo?* on a dream so it is now a standalone book.

ABOUT THE AUTHOR

THOUGH I AM MATURE, I discovered a passion for writing a few years ago. You will see I write with a modern heart and flare. I have on book published on Amazon called *The Key Club Murders*. It has five-star reviews and is doing well.

When writing letters was what social media is today, my family and friends often said I should write a novel because my letters were entertaining. But with raising a family, working full-time, keeping up the house, making a home for my children and keeping up in their activities, not to mention keeping hubby happy, I had no time to write.

Made in the
USA
Lexington, KY